T0129954

Earth Tremors,
Mountain Movements

by

Richard Cullern

Order this book online at www.trafford.com
or email orders@trafford.com

Most Trafford titles are also available at major online book retailers.

Cover Illustrations Richard Cullern

Printed in the United States of America.

ISBN: 978-1-4269-7206-5 (sc)
ISBN: 978-1-4269-7207-2 (e)
ISBN: 978-1-4269-7208-9 (hc)

Library of Congress Control Number: 2011909529

Trafford rev. 06/09/2011

 www.trafford.com

North America & international
toll-free: 1 888 232 4444 (USA & Canada)
phone: 250 383 6864 ✦ fax: 812 355 4082

For
Bernadette, Kieth, Stephen, Michelle.

Contents

Chapter 1

Unwanted Guests

Owl, landed on the window ledge with a hefty thud as he tried to dodge the open window. His whole body shuddered with the force, ruffling his feathers. What had made matters so difficult was the window blowing wildly in the wind, without even the restraining latch being in place. The thought, and then the realisation that it had been left open all night, was an instant irritation.

"What is going on here!" he hooted at such neglect for security. "Brimen!" he shouted as he winged inside to land on the clock. "Where are you?" Rooney came rushing in to the room. "Owl!" he said surprised to see him. "We were not expecting to see you today?"

"I realise that!" hooted Owl sharply. "So, tell me, WHY, has the window been left open?" He hooted disapprovingly watching it still banging uncontrollably against the rock face. His eyes then fell dramatically to the wooden floor, noticing a pile of coiled rope. "What is that; doing down there?" he said with a tone of serious alarm.

"Oh! I must have left it there." replied Rooney rushing over to secure the window and then attempting to pick up the coil. "I., I., I was going to clean the windows from the outside," he stammered. "Holding on to it for support!" he assured Owl. "ER! It's the only way."

"MMM!" hooted Owl suspiciously. "Now where are those lazy Oakmen?" Rooney was too embarrassed to reply truthfully and was about to be diplomatic in his answer when there was a noisy response.

"Don't panic!" sounded a firm voice. "We are here," said Brimen coming through the door that led from the vaults. He was soon followed by Gannon and Olan who were busily wiping their dirty hands on old rags.

"Huh!" was Owls doubtful reaction, surprised to find that they had been working?

"Yes; Well, Mmm..," Bluffed Brimen. "We have been servicing the carts," he replied with a hint of feeble excuse.

"It is just as well!" said Owl with an air of warning. "You will need to be prepared, for what is about to come your way." He waited for a reaction from the three of them then hooted impatiently. "Now where is it?"

Brimen registered the implications of Owls remarks but could only deal with the most obvious of Owls demands with any immediate clarity at any one time. "Where is what?" he replied looking all surprised.

"The golden acorn?" was the curt reply.

"OH; 'THAT' - the gold?" said Brimen searching for a good excuse. "Well! We have been very busy," he said.

"Doing what?" insisted Owl. Brimen was now becoming somewhat preoccupied with Owls comment, 'what is about to come your way'. Gannon and Olan meanwhile were still busily wiping their hands clean whislt staying wisely quiet.

"It has now been weeks since Sprite told you to retrieve the stolen acorn," said Owl accusingly, stating. "It's for sure that you haven't even bothered to look for it!"

"Now that's not fair, we..,

"Don't make excuses!" hooted Owl. "Rumour tells me that you are more distracted with other things?"

"Well! I am not!"

"Then, tell me the real reason?" snapped Owl, goading him.

Rooney felt increasingly uncomfortable; looking for an excuse to leave the room in case he got the blame for the 'rumour'. "AH! Wait a minute I've left the kettle boiling," he said. Then quickly, scurried away to attend to it. Gannon and Olan followed close behind with the excuse to wash their hands, leaving Brimen feeling deserted and annoyed with Owl's usual 'know it all' attitude.

"There!" said Brimen pointing at the ledgers. "If you want them, they are over there," then moved to join the others in the scullery. "Take them and go!"

"Mmm!" hooted Owl, deliberately labouring the point. He completely ignored Brimen's demand and then said with great timing. "It's this 'medal' nonsense, isn't it?"

"What 'medal' nonsense?" said Brimen turning around, fiegning an innocent look.

"Hah!" scorned Owl. "The King - for some pathetic reason - wants to commend the Oakmen for rescuing Culjern from Ersatz's Citadel." He stated sarcastically.

"So what if he does?" challenged Brimen.

"Hah!" scorned Owl again, sounding jealous. "Why, would he want to do that?"

"Is that all you have really come here for," said Brimen. "Too state your objections to our heroic deed?"

"No!" said Owl sounding miffed. "That! Idea is of little consequence; I am here to tell you that Sprite wants an urgent meeting with the three of you, Ankra, and Monk."

"Oh! Not another meeting," whinged Brimen. "What is it about this time?"

"You will discover that when you turn up!" hooted Owl. "If you even bother too." Owl then began demanding that the window should be opened so that he could alight and be on his way. Yet, Brimen was still curious and wanted to ask him what he meant when he had said earlier - 'what is about to come your way.' Then Owl was gone. Brimen watched him disappear over the tree tops as he had done so many times before.

Gannon, who had been listening from the scullery, came rushing back and said. "What do you think Owl meant when he said – What is about to come your way."

"I am not too sure," said Brimen thoughtfully. "Owl didn't give me the chance to ask." Then he decided. "We had better set to work on the carts – just in case."

As Owl had said, the Great King Henved had been so impressed with the Oakmens brave attempt in successfully rescuing his favourite warrior, Culjern that a celebration was to be held at the castle in their honour. Whereupon, each Oakman and Gnome involved in the rescue were too be awarded a citation; to be written in the Oak book roll of honour. In addition Brimen, Gannon and Olan would receive a golden acorn medal for their part in the daring mission.

Days later, back at the lodge on the morning of the celebrations. The expectation of honours, were causing a slight disagreement between Brimen and Olan.

3

"Well, I er..!" he paused a short while. "...think that mine will have the extra gold bar and acorn attached to the oak green ribbon," stated Brimen smugly as he examined his highly polished, buckled, shoes. Prims came into the room with a supportive smile on her face as she fussed with his newly ironed tunic on its hanger.

"WHY?" answered Olan in response as he adjusted his belt in the reflection of the mirror. "Why should you receive a different medal?"

"Because, I am the Leader!" said Brimen proudly. "There has to be a distinction?"

"Here we go again!" whispered Rooney into Gannons ear as he brushed the dust from the shoulders of his tunic. "We know where this could lead?"

"If you think that you are that important!" said Olan flippantly. "Then ask for a knighthood?" No sooner had the words left Olans lips, when he saw a glint of pleasure in Brimens eyes. "NO! NO! NO! Forget I had just said that." He hastened watching Brimen puff himself up with pride. "What I mean is WE were all in this together?"

Olan then glanced helplessly across at Gannon and Rooney wishing he could retract what he had just said. Meanwhile, the two of them were shaking their heads while sniggering hopelessly at the comment.

Gannon soon bought the spat back under control when he then raised his eyebrows becoming serious, showing a more responsible approach to this ideal. He knew full well that Brimen was gullible and at times may just take Olan seriously. "Are you both dressed yet!" he snapped. "We need to get to the castle early."

"Yes! Yes! Yes!" groaned Brimen, dropping the idea of a 'knighthood' dream.

"After all, that is not the sort of thing you ask for - from a King," added Gannon.

"Anyway!" said Olan more realistically. "We've got to persuade the Elders to accept your statue first."

"Mmmm!" said Brimen on reflection. "If Owl had not interrupted us the other day we would have got the plinth finished," he sighed.

"Let's forget about selfish motives," said Gannon getting more irritated with all the cross talk. "We have yet to pick up Eva, May and

Daisey. We also have to make sure that young Tad and his helpers have delivered the harvest food to the castle kitchen."

"I know! I know!" answered Brimen sharply. "Let's make our way to the castle."

To everyone's surprise, unwelcome guests who had not been invited to the castle turned up too, demanding to be let in. Merva and Derva had been a continuous annoyance to their brother Monk and were constantly objecting to their omission from the favoured list. They would not leave his side until he had sorted out their problem.

The two had long claimed that they had also helped in Gannon's rescue of Culjern by not telling Ersatz when they knew what was happening in the dungeon. Rightly so, the two also claimed that they had never, ever given away secrets of the stone seals.

"Sprite made a fuss of us!" The pair insisted. "She threw a party for us and said we were special!" they reminded him. The outrageous demand on their brother was - that he should plead to the King for leniency.

"But, there are reasons beyond my control!" was Monks, consistent yet convienient reply. Monk knew that the sisters could never ever forgive him for being deserted all those years ago. The fact that he claimed he never ever knew of their plight never convinced the sisters. He was also aware that the pair thought that their incarceration in Ersatz tower was not a mistake. Time after time he felt the effect of countless spells cast on him to prove his suspicions were correct. What ever was taking place in the unseen realms of magic; remorse was having a serious effect on his mental state.

"They have changed for the better!" fibbed Monk as he stood at the entrance begging the doorman to let them in. All the while the queue of guests arriving behind them was getting longer and more impatient with the delay. Inside the usher was looking nervous; wondering what had happened to the constant flow of guests and hurried to the door.

"Please! Let them in." begged Monk embarrassed by all the fuss. "They have changed for the better," he said even louder while turning round for support from the waiting throng.

"Just allow the other guests to pass by," said the Usher eager to move the crowd along. "Stand over there!" and then signalled to a runner to fetch the King.

The sisters, acting coy, stood to one side hiding resentful expressions with their ornate, lace fans. They were dressed in what, at one time, were beautiful gowns made from the finest of silk, the best that Evermore could produce. Alas, now the gowns fitted too tight, were so old, frayed and in tatters, to match their worn, booted footwear.

Eventually the King himself appeared and stepped attentively outside the door to face the embarrassingly, awkward situation. "Why were there problems with guests arriving?" He said extending his hand to greet Monk. "Ah!" stressed the King as the sisters stepped out of the shadows of the buttress, where they were told to stand. "I understand now," he said worriedly.

The sisters pleaded in unison:

> "Let us in
> Me and my twin
> Have known you
> From a distance.
> We're justified and
> Seek you, now!
> Let us in
> This instant:"

Flattered by the sister's insistence to be included among the good and the great, the King suppressed his better instincts. "Let them in," he bellowed with great charity, while casting a deep frown of uncertainty at the doorman. Monk bowed submissively and assured him that he would look after them. "Beautiful guests are always welcome!" added the King with a warm smile and gracious demeanour.

The sisters, still hiding their faces behind their fans, giggled softly at the flattery as they both daintily stepped over the threshold into the castle. The King responded by sweeping his arm down as a gesture of welcome and the band continued to play.

Even more promising for the sisters as they listened to the beautiful music from the orchestra, was their instant recall of wonderful past times when they would visit the 'big house' - to play with the young prince - on a regular basis. The chandeliers; the carpet of gold; the grand, central staircase sweeping up to dizzy heights; was just as they remembered.

They recalled the lengthy corridors, giving access to many rooms of different décor; that forever held there mystery. Of course all this was many years ago when they were firm friends with the royal household.

Merva and Derva looked around excitedly, searching out the many faces before them. In the ball room, they were expecting to see the young prince dancing a reel.

"Ah!" said the King noticing their interest for fond memories of past events. "The Prince has had to go away," he stated instinctively.

Monk sighed with a look of relief at this statement. At the same time felt uncomfortable, recalling the moment of the sisters last and final visit when they had terrified their young host.

Undeterred the two swept down the marble steps onto the ballroom floor, completely ignoring the usher tapping on the stone, about to introduce them. "Merva, Derva and the brother – Monk," he stated in a laudible voice.

As the sisters eagerly mingled with the guests, objectionable coughing and gasps of discomfort from behind hand held masks, spread through out the crowd. Comments of: "How uncouth! Look at their clothes? Disgusting! They are witches!" were whispered softly amongst each other, whilst displaying contemptible grins of false greetings.

Monk distanced himself and began to make his way through the crowded hall of guests, leaving the sisters to continue to mingle whilst ingratiating themselves on any who would give them the slightest bit of attention. Even joining in and dancing the occasional reel with young men, who treated them as a figure of fun.

As the evening wore on everything seemed settled. The sisters were happy – at Monk's last check - even Ankra had discarded his inhibitions as he too seemed to find them 'friendly'. The time spent in their company seemed gently amusing. Alas! Ankra was now – without realising – held under their spell.

Monk distanced himself again and made his way toward Brimen, Gannon and Olan who were now standing with Culjern and other highly esteemed persons, all displaying medals on their chests. Obviously grieved by Gannon and Olan's medal being exactly the same as his, Brimen would now be expecting something special from his friends.

As Monk got closer to the group, all he could hear was Brimen giving voice to the idea of receiving a higher honour; to be expected at a later date from the Elders in Oak Village. The remainder of the group began to shuffle about, suddenly feeling uncomfortable by it all and found an excuse to move away leaving Brimen, Gannon and Olan standing on their own.

"Where did that idea come from?" whispered Monk into Olan's ear. Just then Eva and May pulled Brimen and Gannon away to dance. Daisey had to wait for Olan while Monk was awaiting answers, causing a look of horror on the Oakman's face, almost a look of guilty secrets. "Olan?" questioned Monk, noticing his reddened face.

Fortunately for Olan, he did not have to confess any secrets of the statue. Coming to his rescue at this crucial time was a deeply concerned, Tono. He began tugging vigorously at Monk's habit. "Where has Ankra disappeared too?" he said. "Where have the sisters taken him?"

"Taken him?" alarmed Monk. Who then immediately turned to scan the ballroom in search of the twins; they were nowhere to be seen. Straight away he knew there would be trouble. The last time he saw them; and that wasn't so long ago they were talking and laughing with Ankra. Now, they all had an emergency on their hands.

Without causing too much fuss he enlisted the Elves and Oakmen's help and carried out a discreet search of the many rooms. The searchers soon picked up on the trail when one of the sisters, grubby and thread bare gloves lay on the stone floor, at the foot of a winding, narrow, stone stair.

Alighting the steps, eventually led on to a narrow corridor, along which they found another sign of the sisters whereabouts – a broken fan - laying outside the door of a small closet. As Monk bent down to pick it up he saw a light underneath the door and remembered that this was the same spot where the young prince had been terrified by Merva and Derva, all those years ago. He peered through the keyhole but could see nothing. "It's locked!" he whispered, as he gently twisted the handle.

With his ear placed gently against the door, Monk could hear muffled cries of - help! Still, not absolutely sure of why or what the sisters where doing, he signalled to the Oakmen to be careful when they entered the room. He was just about to grip the door handle, intending to barge open the door, when the king and his bodyguards caught up with them demanding to tell them what was going on.

Monk didn't get the chance to explain. He had lost control of the situation and watched as the kings men immediately battered down the door – with axes! What they all saw when they entered the stuffy little room was Ankra, tied to a chair restrained by yellow kord. His mouth heavily gagged with tape stuck tight across his face. His eyes were red and strained, almost popping out of his head.

Every time he tried to yell out for help the vein on his temple threatened to burst. Derva had his head held tight between her hands while Merva dangled his monocle swinging it too and fro across his face attempting to hypnotise him.

On being caught in the act of dark secrets the sisters screamed and screamed as Monk instantly condemned them. "What are you trying to do?" he yelled rushing forward spouting an angry tirade of abuse. Without any thought of kindness to the victim he ripped the tape from Ankra's face. It was so fierce it took most of his moustache away with it. "You are a stupid, Pair!" he shouted. "When will you learn to leave people alone?"

"But, you said you wanted..," screeched the sobbing sisters throwing themselves at him, holding on tightly to their brother for protection.

"Shut up! Shut up!" seethed Monk, forcefully pushing them to the floor to silence their ranting accusation. The King's bodyguard overpowered and grabbed hold of the hysterical pair just as the King rushed in to the closet to take command. "Get them out!" He roared as disturbing memories of the Princes ordeal came back to him. "Get them out of here!" he yelled with little tolerance for their disturbed behaviour.

While Ankra - still held tight by the yellow kord - was crying out in pain and feeling the agony for his lost moustache, Brimen rushed across to free the stricken victim. "Get them out! Get them out!" The king continued to bellow.

The Kings men were now finding it extremely difficult to remove the sisters as they held on tenaciously to any fixed object that they could reach out to. Visciously they kicked; punched; spat; riggled and screeched resistance.

Finally, Merva and Derva were restrained. The pair now held by the yellow kord that had held Ankra tightly in his chair. The sisters were then dragged roughly out of the closet still ranting and raving, spitting words of venom into the face of their captives.

The pair continued their hopeless struggle all the way down the stairs; across the ballroom floor – in front of all the shocked guests. They were then pulled ruthlessly up the marble steps, past the frightened usher, till they came to the doorman who was then ordered to open the port cullis.

The mechanism of the chains responded to the emergency and rattled at an alarming speed. The huge double doors opened and the drawbridge lowered. It sent the rushing wind and rain - of the active storm outside - howling into the opened castle.

An immediate crack of thunder, followed by the immediate bolt of lightening, struck the iron door studs and the sisters were rejected; thrown out into the pervading storm.

Unrepentent! They picked up their rain soaked bodies from the saturated floor then cursed and spat a warning to all:

> "You'll rue the day
> You turn us away,
> We won't let you forget it.
> For we have ways
> To make you pay,
> Inside your heads
> We will target."

As the spiteful words echoed in the Kings ears, he countered the curse with contempt pointing threateningly at them. "Do not come near here again." The chains reversed their course of action and the port cullis lowered 'humming' a sweeter tune of security. The huge, heavy, oak doors firmly come together; closing with a thud of finality.

Chapter 2

Seeking a Victim

After the celebrations at the castle the Oakmen took a well earned rest with their loved ones. It would be some days when the Oakmen returned to the Lodge and duty.

Brimen awoke from his slumbers occupied in his mind with Ankras cruel treatment by the sisters and their subsequent treatment that they endured by the Kings men. Although it was days ago and the curse not aimed at Oakmen it still had a chilling effect, feeling its way through Brimens fears leading on to Owls remark of some weeks before; 'what is about to come your way'.

As far as Monk was concerned D'rasnah and his band of Ner-do-Wells were all successfully chased and banished to the dry, arid land of Drone. "They will never return!" he predicted. He was often heard to boast, on more than one occasion. "There would be no hiding place for goblins in Evermore."

But that was because most of them were now in chains incarcerated in the prison with the renegade Gnomes, put there by Wolverine with the help of Hog - the wildest of Boars - in a relentless task to hunt them down. Of course, they never captured any of the leaders; this meant that D'rasnah and his gang had all escaped from the marsh and were hiding out where nobody could fathom.

So! As usual Brimen's mind would wander into familiar territory as he lay there and soon floundered on the idea of his statue. "Mmm?" he thought after working out some incredible designs in his imagination. "Yet, perhaps we should service the carts and check on our tools first?" he pondered.

His reverie was then taken up again with; "What did happen to D'rasnah?" At first he considered several other options, but none of them made any sense. He then began to worry about rumours of some goblins appearing in several different places over the past two weeks.

'Mmmmm? If that is so then he must still be hiding in Darkwood, possibly they still have access to the dungeons of the Citadel?'

He gave this possibility one moment's deeper thought then realised. 'I must get in touch with Ffelin; if any one would know, it should be him?' Brimen then fell into a Melancholy mood in expectation of the expected terrible winter forecast ahead. "Ah! We will sort it all out, in the spring," he thought and turned over for more sleep.

His extended 'Nap' soon ended as daylight crept into the room through the gaps, defying the heavy drape curtains. Brimen lay there listening to the rhythm of the ticking clock realising that he should make the effort to get up. "Oh! I thought it was earlier than that?" he groaned. First one leg moved then the other and he sat up thinking of Eva, recounting the wonderful evening he had at the castle collecting his medal.

Opening the window he breathed in the fresh woodland air – his usual early morning

Exercise of the day - looking over the tops at the miles of Oak trees, prompted the need in him to find that missing golden acorn. "Mmm! But it looks like rain is on its way."

Even more evident to the Oakman was how late in autumn it now was, stark and dreary with very little sunshine. Some smaller trees had stood bare for some weeks, earlier than normal due to icy cold blasts from the north wind bringing with it ravaging hail storms followed by the heavy rain falls. Daylight hours would soon get less with the encroaching winter bringing long periods of darkness.

The abundance of acorns, holly berries, cotoneaster, early August fogs, rings around the moon, the early arrival of Snowy Owl, were all seasonal signs of a hard, bitter, winter, for the months that lay ahead.

Meanwhile, Gannon and Olan promptly arrived at the lodge tapping excitedly on the door, taking Brimen's attention away from his thoughts. They were bursting with energy feeling renewed and 'raring' to go after the refreshing break with their loved ones and still feeling good from that wonderful evening over the celebrations given in their honour. They bought with them their medals, to be put with the other trophies in the glass display cabinet. Brimen's of course, was already placed on the top shelf, in the center, at the front.

Whilst they breakfasted the three of them were going over the events of the previous months and the eventful conclusion at the castle. All of this led in turn to the growing rumours of D'rasnah's survival and the missing golden acorn:

"We are going to have to find this gold?" said Brimen. "Owl is not going to let this matter rest!"

"Where do we start?" said Olan pausing. "It could be anywhere?"

"I was thinking about that this morning – we need to ask Ffelin!" said Brimen. "They may well be hidden somewhere in that tower."

"Then, let's ask Merva and Derva. They might have an idea where he hid them?"

"Mmm! Can we be sure they would tell us the right place?" said Brimen. He turned to Gannon smiling. "Unless you fancy going into the dungeons again?" then laughed at his mischief. "WHY! You might even get another medal," he added sarcastically.

Gannon took the remark seriously. "If I knew for sure, that, that is where the gold was - then I would!" he replied, willing to accept the challenge.

"Yes! Well, it was only an idea!" grumped Brimen getting up to check on the weather. "ROONEY!" he shouted. "Go and tell Ffelin we want to speak with him!"

"Should we be asking Ffelin to get involved?" said Olan.

"Why not ask him?" replied Brimen anticipating another row about to develop.

"Big Oak should remain as secret. You can't trust Ffelin not to be inquisitive?"

Reluctantly, Brimen had to agree. "You are right! Perhaps there is another way; we need someone who knows nothing about gold?"

"I'll ask Rat," said Gannon. "He won't ask questions and can move around anywhere without being suspect. He will bring it out for us: If, it is in there?"

"He won't know what to look for!" said Brimen dismissively.

"Once we tell him what it looks like and that he cannot eat it, things should be alright" said Gannon.

This seemed a reasonable idea and Brimen immediately shouted again to Rooney. "Forget Ffelin! Tell Rat to meet Gannon in an hour, at the stormwater drain."

Gannon made preperations and set off alone, waiting for Rat as arranged - at the drain. This was the same place they had escaped from when they rescued Culjern some months before. Soon, Rat was squeezing through the grill with two others.

"We've searched everywhere!" he said breathlessly.

"What about the 'torture' chamber?" pressed Gannon.

"Nothing is left in there. It's still a burnt out wreck."

"Did you search every room?

"All, but the room Merva and Derva used to stay in."

"Why?"

"Because Ersatz was angry and thrashed us out! He sets traps and keeps it spotlessly clean, hoping that the sisters will eventually return to him."

"Is there any sign of D'rasnah?"

"We've not seen him or his goblins since the trouble in the marsh!"

"Are you sure?"

"Where ever D'rasnah is, he is not with Ersatz. Ffelin would see to that."

"Rat, take me back in there?" demanded Gannon.

"What now?" he said shocked at the idea. "I., ER! We; have just taken a thrashing from that madman. If he sees us again - so soon - he will set more traps everywhere."

"Oooh, we can't risk that," said his friends, getting nervous and ranting. "We need to come and go and scavenge freely."

"If you don't help me – NOW," stressed Gannon. "Then I will make sure that you and your friends cannot scavenge inside the Castle walls." Rat now had to re-think his motives again. "After all!" said Gannon. "There are far richer pickings in the Kings residence." Rat's gnawing teeth vibrated at the decision he now had to make and he weakened his resolve. "I can take you there!" he said submissively. "But, we must be quick the water level is rising!"

They splashed there way through the pipe eventually getting into a narrow gap between the walls – this was an escape route built in when Culjern occupied the tower. Ersatz never knew of it and it had stayed concealed.

Just like before; at some point Gannon would have to negotiate the long, dark corridors, creaking stairs and niches. Fortunately, there

15

were no goblins around to worry about, even more pleasing - mouse and his friends were rushing past them, off to the kitchen larders reporting that Ersatz, Ffelin and some others had just left the tower.

Back at the lodge, Brimen was striding backwards and forward across the floorboards waiting anxiously on Gannon's return. His ears, getting redder and redder, with each forceful step he took. Every now and then he would peer out of the porch window at the heavy rain falling from the darkened sky; expecting to see him bounding up the steps at any moment.

"Someone should have gone with him." he groaned. "It's getting late. He should be back by now?"

"Oh! He will be alright," replied Olan. "He can look after himself!" Rooney came into the room to light the fire. "Give him a bit more time," he said. "He'll show soon."

"I should not have let him go on his own," worried Brimen. "It is far to Dangerous a mission," he emphasised. "After all it was just a sudden decision that the gold may be in that Tower." A short while later he said to Olan; rather unfairly. "Why didn't YOU volunteer to go with him?"

"You'll think different if he succeeds!" replied Olan, ignoring Brimens provocation. "Then again, if he has not arrived back here soon, we must remember how D'rasnah held Smithy captive and do something about it?"

This idea of Gannon ending up as a prisoner shocked Brimen into immediate action. "ROONEY!" he shouted opening the scullery door. "Go and find Smithy, Rigg, Stretch, Lobe and Tiny. Tell them to report back here!"

"What now?" was the unco-operative answer. "I can't go out in this horrendous weather, its lashing down: Can't it wait?"

"NO! It can't wait!" said Brimen. "In fact, tell them where Gannon has gone and that they need to look out for him." Rooney was furious. He had hardly rested all day due to the Oakman's demands on his time and now this. He wasn't even getting time to enjoy the afternoon tea that Prims had just made and started to huff and clatter around.

"And don't.... slam the door!" said Brimen.., waiting, then hearing it 'Bang and rattle' against its door frame with the force of an angry exit. Rooney lifted his collar against the wind and driving rain and raced down the steps, speeding hastily into the village making for the forge where the smelters were still working.

A little later Rooney returned, soaking wet and exhausted with bad news. "Smithy and his men can't make it. They have been chasing goblins who had been caught stealing tools from his workshop." "Goblins?" questioned Brimen. "Stealing?" he said alarmed. "Did he catch them?"

"No, they managed to escape," said Rooney. "Smithy said – they just disappeared."

"What can they do with 'forge' tools?" said Olan totally perplexed.

"It doesn't make any sense; only that D'rasnah is hiding out somewhere in Evermore and that means we have got to find him." said Brimen. "Now, Rooney go and tell Fisty, knuckle and Bone what has happened: He's to get as many others as he can to search!"

"But I'm soaking...,"

"Take no notice of that," snapped Brimen dismissing the plea. "Olan, its getting late we need to find what has happened to Gannon," he said on hearing the door slam on Rooney's exit. "Bring the oil lamps we will meet Smarty and Smug along the way."

Events had now turned into, a long, cold, wet night of useless searching with no clue as to where Gannon could be. No one in the wood was available to ask, they were all sheltering in their, lairs, dens, setts, burrows, roosts and dreys. In the early hours of the new morning they returned to the lodge.

Exhausted with fears of Gannon being captured by D'rasnah they remained silent. Tired and weary they all sat around longing to get some sleep. It would be daylight soon but they had to decide what action to take next. Rooney and Prims bought in some welcome mugs of tea and scones when there was a polite knock on the door.

To everybody's joy; it was Gannon held up by two not so familiar figures. It was the night fishers that had found him – a small tribe that lived in barges on the water –while they were trawling their nets. Gannon had been rescued about three miles away. He was found wedged between rocks in the river Fastflow on the last bend of the river before it emptied into the huge lake - Oakmere. They bought him back to the Lodge when they returned for the early morning markets.

"I got caught in that raging torrent of storm water," explained Gannon. "It forced me out of the drain and into the river. The more

I tried to swim the harder it got and the weaker I became. I just had to give in and hope for the best. Fastflow had swollen so much that I eventually clung on to driftwood. Then I hit the rocks; wedged tight, exhausted and lost consciousness."

Everyone in the lodge was spellbound at such single minded heroics, Yet even more impressed when Gannon – still soaking wet and tired – said. "But I still held onto this!" Dutifully, he unstrapped from his body a weighty sack and dropped it on the floor. Out, rolled the golden Acorns:

"We've done it? We've done it!" screamed a hysterical Brimen. "At last, at last we can be free from Owl's insinuations. He stooped down to pick them up and started to polish the glistening gold. "This will make them change their mind about the statue!" he added gleefully. "We can now........"

"WE!" shouted Olan. "Gannon did this all on his own," he said supportively. "We did not take any part in this." Gannon was too modest to want exceptional praise and moved nearer the fire as Prims arrived with warm dry clothes.

"Yes… Well..! But I did come up with the idea?" skulked Brimen. Everyone was now feeling exceptionally pleased to have Gannon back safe and sound. Slowly they all dispersed, deciding on getting some well earned sleep.

Although nothing remotely had stirred in Evermore since the victory gained in the marsh there was still a lingering, uneasy peace for most of the little folk; now they had a prison to contend with the like and size of which, they never had to consider before.

As expected Monk was harsh and had brutally punished his sisters for their terrible behaviour at the castle and made them retract their curse; with apologies to the king.

To distance himself even further from their ongoing antics, he made plans to house them in a deserted log cabin that once belonged to a loner called 'Herbage' who was an Alchemist that now worked in the marsh on secrets for Monk.

This lonely hut was situated in an isolated place among a dense forest of Elder. It was covered in moss and lichen, reflecting as bright and green as the many shades of an emerald. This area was once reported to have supported the covens of Ersatz's mother.

From this base the two sisters were given the task of tracking Lurker. Unfortunately this soon became an obsession as it had them forever wandering about Evermore, tormenting and worrying their neighbours. Sometimes they ventured as far as the castle, to remind those who had rejected them, of their curse.

A fine mixture of snow and sleet was falling to the ground as Monk came to collect the sisters on his way to the prison. He knew he would have to move fast before the real bad weather set in and hoped to enlist their help to wheedle out information as to the missing D'rasnah and his elusive leaders. Recently he had learned that one of the captured Sneaks was willing to tell all.

"What shall we do to the Gnome?" pestered Merva and Derva as they raced toward the prison with their brother.

"YOU; won't 'DO' anything!" he stated. "Just scare him a little."

"Can we take one of the Goblins back with us?" begged Merva.

"To our hut, for our friend?" joined in Derva.

"NO!" shouted Monk. "Now shut up!" They both reeled back tearful and fearful from the blast of his words. Whenever Monk raised his voice it scared them.

"But, what will you do with them?" asked Merva insistently braving his wrath.   Monk determined to ignore the questions from the manic pair and the continuing pettiness that followed.

On arrival at the prison Monk thumped determinedly on the iron door with his clenched fist. One of the trolls, who guarded the place, opened the door. On entering this dismal place, the two sisters went eagerly into verse:

> "They have no rights
> Yet still want to fight,
> Let's put them under a spell.
> Then send them to Drone
> To our cousin the Crone;
> She will make them say
> And then make them pay
> Or drown them in a deep well
> But they're all alone?
> So, she'll set them firmly in stone.

"Now, stop it! The pair of you," fumed Monk. "I will decide what to do with them! NOT either of you!" He became adamant in the task ahead. "Your job is to get information," he stated. "We need to know where D'rasnah is NOW hiding!"

The prison was housed beneath the castle walls set in a natural cleft in the rock, a long, cavernous gap that held only a little natural light, coming down from a vertical shaft. The rest of the cave was lit by flame torches. Another of the Trolls, who guarded the place, opened the inner iron door.

The chained up victims, squatting in the damp stench of the enclosed space, excited the sister's passion for suffering. Immediately, Merva reached out to grab and hold onto a frightened, snivelling, little goblin while Derva began searching out a victim of her own to torment.

"Stop it!" raged Monk at the sister's rapacious appetite for suffering. "That is not what we have come here for!" He then forcefully; pulled both of them away from the victims they had chosen. This caused them to harbour resentment for a time at the constant bullying and become sulkily quiet.

"Ask only for information as to the whereabouts of D'rasnah," insisted Monk to his sisters, expecting his simple request to be obeyed.

For a while the three continued to move quietly among the prisoners searching for the Gnome that wants to tell. The sisters carried with them an evil 'air' - an expression of 'execution' menace muttering softly into each vulnerable ear. Its effect created a cold, cold, chill and panic in the breast of each victim.

Eventually; one of Turncoats Sneaks beckoned to Monk that he was the one that wanted to tell where D'rasnah was hiding. In exchange he bargained for his freedom. Monk took him to one side, amid the jeers and cries of traitor, coming from the other prisoners while listening to his betrayal privately.

Monk's terms for the information he received was that he would only release the Sneak on learning first – where Drasnah is hiding. Then second - with the added reward of freedom - on condition that he tracks down Turncoat and brings him back. The shifty eyed Sneak whispered softly. "I know where he is hiding!" Then thirdly and finally – to carry out a very special task; with an award of gold, that he would tell him about later.

On leaving the prison - having got the agreement - Monk decided to keep the Sneak chained at both hands and feet, forcing him to walk awkwardly between the hooded sisters while he walked on ahead. "Where is your leader, Turncoat?" whined Merva into the Sneaks ear. "Mmmm?" She Pushed back her hood, sneered and started nudging him at every step then thrust her face into his, sighing. "You must tell us!" Then Derva, joined in unison with her sister.

The little Sneak, terrified at their closeness, was held tight; crushed between the two of them. Wriggling free, he fell to his knees begging to be released from the, squeezing, poking and prodding of continual abuse that he was receiving. The piercing blue eyes and lumps on their faces were scary; the jutted chins had sores covered in whiskers. From hawk like noses hung warts dangling on threads of skin, now touching the Sneaks fearful face as she forced him to his feet.

"Merva!" harmonised Derva throwing her hood back too. "If he doesn't talk, let's, heat him up at the cottage." She then whispered softly in the Sneaks ear. "We'll cook you in our pot," then screeched with uncontrolled delight as Merva, spat in his face.

Monk became furious at the sisters constant interference and turned brutally on them. He used his staff to prod and threaten them with. "Lurker may be around, listening!" he warned them. "Now shut up, be quiet! And do as I say," he warned. "Let's return to the grotto, slowly and silently. "There is to be no more interference with our prisoner." He demanded.

The force of Monk's anger always frightened the sisters, even the anticipation of it. They strongly objected to his bullying yet mostly did what they were told. This time they both carried on their differences with him, ranting aloud with another rhyme aimed at their brother's intolerance toward them:

"He'll lose his head
If you allow
The Sneak to have his way
Let him come with us
So that you find trust
In all we do and say."

21

"If you don't shut up!" warned Monk. "I will send you both back to Ersatz." His intolerance was such that he then, again used his staff too hurt them. This time they went into a fearful huddle for comfort, whimpering with suppressed anger while gripping hold of the Sneak. Merva whispered softly into Derva's ear her vengeful plan, aimed at their brother Monk:

"Why, is he so Cruel
To make us the fool
I'll surely make him regret it.
With this pin
I'll sink it in,
To his knees
That'll make him decrepit."

"Shut up! Shut up!" Yelled Monk infuriated with their spiteful ways. He then felt the positive tinge of discomfort in his knee joint. The two screeched with joy watching the painful reaction and Merva wilfully cast another of her spells. At once Monk knew he had encountered the Sisters use of evil incantations.

In Monks darker moments, he too could resort to spells, resulting in hurtful and lasting displeasure to his victims. To negate the attack he garbled a protective verse against the effect of suggestive witchcraft, holding tightly onto his cross until he had finished:

"Mischief, mischief - turn about
Turn their spell inside out
Find the spot, make it tender
Then make it rot
And they surrender"

The result of this verse saw the sister's fall to the ground crying, landing right on top of the terrified Sneak smothering his pathetic cries for help. "That will teach YOU a lesson!" yelled Monk to his troublesome sisters, whilst rubbing his knees to ease the extreme discomfort he had received.

When he had fully recovered he pulled the sneak free growling: "Now, I will teach the both of you another HARD lesson in life."

Without hesitation Monk raised his staff high in the air to chastise the pair raining physical blows down on them. It was then that Owl flew by on his way to collect Sprite. The situation was irksome for Monk. It seemed he couldn't move around freely anymore with out bringing attention to his dark deeds and made rapid moves to disguise his actions.

Owl; was no fool as to what Monk was doing and made the most of his 'ariel' advantage. He circled above several times with much louder hoots of objection to the bullying and using of his sisters then swooped down squaking as only an Eagle Owl could. His orange eyes and fearful expression also showed disapproval as to Monks clandestine operations of removing a prisoner without consultation.

Chapter 3

Brimen gets his Orders

Owl had picked up his passenger Sprite and now began making his way to the lodge feeling niggled over Monks furtive movements at the prison. "He really must tell us what is going on," ranted Owl. "He can't just do what he does without accountability. And; the sisters," he continued to hoot. "Surely he has no right to bully them in that way?"

Sprite, could not answer straight away. The speed of Owl, flapping and dipping wildly about, made her journey uncomfortable and virtually impossible to understand exactly what he was whinging on about. Besides, in her mind, she was more interested in putting to the Oakmen their next move.

Owl's landing on the window ledge was softer this time as there was nothing to obstruct his descent; the window latch was firmly secured. His passenger, Sprite was only too pleased to have arrived safely after such an angry and erratic flight and she was sure that this would remain the first and the last time that she ever accepted a lift.

Normally her visit to the Oakmen would be formal, with her entourage. But this journey was an urgent and sudden decision to arrive earlier than planned.

Owl was still seething with conflicting thoughts and suspicions as to Monk's motives with the removal of a prisoner. He added to his own misery by becoming extremely intolerant. In particular to find that there was nobody waiting to let them in.

"Where are they?" hooted Owl to Sprite while tapping the glass franticly with his beak. "Stay here!" he commanded her. Vexed, Owl flew round to the scullery window to get Rooney's attention.

"I don't think they are awake yet!" answered Rooney responding tactfully to the urgency. "I've called them twice but they had a rainsoaked eve..,"

"Let us in!" demanded Owl. "We'll get them out of bed!" Owl swiftly returned to Sprite, anxiously waiting until Rooney opened the window.

Niggled, he entered the lodge landing on the clock. Suddenly the inside door of the parlour opened and in came the Oakmen, wearily dragging their feet.

"Alright, alright," said Brimen sneezing. "Don't panic, we're here!" Following close behind were Gannon and Olan. They all gave a hearty yawn as they stumbled in together, expecting their morning toast and tea to be ready. Owl hooted long and low, disapproving at the Oakmens casual attitude.

"I'll have orange marmalade today!" said Brimen to Rooney, ignoring Owl and not fully aware that he had bought 'special' company with him.

"Make that two!" said Gannon, rubbing his tired eyes and yawning; struggling to wake up after his hectic ordeal of the day before. He too sneezed several times.

"I'll have the strawberry jam?" said Olan, scratching his stomach, while yawning then pulling out a chair to sit down. The three of them sat wearily at the table, with their heads in their hands.

"It's not good enough!" chastised Owl from his perch. "It is now late in the afternoon and you three have just got out of bed. - Why are WE kept waiting?"

As soon as Brimen, Gannon and Olan heard the word 'WE' it jolted them back to the now! Realising that Owl was not alone they concluded that Sprite must be present. As soon as she made an appearance she hovered over them to speak, causing them to quickly change their off hand manner to grovelling politeness. It didn't fool her, she became alarmed at the lethargy; stern and hardened in her reaction.

"Brimen!" she said firmly. "You are spending too much time on your own interests."

"It's not that; I wasn't expecting you to arrive with Owl," he answered floundering trying hard to find his composure.

"Since you received awards from the king, you have been lax in your duty to protect Evermore," she said. "Do all three of you think that there is nothing more to do?"

"Well, ER! No! I.., but last night..,"

"I should not have to remind you that your duty is to keep Evermore a safe and secure place," she stated even more determinedly. "Not, to lay sleepily in bed - idling precious time away."

"But, we had a very late night!" answered Brimen defending his actions.

"You were talking all night, about your statue - I suppose?"

"Statue?" he said surprised at her awareness. "We had to go searching.…." He halted, shocked! 'How did she find out about the statue?'

"Listen to me! There are still great threats from Ersatz and the goblin D'rasnah..,"

"Seriously!" pleaded Brimen. "We have not been wasting our time," he stated indignently. "We have retrieved the golden acorns that were missing; Er! Or rather Gannon retrieved them," he added proudly correcting himself out of consideration for the Oakmans ordeal. "He got them early this morning."

"That is wonderful news!" said an elated Sprite.

"Yes! Well! It's not before time?" hooted Owl sounding peeved over the success.

"What it does show is, that we have not been wasting time," pleaded Brimen.

"So where is it?" snapped Owl.

"In the vaults!" said Brimen.

"I must examine it immediately?"

"Not now," said Sprite intervening between the two. We can trust that it is safe; so it can wait." She glanced across at Owl who had been constantly criticising the Oakmen for laziness, realising that there was more a hint of jealousy with him over the Kings recognition in awarding medals.

Owl hooted with a further show of pique ".…and the statue?" he questioned.

"But, the Elders..," blurted Brimen. "They have..,"

"BRIMEN!" said Sprite firmly, much to Owls pleasure who was now hooting with delight. "YOU must listen to what I say." She stopped briefly to observe Gannon and Olan, who were showing a more receptive attitude. "Since that memorable victory in the marsh, YOU, more than anyone has fallen behind with your commitment and work." She continued. "It is up to all of you to arrest this slide and I want you to spend the winter at Isolate."

"But, we do that every year!" answered Brimen with dismay.

"No! Not just for two weeks – you have some valuable time to catch up on?"

"We had already decided on that, at some time later – ask Monk?"

"I mean with immediate effect."

"But, I still have so many things to do!"

"There are no buts about it," hooted Owl, stretching out his wings. "Listen, to what you are being told."

The actual benefit of any conclusion - due to no helpful discussion before hand - could never be satisfactorily explained to Brimen. Try as hard as he may - not to think about it - he started to feel cheated. Like the time before when he was encouraged to take Turncoat to the Big Oak against his wishes and the consequent results that followed.

"Of course we intend to go to Isolate - after the winter Solstice," reasoned Brimen indicating Olan and Gannon's inclusion with a nod of his head. "We must celebrate that first - with the village?"

"You can do that at Isolate!" demanded Sprite. "Then, return on the March equinox, not a day before. Is that clear?"

"For that long?" said Brimen shocked at the harsh decision. "Why? – It will leave Oak Village unprotected."

"This coming winter will be long and harsh," countered Owl, hooting a warning with a long low tone. "Nothing much is going to happen."

"But I don't understand!" said Brimen, feeling chastised. "Surely you need us here?"

Some goblins have returned and attacked Smithy at the forge. Didn't you Know?"

"Yes!" said Sprite. "You must stay away because of other events that may occur."

"Events that may occur?" repeated Brimen. "Like what?" he said with disdain.

"Strange events, of a deep and serious nature, that may already be in action."

Brimen turned to face Owl and said. "Is that what you meant when you said the other day – "about to come your way?" Sprite looked a little curious and glared at Owl's petty interference in the scheme of things, who in turn glanced sheepishly away.

"If this is so, then we should know about it?" reasoned Brimen. "Not while you have been so selfishly pre-occupied," said Owl deflecting the attention away from himself. "I am not selfish!" boomed Brimen guiltily. Yet, Gannon and Olan were also feeling the same sense of guilt. They knew things had been neglected and had to admit to dismissing rumours of D'rasnahs return too.

"But Sprite..," Pleaded Brimen as Owl was about to leave. "Who will protect Oak Village while we are away?"

"Oh! Don't start that again!" hooted Owl and out of the window he flew. In no time at all, Owl had circled back for Sprite to say. "Within two days. Be ready to go!"

"But Sprite?" yelled Brimen, thumping the ledge with frustration. "Why, do we have to spend so much time at Isolate?" As they flew further and further away Brimen shouted even louder. "What is going on?" When they at last disappeared from view Brimen, turned away looking sadly at the others, wondering what to do next. "We will never know if they don't tell us," he said, shrugging his shoulders.

"Yes! We know that," said Gannon. "But, it's like Sprite was trying to tell you. There are more important things to consider than a statue. Anyway nothing will happen to Evermore until the thaw."

"I know! I know!" said Brimen. "Don't keep reminding me."

"We will soon find out then what's been going on - when we return," said Olan.

"And that is when we will have to sort it all out," answered Brimen. "HUH! Like we did after Big Oak? – Well, I am not taking Turncoat this time!"

"No, one is asking us to," Said Olan then went on to say with a chuckle. "You had now better cancel the Criers visit." To which Gannon responded with a laugh. "I'm sure he will be sympathetic and understand."

"Stop it the pair of you!" snapped Brimen. "This is not funny! You know he'll arrive any moment soon. Now, that's that and all about it!" he warned.

"You hope he will arrive?" said Olan. "Maybe he has found better things to do?"

"I'm warning you!" said Brimen waiving his fist in Olan's direction. Thankfully, a loud knock came on the door before an argument could ensue, followed by several urgent repartitions. Rooney opened it and let in Brimen's expected visitor.

"I can't stop too long," came a hurried response from the Town Crier as he sped inside, seemingly ready to take off again.

"What do you mean?" said Brimen indignantly; striding forward to greet him.

"Only to tell you..," flustered the Crier. "That, we cannot proceed with the plinth."

"Cannot Proceed..?" Bellowed Brimen, but my sta..,

"Well! No, not just yet!" responded the Crier nervously.

"What do you mean – not just yet?" fretted Brimen feeling let down.

"Er.., I can't stop, we will have to talk about it later!" he said turning around to leave.

"LATER?" Shouted Brimen as the Crier moved hastily for the door.

"Yes! I'll see you next year, when you get back from the mines," sounded the determined yet hesitant reply.

"How do you know I am going to the mines?" shouted Brimen shocked at the Town Criers knowledge of current events.

"Er! Well, yes, I….must go!" was the uncommitted answer. With that said, he darted through the opened door that Rooney still held onto and ran down the stone steps, leaving Brimen open mouthed in a mild state of shock.

"Where did he get the information about Ioslate from?" said Brimen, turning desperately to his friends. "WHO told him such things - so soon?"

"Well, I don't know!" said gannon, scratching his forehead in confusion.

"Never mind!" said Olan sounding sarcastic. "After all, it is only a statue, you are sacrificing." He added. "You can at least polish your medal, every day."

Infuriated, with all the disappointments Brimen did not respond immediately and lapsed into a sulk; predictably pacing up and down, his ears getting redder and redder. This fractious attitude soon got out of control and Brimen returned to his difficult self. "It must have been you?" he said accusingly to Olan.

"ME!" replied Olan stunned at the unfair outburst. "Told Him?" he screeched. "How did you work that one out?"

"You MUST have told him!" said Brimen, content to proportion the blame.

"It's not my fault if you can't get your statue made," said Olan. "Don't sulk about it by blaming me!"

"I'm warning you!" growled Brimen. He held his clenched fist up to Olans face and stormed back across the floor. Olan stared back at him, playfully.

"Now, stop it right there!" shouted Gannon coming between them. "Let's be sensible. NO, fighting, other wise Prims might come in and sort us out!" The two begrudgingly decided not to persue their differences and parted. Only because of the overwhelming thought, feeling and fearing at the wrath of Prims. The aggressive image, of a broom held firmly in her hands - made them see sense.

Satisfied that common sense had prevailed and stability returned, at least in the short term, the Oakmen sat down together to organise the long journey to Isolate. The best estimation that they could come up with, in order to meet with Sprite's demand, were at, least twelve carts. Covering two separate locations, working solidly for about, six months. It didn't take them long to work out that they would be expected to bring back an amazing amount of assorted minerals.

Their first stop would be Pewt hill where six carts, Graff and twelve miners would stay under the supervision of Smithy and the Smelters. The rest of the caravan would carry on to the deeper mines at the peaks of Isolate, where Brimen, Gannon and Olan would supervise Grondo and his twelve miners. There, they too would remain for the winter returning the following spring.

"Doesn't Sprite realise the amount of Oakmen and gnomes that will not be around to protect Evermore," said Brimen. "Can we be sure she knows what she is doing?"

"Of course she does!" defended Gannon. "There must be a good reason to this idea."

"Remember, too!" said Olan wagging his finger to make a point. "This is going to be a very sever winter. Nothing is really going to happen until we return," he said wisely.

The inflection in Olan's voice and the pointing finger irritated Brimen. "BAH!" He Grumped. "I'm going off to meet Monk." "Why?" said Olan using his open palms to make an inviting gesture. "Because: I will ask him the best route to take!" "Why? Why not go the way, we always go?" This time Olan raised his shoulders as he made this penetrating enquiry.

"Because; we normally go when the weather is dry, And the day light hours, longer lasting," snapped Brimen. His, tolerance with Olan was teetering on the edge, about to run out. He glanced out of the window noticing another flurry of sleet falling down, took in a deep breath and sighed wearily. "If we are lucky we will get to Isolate before the snow storm starts," he said.

"Supposing that we don't?" was the challenging response. This time Olan had gone too far in his goading of Brimen and the leader lashed out with his fist, just missing Olan's chin.

Gannon, who had found their usual 'Spat' tiresome, had reminded both of them earlier of Primm's own brand of justice in order to maintain discipline. He decided not to get involved as the pair, grunted and wrestled each other to the floor; distancing himself away from the action. Unfortunately, as he moved to get out of the way - in anticipation of Primms entry - he became the first target of her swinging, thrashing broom. In no time at all he sped to safety disappearing down the vault.

The other two escaped punishment because reality took over and they hauled themselves off the floor with lightening reactions making a show of apologising for their bad behaviour, whilst brushing the dust from each others clothes. It gave enough of a hiatus for them to dash down the stairs – following Gannon's escape.

Two days later - as instructed - the Oakmen and Gnomes were about to set off on the long journey to the mines. It was a bitterly cold day for this time of year with more sleet covering the ground. The twelve cart convoy was parked in line, waiting ready to move while the miners stood around in groups talking, swinging their arms and lightly stamping their feet to keep warm.

To see them off on this long sojourn the little folk of Oak village had lined the streets to wish them well and pray for their safe return. The excitement of the day was such, that all the miners became festooned with garland and sprigs of lucky heather, thrown by their enthusiastic admirers.

Although Brimen was enjoying the joyous attention, his mind occasionally wandered over to where the brass band, were assembled. They were situated on the exact spot that he planned to put his statue. His eyes wandered into the crowd assembled nearby, imagining the magnificent site that everybody would see sometime in the future.

Amongst the jostling throng he noticed Merva and Derva, moving furtively among the crowd. Both of them in disguise dressed to look like members of the 'Brotherhood' using Monk's clothing to fool everyone - brown habit with yellow cord tied round their middle. They had pulled the cowls over their heads to disguise their scary faces.

All of the Oakman were quick to spot the pair, only too aware of their bizarre antics when ever the sisters wanted to get close and friendly. Yet! Brimen couldn't escape their attention as he stood alone at the head of the twelve cart caravan for the off.

He just shrugged at the others, resigned to accept the embarrassing adulation in front of the whole village. It would become quiet a shock when the sisters eventually reached their target.

As the two got closer, Brimen didn't detect the sisters usual over enthusiasm. Instead they had become quiet subdued; a more serious side was evident. They pulled back the cowls to display their long white hair flowing freely on the breeze - now free of bird's skulls. In a tone of trepidation they recited:

> "In between
> And underneath
> D'rasnah's kind
> Bring the teeth
> Skelt will return
> And sink them in
> Reynard's red
> And useless skin."

"What do you Mean?" said Brimen perplexed and fearful on hearing the Skelt hound mentioned. He had encountered this ferocious beast before.

"Drasnah never left Evermore," whispered Merva. Her voice was hissing, with saliva dripping, as she got close to Brimens ear. Merva continued whispering. "He is hiding out in the disused flint mine; Do not go that way!" Brimen turned his face to wipe his ear dry. "Do NOT go that way!" she said again with trepidation sounding in her voice.

"No! You are wrong," snapped Brimen. "D'rasnah was banished to Drone."

"But, he has returned!" persuaded Merva. "Returned - too cause havoc!"

"No! He can't come back," insisted Brimen. "We won't tolerate him!"

"Isolate is a long way from the Oakwood and the marsh," joined in Derva, her eyes widening at the threat of great danger. "He and the others will come out of hiding and attack you before you get there."

"Then there are enough of us to deal with him," said Brimen bravely.

"NO! You must not. It is far too dangerous. He has a new plan."

"What new plan?" raged Brimen. At this point Gannon and Olan had become alarmed at Brimen's reactions and moved swiftly to the front to find out what was being said. They reached Brimen just at the time when the sisters had finished speaking their warning.

"What did they say?" said Gannon watching the Sisters huddle together. There was no answer. "What did she say?" pressed Olan pulling on Brimen's arm.

"Oh! Some rhyme about D'rasnah and Reynard Fox," said Brimen dismissing the idea and not mentioning the Skelt.

"What about him?" insisted Gannon.

"Let's worry about that on our return," said Brimen.

Just then Smarty and Smug arrived to join them. "Everybody is ready. We need to get moving before the weather worsens," they said. Brimen reached inside his satchel slung over his shoulder and removed a map. "There! That's the route we'll take," said Brimen determinedly. "First, Pewt Hill then; that way to Isolate," he said pushing his finger across the unrolled parchment.

"Why change the route now?" said Gannon trying to avert the sisters loving gaze.

"That's the long way round," joined in Olan. "Why not go past the, Flint mines?"

"No, no, no," worried Brimen more preoccupied with what Merva and Derva had just said. "We need to take the easier route," he said not wanting to alarm them.

"But Monk said it was the shortest route to Isolate?" queeried Olan.

"I know! I know! But, we can't trust him."

"Why? Is it something of what the sisters told you?" demanded Gannnon.

Brimen took in a deep breath. "Alright!" he decided. "They are saying that D'rasnah is hiding in the flint mines," confirmed Brimen. "He is waiting to attack us there."

"Can we trust THEM?" said Gannon watching the sisters eagerly nodding, yes!

In the middle of the square, the town Crier was coming to the end of his long enthusiastic speech praising the Oakmens resolve to put all things right. He then rang his bell continuously before the band started up amid cheers of support for the cavalcade of miners about to set off on their long journey.

The sisters looked adoringly at Gannon then broke into verse with a smile:

"We leave you now
Just take care
When you return
We'll still be here."

Brimen, found it easier to dismiss any idea of a return of the Skelt hound and felt safer with making a sudden decision to avoid the flint mines. He left the village with the increasing wind and sleet making the start of the journey difficult. With a confident stride he bellowed the command. "Jib up! And pull! Jib up! And pull!"

Although it would be a long haul to the mines at least there would be no Turncoat and his shifty ways to worry about. Unbeknown to the Oakmen, he was a cause of considerable concern somewhere else.

At the same time as the caravan of miners left the village and faded into the distance. Ersatz was eschewing his guilt over Taz's betrayal and purging his ranks of suspected traitors.

Chapter 4

Ersatz Takes a Head

It was Ffelin; Ersatz's favourite dwarf who had informed him of Taz's intended treachery with his ally D'rasnah. Swift to respond Ersatz swore revenge and carried out his own brand of justice in front of his warlords. He was both the judge and jury on the day he confronted Taz, serving the ultimate punishment on him for blood brother betrayal – execution by his own hand.

This horrendous betrayal was the second blow in succession to fall on Ersatz, after he had heard about Merva and Derva's escape, made worse by Culjerns flight to freedom.

Yet! He was bolstered by his favourite Dwarf's loyalty and reckoned this to be a good omen for the coming months ahead.

Not such a good omen was the effect of spectral hauntings and wild imaginings taking place in Ersatz's discordant mind. Since Merva and Derva had left him, this once mighty Neanderthal had become more subdued. Even the phantom – that other part of him that would haunt the wood on moon lit nights - could not be raised. It was almost as if the sisters had taken his powers and forgotten he ever existed.

Dwelling alone in the Citadel was an anathema to Ersatz, who now sat sulking in the skull room, going over and over in his mind spells to get the sisters back. He lit candles to throw shadows on the wall: He burnt incense to please the after-world: He scratched the skulls to awaken ancient knowledge: He rediscovered and practised even darker magic from his deceased mother's almanac - a book still being used in the faraway Covens of Drone. Absolutely nothing seemed to work in his favour.

After all of his endeavours to find a solution, Ersatz fell into a deep sleep lasting for several hours. He was awoken only by the prescence of two shadowy figures and voices whispering. As he opened his eyes the pair turned to look at him and they just as soon vanished. It was just long enough for him to identify his mother and Taz, communicating in a bizarre way. Ersatz was finally convinced that his mother began speaking to him in rhyme. He was sure that it was her voice resonating in his head, advising him of the way forward. At this particular time he was almost certain he could again see her clearly standing in front of him:

"Halt your anger,
Don't go too far,
I am the Mother
Of all your - scars.
The Skull that falls
Will not forgive,
Now that you refused
To let it live."

It wasn't until Ersatz had considered the verse - referring to the beheading of Taz - that he responded to the working out and solving of his nightmarish darkness. The verse had informed him that he had made a mistake in executing his blood brother. To add to this misery, Ersatz could hear and feel the chilling presence of Taz standing near him, as the rhyme might have suggested.

Over the next few days; Ersatz's desperate attempts to deny his violent action and thus interpret the message to his advantage provoked his anger to reckless proportions. It was compounded with the shocking realisation, when news had finally reached him of D'rasnah's failed attempt in the Marsh and the goblins disappearance from Evermore. He was furious and could not contain his rage. Ersatz needed to bolster his deflated ego after dealing with the treacherous Taz and decided he now needed full support from his warlords. He called for a war council to declare his undisputed leadership.

High up in his tower, Ersatz was in a dominating mood impatiently striding across the floor of his stronghold, demanding total loyalty from his warlords. Anxiously he stepped through the arch leading out onto the veranda and leant heavily on the stone balustrade. Grasping it tightly with his huge hands and breathing deeply he let out a long lingering growl of frustration as below in the distance, he watched six riders, in pairs, making their way to the castle. At the head, holding the kings flag proudly was Culjern.

"Once, he was MY prisoner," he seethed. "Now, I have to pretend to be allied to their cause." Feeling the presence and superiority of a much stronger force obstructing him he looked out intently across the vast expanse of woodlands, stretching up to and beyond the King's formidable castle standing proud on high ground. "I will show that King, who has the most power. Culjern will carry MY banner then!"

Meanwhile, Ersatz still occupied Culjerns fortress pretending to work towards a peaceful settlement with the King - Even subjecting his-self under Culjerns command. He had also offered to enlist one of his warlords to support the king's army based in the South where they were constructing Culjerns new castle, too secure that larger region. His brother Miljern would also extend his own influence to another castle in the North.

With disappointment beating heavy in his heart Ersatz continued to growl into the rushing wind. "I was promised success!" He moaned. His grip tightened on the stone, wearing it away. "D'rasnah, was going to get me the gold; he told me that his way was best," he howled with frustration.

Tangsa, his new right hand man, was standing alongside trying to pacify him:

"D'rasnah, will return," he uttered assuredly. "He hasn't yet finished his quest to take over the little folk's world!" Ersatz wasn't listening and turned sombrely away. He re-entered the room shaking his head saying. "Even Merva and Derva will never return."

"D'rasnah, will have to return!" said Tansga again. "If not, send Ffelin to get him." Yet Ersatz was still not listening to reason and turned away. Frustrated by his reversal of fortune Ersatz just could not let go of his resentment. It was as if everybody else had an answer, yet he could not work out the facts for himself.

Instead, he instinctively and furiously grabbed hold of the dwarf that was carrying a barrel of wine into the room and sent him sprawling. "Where's that little wretch?" he growled kicking and pummelling the little man to the floor. At that moment, the deformed jester - that entertained when guests were summoned - excitedly intervened with a cruel boast. Dancing and tumbling with an air of annoying conceit he landed on Ersatz's shoulder:

"Puzzle, puzzle,
All you like.
I know the answer
Too D'rasnah's, spite.

Ersatz fumed at the jester's Rhyme. "He never did show me the golden acorns!" and then pushed the deformity to the floor stamping on him with the heel of his hefty boot. "Now, D'rasnah has made off with them," he growled and continued kicking the defenceless fool. "….and keeps them for himself!" He ranted on as he watched the jester crawl away hurt and sobbing.

Ersatz looked around the crowded room, for someone else to blame. "Those magical, golden acorns," he lamented appealing to his followers. "Now they are lost forever!" His challenging stare searched out a weakness among the warlords; perhaps a hidden sympathiser of Taz may still be lurking? His glare only found a united wall of resistence. All stood in defiance with hands placed firmly on sword hilts. Ersatz turned away and filled a goblet from the keg of wine, while signalling to Ffelin to place more barrels around the room. "I nearly had them in my hands," he persuaded his guests while grasping the air in a lightened mood.

"We will get the gold again!" said Tansga appealing to the warlords to ease the tension. "Spread out the food, Let's eat!" Into the room came dancing maidens and musicians and soon the whole room erupted into merriment and accompanying games, with the dwarves bringing in more food and wine at a constant flow.

The Warlords were never really sure of whom Ersatz was talking about when ever he mentioned D'rasnah. They could never grasp why he depended on these 'Little folk' to get him what he wanted. They had often heard about and knew the folklore of Evermore but had never seen any little folk or had any proof as to their existence. Their only way – in any situation – was to use direct force and brutality.

They found it easier to agree with Ersatz's random choices, as they did on the night that Ersatz took Taz's head with the victims own sword. At this particular moment they were really only interested in wild abandonment.

As the long night wore on; bawdry entertainment and merriment increased unabated, until suddenly the drunken revelry was halted by an oppressive atmosphere spreading throughout the room. It signalled to the Dwarves, musicians, singers, dancers and Tether – Ersatz's faithful wolfhound, that the night of excess was over. Frightened, they escaped to the safety of another location.

The pervasive atmosphere commanded ultimate attention and everyone was gripped by the effect of someone or something voicing numbers out loud: 'One-Two-Three it sounded then paused leaving a cold lingering draught. Four-Five-Six it continued with a deeper guttural strain. When it finally reached the number twelve the counting stopped with a heavy, sounding sigh of a last exhausting breath.

Everyone that was left in the room knew the significance of the number twelve. It was the amount of cut and thrusts it took to kill Brumma - the ancient warlord – in his last major battle. His skull, hanging on the wall started to groan.

Ersatz's black, sunken eyes searched the stillness of the chilling room for unusual movements. Then just as suddenly the oppression lifted and the room quickly warmed to a comforting passive state. It was then that something else took Ersatzs attention. It had moved so fast that at first it was difficult to focus on. Nobody else had noticed and after a time the warlords returned to heavy drinking and reverie, dismissive of what they did not understand.

It was just a glimpse but Ersatz definitely saw the movement. The space around him went immediately cold and deathly silent, but did not disturb the revellers. Suddenly the shimmering image of Taz broke through and taunted him. It was laughing, scorning; mouthing words without sound. Touching him, yet! he didn't feel the contact. Ersatz was transfixed, then it was gone and the excitement of the room returned to his ears.

The Jester, with his uncanny gift of knowing sensed this other presence when others couldn't. He limped back across the room resentful with the beating he took earlier. Shrieking a warning into the vulnerable ear of Ersatz:

"Taz is here
He won't go back
He's going to
Make sure of that."

Confused and tormented, Ersatz violent streak took control of
what he did not understand and he again hit out at the Jester sending
him flying across the room. He then lashed out with his fists and
kicked the wall panel, the force sent out shock waves knocking off
and destroying the glass case that housed the skull of the ancient
warlord.

The Jester, in agony after landing on his back, painfully crawled
back to Ersatz adding more misery by insisting on being heard
again:

"Not one, but two
Is a big mistake.
And if you won't listen
Then you must take,
The consequences."

As the skull lay on the floor, smashed into pieces, the warning
of Ersatz's mothers rhyme went coursing through his mind. The
effect made him fly into another insane rage, so fierce, that no-one,
had ever witnessed such a force before. He thumped his head against
the wall as he continued to hear, louder and louder in his head, the
repeat of the message; echoing, again and again. 'The skull that falls
will not forgive."

With vengeance weighing heavy in his heart he cursed the skull
of Brumma vowing once again that one day Evermore would all be
his. "Nothing will stop me!" he shouted repeating. "Nothing will stop
me. I don't need this Skull to threaten ME!" he boasted as the wine
increasingly took effect of his emotions.

The disowning of a warlord was unfathomable: Discrediting a
warlord unimaginable: Causing damage to its skull unforgivable.

The warlord Tansga was mortified and darted across the room
- as he had done months before - to rescue the sacred relic that was
held in such high esteem. The other Warlords shrank back in horror.

Even in their drunken state they could not blot out their superstitious beliefs. Tansga was then determined to stop Ersatz going any further; shouting at him. "Enough, is enough! Stop it now!" he then tried to restrain him forcibly. "This is a TERRIBLE omen," he gasped with trepidation.

The tension in the room now turned violent as the warlords; with swords drawn, moved to support Tansga. "We need to rethink our plans," they emphasised halting Ersatz's reckless behaviour. Ersatz fell to the floor and brooded for a while, struggling to dismiss the fragmented skull from his mind and feeling bad over his actions,

Just as suddenly he then sprang to his feet accusing everyone and everything for not doing enough to support him. No matter how much his supporters pleaded with him he became insane, dominating them with murderous intent to look for another victim, somebody who would bear the blame and pay for his failure. "I will have someone else's head for this," he threatened in deep growling undertones.

Turncoat and the Sneak, who had begged for freedom in the prison, were both pushed into the room by a knowing hand while all the madness was going on. Keeping very quiet, fearing that the worst would fall upon them, they hid them-selves from view hoping to seize the moment and escape this ugly scene.

They both moved slowly and quietly toward other door, only to be stopped by a snarling vicious wolfhound when they opened it. It was Tether, on guard for his master.

Far from remaining hidden, the two had bought attention to themselves. "Where is he?" snarled Ersatz, moving across to grab hold of Turncoat's arm. His massive hand gripped tight the skinny throat. "Where is he hiding?" he demanded.

"He's in the L., L., Land of Drone!" stammered the choking gnome.

"Do you mean he is helping Rager?"

"NO! I'm n.,n.,not sure," he stammered. "I think he remains loyal to you!" Ersatz let go of the gnome's throat and turned toward the spooky, shimmering image of Taz that was now taking on a frequent and clearer form.

"I shouldn't have listened to you," seethed Ersatz without doubting its presence. "I created these demons on your advice, and yet! I've still been defeated." Holding his breath with a fury that created more fury within him, he continued to stare and talk at what was, to the others in the room - a blank space. Turning a shade of deepest purple, he started to shake himself violently until he again heard, felt and could see his blood-brother clearer than ever. Tansga was spellbound; thinking he too had caught a glimpse of the murdered Taz and shuddered.

For the first time also, the Warlords could now see these strange little beings that lived in the wood. Transfixed by their existence they delighted in them, arousing jealousy in Ersatz as he shielded them from further inspection.

Taz's spirit, now stood boldly beside Ersatz, whispering soft, encouraging tones in his ear knowing that he could see the warlords but they could not see him.

"Think of it this way," said the voice. "You now have the opportunity to make war, attack the king. Your men could overthrow Culjern. "See! Look at them," he said pointing to the warlords. "They are begging; only waiting for your decision. But who can you trust?" he added casting doubts. "Someone is looking for YOUR head!"

"I've heard all this before," growled Ersatz blocking his ears with his hands, but the spectre carried on his commanding pursuit of evil suggestion.

"Brimen and his little spies have had their time taken up looking for D'rasnah and any survivors that maybe hiding out in the marsh. He can't rest until he has tracked them all down. The gold, it must still be out there, somewhere?" emphasised the spectre with great persausion. "D'rasnah knows where it is - listen to me! These have come to help you." He beckoned for Turncoat and the Sneak to draw closer.

Turncoat, angry at being forced to answer for D'rasnah's failure, was now expected to give a thorough account of events in the marsh. In doing so he wanted to protect him-self and decided to betray D'rasnah in vivid detail, also tell Ersatz the truth about Merva, Derva and the power of the seals.

Smirking at his-own mischievousness, while enjoying playing out his real deceitful self, Turncoat demanded everyone's attention and started to speak slowly as he unravelled the disastrous events. "I have to tell you," said Turncoat stretching up to whisper in Ersatz's ear. "There were two acorns taken from Squirrel, not one." "Two?" said Ersatz puzzled. "So D'rasnah now has three?" he held out his mighty fist and uncurled his blunted fingers one by one - counting.

"No, he had a lot more," sniggered Turncoat. "Some of the gold Brimen took back with him, when they attacked in the night at Hollow oak." He added casually.

"Where's that?" quizzed Ersatz. "He never told me about that place?" Ersatz thumped his mighty fist on the table sensing the deceit of a little man that is now completely out of reach.

"Yes!" blabbed Turncoat. "D'rasnah intended to make his crown first but Smithy was rescued by Gannon." Ersatz looked furious and was sure he caught Taz trying to deflect the gnome from saying more. Unfortunately he raced on to say. "Smithy has the secret of the forge. It is only he that can make the crown of power."

"Crown of power?" floundered Ersatz oblivious to the facts. "WHO, Is Smithy?" he demanded. Glaring wildly at the ghostly image of the blood brother he beheaded, Taz could only shrug his shoulders as if it was the first time that he had heard of such a thing and then vanished.

Turncoat was spared further inquiry as Ersatz waited anxiously for Taz to reappear and explain. In the quiet time that followed the Sneak nervously peered out from behind a large backed chair. Getting nearer he climbed onto Ersatz and whispered. "I've seen the monster; he's frightening. It disappears and then comes back - like magic!" The weird effect of what was said penetrated Ersatz's curiosity distracting him from the golden crown.

"MAGIC, what kind of magic?" roared Ersatz pushing both of them away, yet fascinated by such an idea he quickly grabbed them back. Confused and angry, he stood the two together and fixed both with a quizzical glare.

What the Sneak had just said now captured Ersatz's muddled imagination, becoming absorbed by the way it was put across. "What did you mean by that?" he said glancing several times between the two. "MAGIC?"

The little sneak could not keep the information to himself any longer, he felt that Ersatz would detect a conspiracy to fool him and spluttered out of his trembling lips. "It is black powder that holds a tremendous force, sparks fly, then turns into fire, it destroys everything," he sobbed.

"Destroys everything?" repeated Ersatz, glaring harder into emptiness expecting an answer from the faint re-appearing image of Taz. The response, sounding inside Ersatz's head was a call for vengeance. "Do it!" echoed the silent demand.

The Warlords were getting restless, trying to make some sense out of it all. None of them could see the spectre of Taz yet noticed how Ersatz appeared to interact as if someone else was present. Tansga too was getting impatient with the dramatics; his curiosity began to demand an answer from all the disjointed talk. He spoke up for them. "What do you mean, destroys everything?" he demanded from Ersatz, for which he never received an answer.

Ersatz only response was to look over his shoulder then move the two gnomes away to the corner of the room turning his broad back on his warlords, standing close almost smothering the pair. The spooky image of Taz looked on. The two blood brothers were now appearing to study Turncoat and the Sneak intently.

"But it's what else, that is still out there?" suggested the Sneak, the pitch of his voice becoming significantly higher fearing the effect of being smothered. "It's some kind of new invention. It sunk our boat and there were lots of them." The Sneak was clearly getting distressed yet eagerly trying to keep Ersatz's interest alive dreading that he might become enraged again.

Ersatz paced slowly across the floor and reached up to remove a large sword from its mount on the wall. It was a double handed, blue bladed monster with a razor sharp edge. It still held blood stains of former executions. The latest being – Taz!

While caressing the blade with his hand; Tether, his faithful dog howled. Its black eyed, hunting instincts targeted the Sneak. Yet! The Wolf hound would have to wait a little longer for the anticipated chase.

"Why didn't we know about this before?" said a more composed Ersatz, now totally taken up with events that lay completely beyond his control.

Frightened at the prospect of Ersatz's sword and of losing his head, the Sneak went on to plead their innocence. "We never ever knew, nobody ever knew what was happening out on the marsh, it was kept a secret; The Elves who guard it had kept it a secret." He paused with a pathetic look of helplessness, begging some kind of understanding. "Nobody had ever come back that ever went in there," he said falling to his knees, hands gripped together, pleading for sympathy. "We all thought it was just reed beds and mud." The Sneak had the idea thinking that by preoccupying Ersatz with as much information as he could that he would be left alone. Ersatz had other ideas and put more pressure on him; amused to watch him squirm.

"Where is D'rasnah?" said Ersatz intoning his enquiry to sound threatening if he did not receive the correct answer. The thought of a little man getting the better of him made him fume. Tether snarled at the mention of his name then whimpered at his master's feet.

"I., I., don't know! Perhaps he couldn't escape," replied the Sneak confused. "Perh..,

"But Turncoat came back, didn't he? So did you!" added a suspicious Ersatz. The glint from his eyes set deep in that menacing skull penetrated into the Sneak making him go rigid with fear. He did not have the answer.

Turncoat's eyes flashed with alarm, not wanting to be drawn into any misunderstanding, yet! Felt that he should try to explain: "D'rasnah had an escape route already planned," he revealed, hoping to throw all the blame on D'rasnah. "He's gone to the land of Drone."

"Do you have anything else to tell me?" said Ersatz after a long pause spent in silence. In a softer, encouraging tone he continued a more passive, understanding line of questioning. The frightened pair could not give an answer so what followed was yet another very uncomfortable silence.

The spectre of Taz had now sat down, drumming its fingers on the table, watching Ersatz very closely, urging. "Do it! Go ahead and do it!" Tansga and the Warlords sat around getting agitated, how much longer would this insane show go on?

While they were struggling to make some sense of it, a sinister sneer spread right across Ersatz's heavy, tattooed features. He then picked up the grovelling Sneak from the floor and began jabbing his sword at him, bringing him to the centre of the room. In an instance Ersatz face was set like stone.

"Do you have anything else to tell me?" he asked again, while looking at the warlords. It was at this point that Turncoat would have liked to save the Sneak from further questioning but he let him carry on.

"Spare me!" cried out the Sneak. "Please! Please! Please! I have got something else to tell you." Ersatz did not take his eyes off the rejected individual and continued to torment him by running his fingers along the bloodied, blade, feeling the sharpness and then displaying a smear of red from his thumb. Next, Ersatz split a fire log in two as a demonstration to add to the gnomes fear. "Merva and Derva are really Monk the Elder's sisters," he squealed wide eyed and tearful.

"Who?" said Ersatz feeling duped by yet another cunning move made by D'rasnah. "Monk the Elder - is he that little man that escaped from the abbey?"

"Yes!" blurted out the Sneak. But, it was D'rasnah that kidnapped them and left them at your door." Turncoat cringed with fear knowing that Ersatz could not work things out very quickly and would react violently to this information, but it was too late to rescue the Sneak from his loose tongue of information.

Ersatz could not take another twist in the turn of events, but the Sneak would not stop his whining. "D'rasnah was after the stone seals!" continued the Sneak "And he had just started to boast about how he will take over Evermore with knowledge more powerful than gold."

"Stone seals? I know nothing of this!" said Ersatz. "He has never told me, of any SEALS! I didn't know such things existed," he raged. Confused and angry Ersatz breathed heavy in total disbelief of how he could have been fooled by all these conflicting events. He looked across at the faint image of Taz that now seemed supportive to his every move. "Did you know anything about this?" he asked. The spectre shook his head slowly and remained silent. Only a louder urge of, "Do it! Do it!" sounded through out Ersatz's mind.

"Monk said, that I could go as soon as I had told you," said the Sneak innocently about to dismiss him-self from further enquiry. He then moved boldly toward the door intent to leave. As he gripped the door handle he couldn't resist a final shock of truth and turned to face Ersatz. "Monk had one seal and Merva had another," he blurted and went on to say. "She kept it on her person all the time that she resided in the Citadel – That is what D'rasnah was really after!"

Turncoat, now fearing for his own safety moved closer to the Sneak, hoping that both could force the door open – but it was stuck. Yet! the Sneak had now become so frightened at the sight of the sharp steel blade in menacing hands while not being able to open the door that he couldn't remain quiet. "D'rasnah stole the necklace from Derva. He knew it was more powerful than the gold." he repeated.

In distracting Ersatz Turncoat felt that he should continue to try to give a better account where the Sneak had obviously failed. "It was Monk the Elder, he knew the way into the marsh," he said in a panic trying to move Ersatz's attention away from the seals. "Oh, he knows everything about Evermore," said Turncoat casually to lighten the mood. "He gets help from Sprite"

"WHO is Sprite?" Ersatz was about to explode, his mind had entered into a fog.

"They say that she is the Spirit of truth," said Turncoat now feeling trapped by what he was saying.

Caught up in a maze of ideas, while occasionally, seeing his blood brother move around the room. He was hearing strange names, that he couldn't fathom, or had even heard of before, Ersatz snapped. "The Spirit of, T., R.....!" stuttered Ersatz. It was no good, after several attempts he just could not say the word nor even admit of such a thing. The working of his mind came to a halt, like throwing salt on a Snail, which melts into a foul jelly, it just disintegrated.

"Spirits," he shouted. "I have the Spirits, from the skulls, there is no other way – Now bring the Sneak here," he beckoned."

Tansga knew exactly what was going to happen next and moved closer to calm Ersatz before he went completely insane. "Stop all of this madness," he shouted. "We should be concentrating on war!" Meanwhile, Turncoat was yelling at the Sneak, to calm down, while pulling him away from the locked door.

Ersatz moved menacingly towards his victim looking determinedly into, the terrified Sneaks eyes. Without further hesitation he took one almighty swipe with his sword and removed the head clean off the Sneak's shoulders.

Turncoats eyes shut tight as he felt the force of the blade cut through the air then shrank back in horror as he felt the spurt of blood reach his face then heard the head fall and roll across the bare wooden floorboards.

The circular movement of the thrust continued its momentum, slicing through the leather vestment, Tansga was wearing - narrowly missing cutting him in two - and he fell to the ground.

Turncoat, scared that he would be next dived behind the chair to avoid the headless torso that was jerking around in circles. He then watched in horror as it fell to the floor writhing in convulsions.

Thinking they were all under attack the Warlords; as one voice, gasped at the violence. Jumping up from their seats with swords drawn they moved in closer on Ersatz intent to stop him from destroying everybody else in the room.

Tansga, was back on his feet in a moment, wild eyes locked onto Ersatz with sword drawn in anger. "This is another bad omen," he raged. The moment he said it, he caught another glimpse of Taz's shimmering presence standing alongside Ersatz. Mystified; he haltingly stammered. "Blood brothers should never attack each other." He then shook his head in disbelief to dispel the image, looked again and the spectre was gone.

"I've been tricked, I've been fooled!" screamed out Ersatz pushing Tansga away ready to take them all on in a fight to the finish. He then pulled Turncoat out from his hiding place gripping his neck while forcing him on to his knees "Where is that deceitful little man, Drasnah? He must have been planning all along to have the gold for himself," and went to take Turncoats head too.

"Calm down, calm down," begged Tansga. "Leave him alone." He rushed at Ersatz gripping his arm to disarm him as the warlords also moved in quickly to restrain him. "Little folk can't fight our battles."

When things had quietened they started to put together the facts. "It's like I said, NOW! Is the time to prepare for OUR, War. This coming winter will give us time to build our armoury. WE will then attack them and take away this –'MAGIC'." Tansga then stated with determination. "Let's get help from Rager?"

"Rager? Ah! yes." said Ersatz picking up his sword to replace it in its sheath. At that moment he felt the return of a sharp pain piercing his gut again. "Let's get help from Rager?" he gasped. "He has the best siege weapons; we will throw down the challenge." He defied the pain, roaring. "Culjern hasn't got his little men to help him, they are far too busy searching the marsh. It's like you've been saying we now have a great advantage." Ersatz's troubled mind went from one extreme mood to another, finally becoming subdued by the continuing pain and spent some time in silence.

An uneasy peace restored, Ersatz and the warlords settled back to debate their next move. Tansga lit a torch and jumped up onto the long table, chanting with sword in the air supporting Ersatz's leadership. His lungs filled with triumph sent out a loud, war-cry that could be heard echoing throughout the woodland, sending out a chilling warning. "Let's prepare for war!"

This positive move of another chance to win Evermore revived Ersatz; moments later he echoed thoughtfully. "Let's prepare for battle." It cooled the explosive atmosphere enabling the warlords to put away their weapons and find a new way forward with fresh support for their leader.

Chapter 5

Tethers Instincts

As everyone in the room calmed, several dwarves swiftly entered the room to clear up and remove the Sneaks messy torso; spiking the head to add to Ersatz's - skull collection. Using this peculiar time Turncoat took his chance and crept over to the unlocked door, ready to make his escape. On opening it he bumped straight into Ffelin. "I think I can find D'rasnah," he stammered nervously in a desperate play for time. Turncoat then tried hard to bargain and avoid being the victim of a second decapitation. "Let me go and bring him back – as a prisoner?" he begged.

By showing Ffelin that he still had a use, Turncoat pleaded again. "Let me go and get him, D'rasnah will have to give Ersatz the gold if he wants to regain his freedom." This sudden and unexpected idea had Ffelin thinking 'Perhaps HE! – himself, should bring back D'rasnah' as a prisoner and lock him in the dungeon; if he knew where he was? Then he would be the hero in Ersatz's eyes.

Ffelin raised his dagger to Turncoat's throat and threatened him. "Why, shouldn't you be next? YOU Have more cunning in your little head, YES, Master could use your little skull."

"AGH!" shrieked the Gnome. "P.,P.,Please, don't hurt me. Wh.,wh.,what is it you want!" He started to panic, going into hysterics. Ffelin slapped his fat hand over his mouth and squeezed it tight until he stopped in case it alarmed Ersatz.

"Then you! Must tell me where this 'golden' Oak tree is?" he demanded, glaring into Tuncoats frightened eyes. "I will bring back this power for master - Not YOU."

Ersatz suddenly called out demanding Ffelin's attention, distracting him from further interrogation. When he opened the door in response, he signalled to Tether to come over and guard the Gnome who was stood shaking with fear in the corner of the room.

Tether's chest was heaving with excitement, waiting only for his master's command, or any command to hunt and run down the distraught gnome that he now held at bay.

Listening and watching through the door ajar in case his prisoner escaped, Ffelin was not paying full attention to Ersatz's needs and took a 'whack' from his mighty hand.

"Get me more wine!" he bellowed. "And more Hog!" Ersatz raised his hand again but the dwarf moved fast. "And bring more logs for the fire." Soon there were many dwarves running about all over the place serving up food and entertainment as the warlords continued to divulge their rapacious appetites. With each bone of meat thoroughly gnawed, it got discarded on the floor - leaving Tether hungrily anxious.

All the while the door's were continually opening and shutting as the dwarves kept up the frantic demand to supply food and wine. The tempting smells wafted stronger and stronger tormenting the hungry hound, until at last some chunks fell off a plate. Tether wasted no time to gather it up. "Go get it!" encouraged Turncoat. "There is more over there," he pointed to distract him.

It was then that Turncoat saw his chance to escape. He took it then ran.

"GET HIM," ordered Ffelin kicking Tether as he raced out the door. The Wolfhound responded with a painful yelp! being lifted off the floor by the force. "Bring him back to me dead or alive and Ersatz will reward you," growled the Dwarfe. The cur went chasing after the terrified Turncoat, snarling and hungry to do justice for his master.

Turncoat had wasted no time in getting away; hurling him-self at such a speed down the cold stone steps of the tower that he lost his balance and fell. He had just bounced to the bottom when Ffelins words echoed in his ears.

In his bruised and giddy state he desperately tried to block and bolt the outer door to halt the hounds advance but didn't have enough time to secure it properly. With his head still spinning his only option would be to keep running as straight as he could, into the snow covered, unknown paths and byways of Darkwood.

"Help..! Brimen, where are you?" begged the shivering, frightened gnome, feeling his head about to burst. "Don't let him get me… don't let him get me! Please, don't let him get me!" he whimpered as he ran for his life through the dank and lifeless vegetation. The putrid smell and yellow haze caused his eyes to sting and water. "I'm sorry… I'm sorry… I'm sorry. I am so very sorry!" he continued to groan into the gushing wind bringing more flurries of snow. Wanting a benefactor to grant him forgiveness for his changeable ways, he promised the invisible Deity all sorts of sacrifices to end his troubles. "I'll change my ways; I'll be good!" Eventually he found his way out, into the healthier woodland and purer air of Evermore.

The chase had sent Turncoat crazy. Stuck in his mind was the sight and sound of the Sneaks decapitated head bouncing and rolling across the wooden floor; then the dwarves spiking it for Ersatz's skull room.

Fearful that he was going to be snared and devoured at any moment, his instincts told him to run 'zig-zagged'; then in circles; jump over boulders; leap over bushes; wade through a stream; back-track, to fool his enemy and then the impulsive idea to take off in another direction, his legs wet with steam rising from his overheated body. Even climbing a tree and balancing while crossing its boughs seemed a good option.

Yet! Again, he zig-zagged; ran in circles; jumped over more boulders; leapt over more bushes; waded through another ice, cold stream and again, back-tracked.

Confident that he had masked his movements he stopped to watch and listen for his pursuer. Apart from the icy wind, whistling through the bare branches rustling the remaining obstinate leaves, the silence in the wood disturbed him. Breathless, tired and weary he rested under a large Horse-chestnut tree, sheltering from the biting cold air in a niche of its huge twisted trunk.

Turncoat had only sat down for a minute and barely got his breath back when he began to hear and feel a prescence, sniff; sniff; snuffle; snuffle; getting nearer and nearer to his hideaway. Traumatised, he froze: He could see his own footprints in the light snow giving his hideout away. Pressing his back further into the recess he held onto his panting breath in case it signalled he was there. With eyes shut tight, he could imagine huge hairy paws gripping him tightly as massive sharp fangs ripped into him.

Suddenly a wet nose nudged him on the cheek. To Turncoat's horror he found he was staring, eyeball to eyeball into his greatest fear. "Agh!" he shrieked wishing he had wings to fly away. All he could do was to cover his face with his hands while sobbing. "I'm sorry; I'm sorry; forgive me; forgive me; forgive me; Oh, please..,"

"It's me! It's me," said Fox shaking him. "Reynard - I've been trailing you for miles." He shook him again until Turncoat opened his fingers to take a look. "You can certainly run when you need to," laughed Fox.

"Phew! Thank goodness," eased off Turncoat, blowing long and hard. He relaxed to take a better look then breathed on his hands to warm them. "That's not who I thought you were!" he said trembling all over. "That cur was instructed to kill me!"

Fox shook his head with a rye smile. "Trying to run away from Tether is impossible, you need my help," he volunteered. "Nothing would give me greater pleasure than to outwit that Wolfhound.

"What should I do?" whined Turncoat not listening to offers of help. "Ersatz wants me to bring him D'rasnah and Ffelin instructed Tether to kill me.......and Brimen has gone to Isolate – for the winter," he added despairingly.

"You will have to stay low for awhile, until the Oakmen return," advised Fox. "Brimen will have the answer."

"How long will that be?"

"Mmmm! It is going to be a long, snowbound winter. I can hide you safely?"

"Why, would Ffelin want me dead?" said the distraught Gnome still not listening to good advice. "I heard him tell that hound to get me!"

"It's just as well he didn't." grinned Fox. "We can't let the wolfhound think that he is the only one to know his way around the wood."

"Did I manage to fool him?"

"You are lucky!" said Fox. "He lost your scent in Darkwood and it has delayed him."

"Phew! That's good," gasped Turncoat. "I can relax a bit now"

"Not with footprints in the snow, to give you away!"

"What shall I do?"

"Well! He's not that far behind, come on follow me!"

Some days later, Reynard Fox was suddenly awoken from his intermittent winter sleep with a jolt, his rested yet weary body not yet ready for immediate action. As he lay there stretching out in comfort, the thought of helping Turncoat to outwit Tether still continued to amuse him. Then he heard it again; clanking, jangling, threatening sounds, vibrating and echoing throughout the lair. His eyes opened wide in response looking straight ahead toward the entrance. "Something is digging into my home," he thought moving stealthily forward to investigate.

Framed in the light, looking into the Lairs entrance was a site he did not expect to see. "It's D'rasnah!" he muttered softly at seeing the goblin so brazen, standing together with Trypannon and Nescient. "What have I done to deserve this?"

Although Fox had stayed aloof from all the events that had happened earlier in the summer, he was fully aware of what had taken place. Therefore; surprised to hear D'rasnah's voice bellowing out his orders, in freezing weather.

"Come on out - Reynard," ordered the goblin. "Or we will dig you out!" Fox could now clearly see the mesmerised gnomes that had changed sides and were supporting the goblins. Most of them were miners led by Grindle; they began to hack speedily into the earth. Courageously Fox went forward and stood defiant at the entrance, nuzzling the frenzied workers away, howling and nipping at them.

"Keep it friendly!" warned D'rasnah standing astride with a pickaxe handle held menacingly over his shoulder.

"What do you want?" asked Fox, his chest heaving with fearful excitement. "You are acting far worse than any hound?"

"Where did you hide Turncoat?" bellowed the goblin. Trypannon bent down and picked up a handful of stones then began throwing them at Fox. "It's THEM or US! Brimen or ME," was the only ultimatum.

"I'm not on ANYBODIES side," stated Fox bravely, avoiding another missile aimed at his head.

"Then you had better decide where your loyalties lie!" hissed D'rasnah. "Where have you hidden Turncoat?" While Fox was distracted; Nescient had moved sneakily into a position to snare him with the noose on a rod. "Easy catch!" he said gleefully, snatching hold of Reynard's neck and pulling on it. "We asked you, where did you Hide Turncoat?" spat the nasty little goblin.

The more Fox struggled to free himself the worse the situation became, the noose tightening around his throat until he eventually passed out. It was only for a moment but when he came too he saw the spiteful look in Nescient's eyes reflecting the enjoyment for torture. In his semi conscious state, Fox was rueing his decision to conceal Turncoat. More than anything he was trying to fool Tether. Yet, he couldn't stop thinking: 'How did D'rasnah find out that he had hid Turncoat?' Then he realised; the only other 'predator' who would have been watching when the gnome was being hunted would have been Lurker. He must have told D'rasnah yet, didn't know where Turncoat was hid. Tether's presence would have kept him away.

Yet, If Lurker did have any idea where Fox had taken him then he would not speak about it or go anywhere near it. The fear of seeing Badger turned to stone, at the entrance of his Sett would deter the superstitious goblin; frightened that it would re-awaken the wrath of Merva and Derva which could come back to haunt him - He knew; that more than anyone the sisters would do the same to him, if they ever catch him. It was he who spied on the sister's whereabouts which led to their eventual imprisonment in the Tower. This sly goblin had every reason to fear for his safety and bide his time.

"I'll ask again," screeched D'rasnah using the pick handle to ram it forcefully into Reynards side. "Where did you hide Turncoat." He then whipped into Reynard trying to arouse him but Fox lay motionless. "Loosen that noose," D'rasnah demanded of Nescient. "I want him alive, not dead. Sick! Yet, Alive!"

Tether hadn't given up the hunt for Turncoat and was still roaming the wood for another try at finding him. Again he returned to the same spot where he first lost the trail in the hunt for his quarry. The snow covered, frozen hard ground was making it difficult to trace anything.

Taking a different route this time, he soon picked up on another scent. A familiar taste was in the air, stronger than normal; yet he felt disappointed in a way because it indicated a kill about to take place without his involvement.

There wasn't as much natural cover at this time of year, only a few stubborn patches of bracken waiting to surrender to the harsh coming months ahead. Crouching low Tether crept closer to the noisy scene.

Peering through the ferns he could see what was happening and watched in amazement as Fox struggled to get up from the floor. Stood weakly, shaking his body, Fox was trying to rid himself free from the noose that the spiteful goblin held onto him. He could clearly see D'rasnah hit Reynard again with the pickaxe handle and the tormented Fox fell down, groaning in a pool of blood.

Tether, was overcome with injustice; Fox was his natural enemy, yes! But losing his dignity in this manner - to D'rasnah and his Ner-do-well goblins - was not right. Wolfhounds had honour too and Tether knew that if D'rasnah got his way all animals would be treated in the same shameful manner. Much bigger and naturally more aggressive than Fox he snarled his support and alarmed the attacking mob.

Trypannon and the others quickly responded to the threat and surrounded Tether, pocking and prodding his ribs with sharp pointed sticks to intimidate him. D'rasnah soon took control thinking that he could easily master the hound under the direction of Ersatz and ordered him to do as he was told. Little did D'rasnah know that the hound was aware of inner turmoil beating in the breast of his Master Ersatz.

D'rasnah, his wild eyes straining excitedly in their sockets, ordered Nescient to remove the noose from around Fox's neck, indicating that he would use the noose on Tether if he did not agree to force the information he required, from Fox.

After some deliberation the Wolfhound got close to fox and nudged him several times to revive him. As Fox lay panting, helpless on the ground, Tether whispered assuredly. "Tell them anything!" Fox understood but couldn't get up, yet managed to tell the Goblin from where he lay, what he wanted to hear

It was enough to convince D'rasnah, that it was the truth. After all, why would Fox lie? Why would he be so prepared to pay such a high price to defend Turncoat? When he was so near to death? The Goblins wanted more entertainment and called for a 'chase to the death'. Turning to Tether they ordered the hound - 'in for the kill'.

"We'll give you ten seconds start," said D'rasnah jubilant with Fox's admission. "Of course, when you get your breath back - We want to be fair" he mocked.

Fox was used to persecution; he had been hunted many times before. Now, however he was at his lowest ebb. He had never been hit with pick handles before but felt he could still out run any hound. He bravely got to his feet.

"Run Fox, RUN" screamed out D'rasnah, releasing the whip from his belt and using it to stir the tortured animal.

Tether howled defiantly, then turned and pounced on D'rasnah, bringing him to the ground and adding a painful bite to his leg. Shocked, by the unexpected move, the rest of the goblins ran off in fright, except for Trypannon who whacked Tether with a hefty club.

Tether could take more punishment than Fox and retaliated with a bite on his neck, he then shook Trypannon senseless and tossed the limp torso in the air. As Nescient tried to retreat in fear of being savaged, he tripped and fell giving Tether another easy target to maul. Biting hard into his foot he then dragged him over the rough, stoney, ice cold ground. Snarling and growling, Tether then set about the gnomes, attempting to come back under D'rasnahs frantic orders. Grindle was first to suffer; tossing him high into the air then the other miners followed, one by one.

Fox, revived by the sudden turn around in his favour, tried to bite D'rasnah as he was about to replace the noose around his neck. "Help me move this 'scabby' Fox," screamed D'rasnah to the retreating bullies. "Get back here and fight!" he screamed again and again. Although he got the noose over Reynards head, Fox managed to sink his fangs into D'rasnah's wrist, and he had to let go.

The goblins and gnomes had again dispersed, leaving D'rasnah alone still screaming for them to get back and fight. Yet, dire for him Tether now had the taste for goblin blood and it tasted good. He went in quick pursuit of D'rasnah, as he limped away, attacking the goblin in the most viscous manner. It left the goblin humiliated and sore with the bites from the rabid hound, leaving Trypannon to pick him up and hobble awkwardly away from the scene to join thier beaten, bitten, friends.

It made Tether proud to have scored a massive victory in such a short time and howled the triumph endlessly, bringing unexpected support to the rescue. The noisy commotion had bought attention to Fox's plight from high up in a tree.

Staying out of sight and out of reach; Squirell with others had been watching every move of Tether's victory. It incited them to join in and bombard the defeated goblins with acorns and large branches that he and his friends had franticly gnawed through.

"That's what I owe you!" shouted Squirell hurling one at D'rasnah as he cowered, nursing his wounds in the wood. It found its target crashing into his weary, bitten legs.

"RODENT!" seethed D'rasnah catching sight of him, while he painfully limped around looking to find protective cover. "Go and get him!" he screeched through tight lips at Trypannon and Nescient. Another hefty log was hurled, this time catching Drasnah on the arm. "Go and get him!" he continued to scream. "Up there, You idiots!" he ordered pointing up at the tree.

As stupid as the two of them were, they both knew that that they could never catch hold of Squirell in his own element, even if they hadn't received so much punishment to their legs; they were never good climbers of trees. The pair still dazed and in pain were trying to recover from the rough attack they had received and slow to respond at least until they had recovered.

Under pressure the two started to hurl logs into the air aimed at their aggressors and then had to dodge them when they fell back down to earth. D'rasnah was furious at their weak attempts. "Get up there - you idiots!" screamed out D'rasnah pointing franticly at the tree. "Climb up and get him."

Cretchin, D'rasnah's latest, closest friend was a Hobgoblin from the land of Drone and an observer at the current debacle. The Hobgoblin was now making preparation with D'rasnah to move into Evermore before Brimen got back from the mines. He had pledged loyalty to D'rasnah - on making his return - in exchange for the Yewman's territory and a share in Darkwood for his tribe, Yet There was an even more sinister reason for this sudden pairing. Merva and Derva had kidnapped and still held onto, one of Cretchins loyal and favoured supporters and he intends to get him back again. An agreement was made with Drasnah to also recapture the sisters and return them to Ersatz then install the Red witch of Drone as the occult leader of Evermore.

Cretchin, stepped forward with a leather flail and threw a second one across to D'rasnah. "I said climb up and get him. I too want that rodents head!" he yelled lashing out and cracking his whip in the air to enforce his demand.

Nescient resented being told what to do by this newcomer and glared across at D'rasnah who just sneered back, indicating to him to get on with climbing the tree.

Before long Squirrel and his friends, had descended below the cautious, climbing goblins and were perched just above but out of reach of D'rasnah. They began shrieking, snarling, spitting abuse into the Goblins and the Hobgoblins face demanding that they all stay away from Fox, and get out of Evermore.

Almost immediately the Wild cats of the forest appeared and sprang up behind Trypannon and Nescient, causing them both to lose their balance and fall out of the tree; landing on Cretchin, crushing him on to the hard, icy, forest floor. The attack was so ferocious and unexpected that D'rasnah and his mob ran for their lives, threatening.

"You will regret this rodent, remember what you got the last time? One last chase from Tether and Wild cat and they were all dispersed.

Badly weakened, Fox was stood feebly on his feet shaking and confused at all the noise. He couldn't see any of the action then suddenly the wood fell silent. Watching Tether and wild cat make their way toward him meant that the Goblins had been beaten.

His saviour – Tether, never said anything. He stared at Fox for awhile, with an understanding look before moving slowly away then briefly glanced back before vanishing into the wood.

Relieved, Fox lay down and licked his wounds wondering how he was going to remove the noose that still hung from around his neck. Minutes later he was joined by another unexpected sympathiser – Squirrel and his friends. Normally Fox could never get near him. The two had always enjoyed tormenting each other from afar.

"Let me help you Reynard?" said Squirrel. "That noose looks painfully tight!"

"Thank you Squire," answered Fox affectionately, using the name he always called him by. "This evil contraption is a curse." Eventually he was freed from the loosened noose grateful that he shared something in common with Squirrel – the removal of D'rasnah and his goblins from Evermore. Something inside his heart suggested that he should somehow repay the debt not only to Squirrel but also to Tether.

Chapter 6

Ffelin's perfect plan

Reynard Fox wasn't sure how long he had remained still; getting his strength back would have taken days – maybe weeks. Alert to every sound, his eyes flicked open on hearing his name being called. "Are you there?" said the soft voice. Straight away he knew it was Ffelin - Ersatz favourite Dwarf. Fox could trust Ffelin so responded without worrying about what he wanted.

"Is it true that D'rasnah attacked you over Turncoats whereabouts?" he said anxiously as Fox came to greet him.

"Yes!" answered Fox. "That is why I am in this dreadful state. If it hadn't been for Tether I …….."

Ffelin's, anxiety heightened not giving Fox a chance to finish his self pitying plea.

"Where did you hide Turncoat?" he demanded.

"AH! Why, does it matter?" said Fox at first disinterested in Ffelin's motives.

"Yes! Because I have a plan to capture D'rasnah – return him to Ersatz who would then keep him locked up in the dungeon where Culjern was kept."

Fox had to think long and hard for awhile then stated. "But you sent the hound to kill him?" said Fox. "Well, at least that is what Turncoat told me!"

"Oh! No, no, no!" said Ffelin, his face slightly reddening. "That was because he was going to bring back D'rasnah and be the hero." His face got redder. "That would push me out!" he claimed.

"Ah! So you are jealous?"

"NO! There are other reasons?" he said embarrassed.

"So what is different now?"

"Well, Ersatz is accusing me of letting Turncoat escape!"

"And, did you?" asked Fox.

"Of course not!" answered Ffelin indignant at the suggestion. "WE, cannot have D'rasnah coming back on HIS terms: NO! If I capture him and force him back, Ersatz will lock him up – if I manage to get the gold too?"

"That sounds good to me," said Fox with a smirk. "It will give me the chance to return the noose on a rod to its rightful owner. For a short while Ffelin remained motionless and silent. He was concerned that possibly he was missing out on some detail or fact that may outwit his plan. Staring intently at Reynard, he looked dubious at what might happen if he misjudges the situation, eventually he had to concede to his own fretting conscious that he was doing the right thing.

"So what is this, PLAN?" said Fox prompting him.

The Dwarf was nodding his head slowly still mulling over whether his plan would work or not. He eventually said. "D'rasnah and his Ner-do-wells are now camped over at the old flint mine The other goblins and their allies will join him later, so it gives us time to fool him." Clenching then grinding his teeth magnified the tension while glaring wide eyed at Fox. He then carried on, suddenly consumed with the idea.

"Now, listen to me closely," he said. "The goblin still has the prison cart in his possession; if he can be persuaded to bring it to wherever you hid Turncoat, we can then - TRAP HIM!" As soon as he heard himself say these words he became ever more eager to get on with things. "…with the noose on a rod!" he concluded.

"YOU! want ME, to TELL..?" fretted Fox, alarmed at the idea. "..Go back to D'rasnah, after what he has done to me?" he stammered, halting. "Are you stupid?"

"YES! I mean no, of course not," flustered the dwarf sighing. "It is the only way to GET him," he pleaded. "D'rasnah desperately wants to know where the Big Oak is and Turncoat was on that last trip he is the only one that could tell him."

"But D'rasnah wants to kill me!" said Fox. "Don't you understand?"

"He won't, kill you," insisted Ffelin. "If you just tell him that you want to be friends. Tell him that you want to be left alone. Tell him that you want to come and go in Evermore, as you please. Tell him anything – tell him where Turncoat is hid."

"Oh! I'm not sure," replied Fox wondering why Ffelin did not grasp his fears.

"Explain to him," encouraged Ffelin. "That you only hid Turncoat to fool Tether."

"Are you sure that will work?"

"Of course it will. He is not after YOU! He's after gold."

"The trouble is I had told him a different place to look for Turncoat."

"This time you would offer to stay with D'rasnah until he has seen him."

"Then you had better include me in the plan, I can't wait to see D'rasnah caged up."

"Good! Now look, Tether is going to join us too. "

"Oooo! Now ease back," worried Fox. "It's all too much, too soon."

"WHY? I will need Tether to distract Lurker, so that we can lay in wait."

"I know he's helped me out this time," reasoned Fox. "But will he do it again and then leave me alone?"

"Of course he will. Has Tether, ever harmed you before?

"He has, when he and Hog used to enjoy digging me out of my home."

"But, that was when he was younger!"

"And he used to chase, me and lady when we were together!"

"But, that was when he was younger!"

"And he..,"

"Now look!" said Ffelin. "He doesn't do any of that now."

"Well! I er! NO."

"Good! Then you must tell D'rasnah that you want to be left alone and make a deal to hand over Turncoat," he said seeing the plan run through his head with great clarity. "Take the gnome to a new hiding place at Never Halt – Tether will make sure that Lurker is kept away by alerting the sisters, who as you know are looking out for the goblin; with ideal planning they will capture him too – Now," he continued without pausing for breath. "Before D'rasnah arrives with the prison cart, I will be hiding, waiting with my friends, ready to pounce on his arrival...With the noose on a rod.

Turncoat, as bait will make himself seen. So you needn't worry. It will work."

The sisters were more than pleased to go along with the idea to set a trap for Lurker. This was the one thing that would really unite them to their brother Monk, or so they thought! It was also evident to them that the goblins had plans to bring into Evermore the Red witch of Drone.

The ideal plan that Ffelin had in mind was for Merva and Derva to set a false trail to encourage Lurker's interest. It would be set along the same lonely track, at the same lonely spot, where the sisters had been kidnapped all those years ago.

When the net fell - securing their prey - the sisters bent over and glared at Lurker while laughing at his pathetic attempts to wiggle free. Spitefully, they then began to arouse his anger by hissing and pocking him with his own silver topped cane. All the while the goblin had to endure their singing, until he was exhausted:

> "You know this meeting
> Is long over due,
> When we last met
> You never knew
> That we'd strike back
> And get at you
> In our home
> Sleeps - Blugoku.

Blugoku, was the sisters name for their 'Guest'. He had been captured and now held prisoner in the cabin; he was of course the Hobgoblin that Cretin had been searching for and now intent to liberate.

Protesting his 'unjustified' treatment, Lurker found just enough strength to hurl more abuse back at them; threatening revenge to the pair when D'rasnah finds out he's been captured. The Sisters only spiteful response was to drag the unrepentant goblin along the bumpy track singing, "We have a friend for you," until he stopped the verbal abuse and fell silent.

When the sisters eventually arrived back at the cabin they immediately stripped Lurker of his shiny buckled shoes; striped trousers; fancy coat; frilly shirt; and his 'Top hat' that they then deliberately squashed and discarded. This was followed up with mocking laughter and nasty threats. "Retribution means execution!" they squealed with delight. They then forced Lurker to wear only sack cloth and sandals.

Scared and trembling the goblin was dragged to the cellar door then pushed firmly down the stairs. "We have a friend for you!" the two whispered into the blackness, to whatever dwelt below.

When Lurker came to his senses, there was only a little light from the moon shining through a small barred window set at ground level. All he could hear was heavy breathing and movement of straw being pushed around the damp stone floor - fom the 'thing' that shared this dark and gloomy space,

Ffelin had created and put forward an excellent idea and it went exactly to plan. Drasnah never suspected Fox's involvement or Tether's role in fooling - not only himself - but also Lurker, whom the sisters now had under their control until it was too late. Humiliated and extremely angry with being outwitted; D'rasnah's immediate response was to seek revenge. Plotting something that he knew; Fox and Tether would never recover from.

"Ah! So you return as my guest?" said Ersatz tugging on the chain attached to the spiked collar strapped tight around D'rasnah's neck. Ffelin pushed the other two; Nescient and Trypannon, so hard into the room that they fell over entangling themselves in their manacled chains.

"Sire! - These he had hidden," said Ffelin passing over two golden acorns.

Drasnah, squirmed. "It's not true I was bringing them to you!" At this moment Ffelin was confident that he had regained his superior position over D'rasnah and continued boasting, in vivid detail to Ersatz, how 'HIS' plan snared the goblins to bring them back here. Pleased with his good work, the cocky, stocky figure of Ffelin praised and patted Tether, who was wagging his tail whimpering for praise from his master too.

"Good work! Good work my trusted friend," said a delighted Ersatz as he grabbed hold of the snivelling D'rasnah.

"Please! Listen," begged the goblin frightened by the crushing power of two mighty fists that held his arms tightly to his side. "I have bought with me untold knowledge that the king - your enemy has access too."

"You have told me that before," said Ersatz staring hard into his face. "Here there are only two? Where are the other Golden Acorns..?....There are more?"

"I have them hidden!" Was the lying, deceitful answer to the, question. Ersatz was now so close that his bad breath was suffocating the goblin. The spittle, spat from angry words, sprayed onto D'rasnah's face.

"The Sneak told me something about, Smithy; the Oakman; and the crown of power;" said Ersatz. "What did he mean?"

"I., I., do., don't know!" fretted the goblin, shocked that Ersatz knew so much.

"Why did you not tell me – that only HE could forge its power?"

"I., I've only just found out, NOW!"

"You're lying! Where IS Smithy?" he growled. "Did TAZ know about the crown?"

"NO!" Squealed the goblin, feeling the leather collar, around his neck - tighten.

"But you both set out to betray ME!" shouted out Ersatz.

"I would not do what he told me!" squealed D'rasnah, squinting at Ffelin who was enjoying watching him suffer. "I still have Smithy as a prisoner – for you!" he bluffed.

"He is lying Sire Smithy is free, Lock him up!" said Ffelin casually thinking that he now had the advantage over D'rasnah. Tether growled and nipped at the goblins feet.

"This time it is different..." whined D'rasnah not looking into his eyes. Instead his gaze went over Ersatz shoulder where he saw the ghastly sight of the Sneaks decapitated head mounted on a spike above the fire mantle. The grisly skull room came to mind and he panicked, looking all around for the tapestry door, expecting to see Merva and Derva appear from the grimness.

"Yes!" grinned Ersatz seeing his discomfort. "IT could be you next!"

"But this time it is different!" pleaded D'rasnah. "What I have to tell is of great value – a great power that destroys things then disappears like magic."

"That is what Turncoat and the Sneak claimed," said Erastz moving over to examine the withered head. "But you do not have enough gold with you." He removed the grotesque object from its mount and thrust it in the goblins face. D'rasnahs eyes shut tight at the sight of it. A blackened, bloodied head, with the look of fear, etched on its face. Ersatz then thrust it at the other two, who were left cringing on the floor. "There is a spike reserved for all of you!" he said.

"I can prove it," chocked D'rasnah as the collar got ever tighter. "I can prove it! Honest! Let me go now and bring it back?"

"Do you think I'm stupid!" growled Ersatz tugging harder on the chain. He dragged all three goblins close to his thunderous face, snarling like a beast.

"L.,let, Ffelin take me there," stammered D'rasnah. "I can prove it!" he claimed feigning, sobbing and apologising, as if he was sorry for his failures. "I promise I will bring back the black, 'MAGIC' powder for you!"

Ersatz quickly turned to face Ffelin, who was beaming a smug look content to see D'rasnah squirm, only now there seemed a sudden turn in events. "Do you know anything about this – 'MAGIC POWDER?" he asked curiously.

"No! Sire, he cannot be trusted," emphasised the Dwarf with a changed expression, doubtful that maybe his plan to trap D'rasnah was not working. "No! No! No! He can't prove it!" assured Ffelin who then took a firm grip of D'rasnah's arm. "Come on! Down to the dungeon," forced the dwarf. "I'll lock him up Sire, with the other's too."

"Wait!" shouted Ersatz. "I want to hear more!" With a wide eyed glare Ffelin realised that D'rasnah's claim was having a sympathetic effect on Ersatz.

"He can't be trusted, Sire, Lock him up!" he said. "I can get this powder for you!"

"Of course he can't be trusted," growled Ersatz. "But the Sneak also told about this BLACK MAGIC POWDER."

"Take these chains off," squirmed the frightened goblin offering up his manacled hands. "I can prove it, NOW! Take the chains off,

I have some in my pocket." Ersatz thought for a moment, he wanted gold not powder. Perhaps he will get both. He looked at Ffelin unsure what to do.

"Lock him up, Sire!" urged the worried Dwarf. "Lock him up in the dungeons." Again, he grabbed hold of the goblin to remove him saying. "He can't be trusted! Take his head, Sire." Finally, Ersatz held up his hand to silence Ffelin. "Undo his chains," he ordered.

"You could regret this, Sire?" said Ffelin letting go of his prisoner. "You could regret this," he muttered.

"Silence!" shouted Ersatz. "Give me the key."

Reluctantly, Ffelin produced the key to unlock the prisoner's chains. D'rasnah's threw them firmly to the floor, leered at Ffelin and removed his collar. He then dipped deeply into his trouser pockets, grubby palms opened to reveal a handful of the black powder.

"See! I can make it work," and placed it on the table. From another pocket he took more powder and a piece of string repeating, "See! I can make it work."

"Don't listen to him Sire," begged Ffelin. "It's a trick!"

Ersatz was fascinated and raised his arm to Ffelin, again ignoring the repeated objections. Curious he started to feel, then smell the dark, gritty powder, finally prodding his stout, wet finger in it for taste, then spat out the putrid stuff. "Show me what you mean," he eventually said.

"I'll put it in that pot and prove to you it's magical power," said D'rasnah eagerly beginning to fill and prepare it. "There that should do!" he fussed, attaching the fuse string. Keeping Ersatz in suspense, He crossed the room to place the prepared device - at a safe distance - carefully on the floor. "Now light the string," he ordered Ffelin. "And stand back." Ersatz watched in awe as the flame crackled and spat, along the string, chasing its length to the pot.

Then, BANG! The earthenware exploded sending shardes of pottery everywhere, one hitting Ersatz with a force that excited him. When the smoke had cleared Ersatz began a frantic examination of every fragment that littered the room. This amazing, effect was beyond his understanding. "Again., again," He urged excitedly.

D'rasnah produced more powder this time from Nescient's pocket and hurriedly placed it in Ersatz's hand. "You see," he encouraged.

"The force is powerful and will bring you victory – with more powder; larger pot; a bigger exlosion."

Ersatz displayed a rare smile of satisfaction. He now had gold, with the promise of more. He also had the magic powder of destruction, with the promise of more. A warm, contented feeling crept all over his body ensuring him the promise of success with a powerful new weapon. "But I want more?" he said.

"I will get it, next time I will show you an even bigger bang!" Bragged D'rasnah.

Ffelin, frowned at D'rasnah's claim and the latter sneered back knowing that he would now get his own way. "Master, I can get as much of this as you want." he added while still eyeing the Dwarf. "Let Ffelin take me there now! I have learned a lot about the marsh and other secrets"

"SECRETS!" scowled Ersatz. "What other secrets?" D'rasnah got close to his ear whispering. "They have what they call, a cannon barrel, it fires iron balls to destroy castle walls."

"I still don't trust him Sire," shouted Ffelin straining to hear what was being said. Knowing that D'rasnah had now gained his status back, Ffelin protested. "If you make me go with him he will have to remain chained."

"But I need this magic," roared Ersatz.

"Then his friends can bring it to you." said an irate Ffelin, pushing Nescient and Trypannon forward. "Lock him up sire, lock him up!" urged Ffelin. "Let me take these two to fetch to it.

"It is only I that can talk with the gunpowder fairy," claimed D'rasnah calmly holding the tension in his favour. "We have something in common," he stated firmly.

"What is that?" snapped Ersatz.

"The destruction of Monk the Elder!" said D'rasnah aware that he now held the balance of power in Ersatz's world.

"Monk the El...! Ah! The little man, that ran away from the Abbey?"

D'rasnah nodded excitedly in agreement. "Kordi wants to blow him to pieces, and when he succeeds, then the king will not have anyone to help him and that clever Oakman – Brimen - will not be able to keep control of Evermore. YES! This time we WILL be able to get the gold – from the vaults - all of it."

"Sire, Think about what you are doing!" pleaded Ffelin.

"I am thinking," growled Ersatz. "I want more gold! and more explosive powder."

"You can't trust him, Sire. You can't..,"

"Silence, YOU will go with them and bring it all back,"

"If I have to go then they must remain chained," insisted Ffelin, frustrated and trapped by his own plans.

"I will agree to that," said D'rasnah surprisingly. "Sire, I only want to serve you!" He cast a knowing glance at the other goblins, narrowing his eyes as he shifted to look at the dwarf's reaction then added. "We'll meet with Kordi at the creek and load the prison cart with the powder. Later we can go back and get the cannon.

"I will not feel safe, Sire," said Ffelin shaking his head worried. He was now wishing he had paid more attention to his doubts and fears of earlier on. "I won't feel safe." He repeated sadly and stared at the floor fearfully.

"No one would dare challenge us," carried on D'rasnah with total mastery of the situation. "We could even come back through Oakwood, while the Oakmen are away, in the dead still of night,"

"Of course!" encouraged Ersatz. "And you will have your friends to protect you. Now go!" he shouted as he sat down exhausted by it all. The three goblins huddled together pleased with the out come, whispering and sniggering at the dejected, red faced Ffelin.

"Oh! Sire," said D'rasnah turning round with a lightened voice, as they were about to leave the room.

"What do you want?" said the now drowsy Ersatz. His eyes closed, about to fall into a deep sleep on hearing his demons calling him to another place.

"May I have my pipe and tobacco back?" pleaded D'rasnah. He deliberately stared, sneering in Ffelins face as he said it knowing what took place when Culjern escaped the dungeons. "I lost it somewhere!" he added with a sarcastic tone in his voice.

"Yes," replied the sleepy Ersatz not bothering about the implications of the request.

Ffelin, got his wish, locking up D'rasnah, Nescient and Trypannon in the dungeons. Even, if only because of the horrendous, heavy, snowfall. That way Ersatz was double sure that they couldn't escape.

Come the spring, he was sure that he and his Warlords would have produced enough formidable weapons to destroy the castle. In Evermore, at this time of year nothing could move about with any ease, yet! Ersatz expected to receive an endless flow of black powder and even more information about the cannon so that he and his warlords could carry out experiments, calculate and be prepared for their intended attack on the King. For now they were were building up an armoury of hand explosives that D'rasnah had demonstrated from secret caches, that he had stored.

This situation infuriated Ffelin. He had become a virtual slave to the goblins, having to wait on their every need – Ersatz instructions. It got worse when D'rasnah had suddenly remembered, other hidden caches, but, only admitting to there whereabouts, when the worst of the weather had arrived. It made Ffelin livid with suppressed anger to be sent out in blizzard and gale - at D'rasnah's beck and call.

The torment was such that even the 'need' to retrieve plans that had been stolen from the marsh on - 'how to load and fire a cannon'- were suddenly missing when Ffelin arrived at the various locations to collect them. In order to get even with the goblins surely manner, Ffelin would often goad them about Merva and Derva's capture of Lurker.

He knew it riled Drasnah personally, because he relied on Lurkers information so much. Then Ffelin would taunt him that it was he that had planned the capture and that when they return from the marsh - with the cannon, powder and balls – after the thaw, that he would hand all three of them over to Brimen. That time was now a lot closer, the long ordeal of winter finally coming to an end.

The evening sun was setting over the marsh as they waited for their contact to arrive. The whole sky looked aflame with orange melting into deep red and purple streaks, yet! still not warm enough to melt the ice remnants in river, stream and lake. The whole effect produced a strange and eerie calm among the gentle rustling of the dried reeds. The moment had arrived to retrieve the weapons of war.

D'rasnah's heart began beating faster as he sat, chained to Nescient and Trypannon in the back of the prison cart. Excited, yet worried, all of them hoping that nothing would go wrong with the plan to supply Ersatz - with explosives, cannon and ball. There still lurked the fear within them of what took place at Tump Island.

As it got significantly darker, the three of them were now feeling trapped. Drasnah peered awkwardly through the bars of the prison cart, asking the nervous Ffelin to undo his chains. "It will look terrible for you if Kordi finds us like this! - prisoners?" he claimed. At first, Ffelin refused his requests but when wandering lights, seen in the far distance unnerved him, it provoked a change of heart.

Shafts of light, reaching out at great lengths were bouncing off the dark, low laying clouds of the night sky. The lights then appeared to flash and shoot across the marsh, forming irregular patterns, circling the blackness and penetrating into the reed beds. At brief intervals they would appear to vanish completely. When they reappeared they seemed to be a lot nearer.

Ffelin, weakened and unlocked the chained goblins, then he became aware that something in the nearer distance was also stirring. Something uncertain, with inflamed red eyes was watching his every move as it too darted about in the night time air. It began to make that awful whirring sound, familiar to those who had experienced it at Tump Island, but a strange experience for the startled Ffelin and his nervous dwarves.

As the gunpowder fairy got closer, the whole effect was accompanied by a powerful after shock. A loud bang followed by other 'snappy crackles' in quick succession. It then continued with a dazzling Ariel display by the Naughty Imps. The colourful, noisy event bought a marvelled response from the other Dwarves, lighting up their smiling faces in wonderment.

"Kordi!" greeted D'rasnah showing him humble respect. "We have come for the powder," he reminded him. "This is Ffelin, he is going to help us." There was no answer from the gunpowder fairy only a close examination of this large, squatty figure and his friends.

"I had to bring him along, to lift the heavy cannon," explained D'rasnah. "Can we use that other cart too?" he asked pointing at it. "It will save us time." Kordi, considered the request then cast a familiar burning smell into the air, indicating to Nescient and Trypannon to fetch it.

Suddenly and alarmingly, there was a flurry of activity around the gunpowder fairy. The Naughty Imps were telling him something of real importance. Next came the clear indication for all of them to follow: "Hurry up! and follow silently" came the order as further into the marsh they sped.

Ffelin led the way with the goblins pulling the prison cart. Close behind, the rest of the Dwarves were nervously spread out in single file, pulling the other cart along the winding path. Eventually they came upon a small brick building, compounded in a secure area protected by a locked gate.

Kordi handed Ffelin the keys to open it, urging him to hurry up. Once through the wired gate they noticed the heavy iron cannon, supported on wooden blocks, laying outside the doors of the small brick shed. Stacked up next to it were cannon balls arranged in the shape of a pyramid. Inside the shed were the sacks filled with the gritty black gunpowder.

"Hurry up! Hurry up! they were urged. "You must hurry up!" It then went ghostly quiet as Kordi and the Imps, swiftly left the scene.

All hands were needed to lift the cannon and iron balls onto the cart. As soon as it was loaded and secured with rope, Ffelin and his dwarves wasted no time in grabbing hold of D'rasnah, Nescient and Trypannon, forcing them back into the prison cart -among the sacks of powder - hastily chaining them up again. "We just don't trust you, WE just don't trust you!" They kept on repeating. Finally, they closed the doors to the shed and were about to leave the compound, when they got a terrible shock.

"STOP, STOP! STOP! What you are doing," shouted the surprise demand from a commanding voice. "WE, Have you surrounded," it bellowed through a loud hailer. Powerful lights lit up the whole area freezing the thieves in action. "I say! Put those sacks back," screeched Ankra, commander of the marsh. His monocle dropped from his eye with amazement. "You are stealing the King's property," he screeched. "THAT! C., C., Cart must not leave the marsh."

Ankra deployed his elves to put a stop to what was happening. "TONO!" he yelled.

"Snatch back that cart," he ordered pointing the beam from his torch at it. "You f.,f.,four!" he stuttered indicating to others. "G.,g.,grab hold and rope the big one." He then anxiously looked around for more support. "Where's Kordi?" he shouted. "Has anyone seen K.,K.,Kordi?"

Soon there were many Elves, each with a torch and yards of rope, swarming about all over the place. "I will have to r.,r.,report you all," threatened Ankra expecting the gunpowder fairy and the Imps to come to his support at any minute. "Now re.,re.,return everything this instant."

Confident that he had everything under his control while watching his elves go into action. Ankra quickly removed the monocle from his eye, breathed on it and wiped the glass clean. Replacing it over his left eye he quoted the rule book to his captives: "Memo 66; sec 3a, states…"

Unfortunately, rules and regulations were of little use as a threat and meant nothing to his clandestine audience. The dwarves were far too powerful against such slender, defenders of the marsh and pushed them easily out of the way.

"Where's K.,K.,Kordi?" shouted Ankra again, desperate for support. "Doesn't he re.,re.,realise we have intruders?" A huge fat hand suddenly grabbed hold of Ankra's face, pushing him backwards into the boggy marsh.

The force sent his baton one way and his beret flying in another direction. As he was falling, uncontrollably to the ground, his monocle 'popped' from his eye and he splashed down in the mud, taking in a mouthful of the horrible stuff.

Ankra, covered from head to toe, struggled to his feet as his aggressor turned away. Defiantly, he began spitting out: "Memo 66; sec 3a; sub sec 4; para 4; clearly condemns trespassers." He then raged. "I know who YOU are," while pointing a condemning finger. "And 'you' Goblins!" who he couldn't really see clearly, but instinctively knew who they were. Ankra then reminded them all with another code from the rule book: "Memmo 1; page 1; sec 1; para 1; That no goblin shall be allowed..," his finger became even more extended, jabbing away in anger until!!

The same 'fat' hand grabbed Ankra again and spun the leader of the marsh in circles several times. Letting him go with a hefty push, Ffelin stood laughing to see Ankra stagger around disorientated, landing once more into the boggy substance of the marsh.

As the cart, with the heavy laden of cannon and iron balls made off into the distance, Ffelin promptly shut and locked the gate on the prison cart and then proceeded to make off with their bounty. His greatest joy was in smashing the search lights and laughing out loud as they left.

When the robbers were clear of the marsh they had slowed down to a halt and rest. They all gathered around the prison cart to decide the next move. Ffelin already had the idea in dealing with the captive goblins and couldn't wait to tell them. "We have no more use for you now." He gloated. "You have served your purpose." he said with strong conviction to condemn. "In fact, I am going to do what I said I would always do – give you over to Brimen. He should be home soon!" At that the Dwarves all broke out in joyous laughter.

"Any day now," they all chanted. "Brimen will be back and you'll stay in chains, forever!" echoed Ffelins friends. The dwarves enjoyed this idea and began to taunt and mock D'rasnah, Nescient and Trypannon, reminding them that Cretchin, who D'rasnah put so much trust in, was now on his own and they would deal with him too.

"You can't do this!" seethed the hate filled goblin, rattling the bars with fury.

"What can you do about it!" challenged Ffelin. "When we finally drive 'Cretchin' out of Evermore you will be in chains."

"You will not get away with his," warned D'rasnah.

"OH, and why is this?" said the over confident Ffelin feeling invincible.

"I am the only one that can show Ersatz what to do," said D'rasnah. "The only one he will listen too," he claimed.

"So you say!" responded Ffelin smugly inviting his friends to support the idea. "We have all learnt as much as you, about 'gunpowder'." he said, confident in his mind that he would come out the winner. "Also... Remember this!" said Ffelin. "You left all the plans of 'explosive devices' back at the dungeon. And the detailed plans for firing the 'cannon'. I have made sure, that in you – and your friend's absence – I will now have total control when it comes to knowing about explosive devises."

"Consider this then," said D'rasnah angrily. "YOU, will have to explain to Ersatz why I haven't returned."

"I'm sure I'll manage that," chortled Ffelin, smirking at his friends for assurance. "You and your friends have run away before, so Ersatz will not be surprised!"

"Now, face it! You and 'your' friends are on your way to meet Brimen. He should be returning very soon," he remided them. With that said the dwarves prepared to return home.

"AH!" emphasised D'rasnah holding there attention. "I have another secret to tell!" he yelled assuredly, stopping them all in their tracks. "And have left it with Atropine to tell Ersatz in case I do not return."

"Hah! We can deal with Atropine!" replied Ffelin dismissively, shouting back at him, while enjoying, the jeers of support from his friends ringing in his ears. By now the Dwarves had heard enough and were eager to return

"But, it's about this!" said D'rasnah stopping there advance. "Look!" he said. And produced from his tunic an item wrapped in cloth. Straight away the object held their curiosity and they re-gathered round the prison cart. "Open the doors," he said. "And take a closer look," he offered.

Tormentingly and slowly, D'rasnah, unwrapped the mystery item to expose a flintlock pistol that Kordi had quietly concealed for him inside a powder sack.

"This is a hand gun especially for Ersatz," said D'rasnah getting their attention. "Even now Atropine would have told him about it." The Dwarves all went sullen for awhile not sure of what this item was. "It is only 'I' that know how to use it!" boasted the goblin. He enthusiastically rammed the powder then the ball into the barrel pulled back the flint, of the already primed pistol and fired off a shot. "You see it works!" The sudden flash of sparks and plume of smoke took them all by surprise. The dull thud of the shot hitting into a tree had them all in awe. Exasperated, Ffelin quickly grabbed hold of the pistol before D'rasnah attempted to fire another shot then herded the dwarves together and began considering some agonising options:

"What is it?"

"It's another secret weapon?"

"If we don't take it back - with D'rasnah, Then Ersatz will wonder Why?"

"If we do take it back – without D'rasnah, he will still wonder why?"

"We could say D'rasnah Escaped?"

"But I asked Ersatz, to let me keep them chained?"

"Mmmmm! he will think this strange."

"If Atropine has already told Ersatz about it, what can we do?"

"If WE, Do not return, with this 'hand gun' what can we say?"

Waiting patiently on there decision, D'rasnah, shouted out at the huddled mass of problematic Dwarves: "Have you decided - Yet?" Infuriatingly, nobody responded to his plea. "If 'WE' do not soon return, then Ersatz will be disappointed." added D'rasnah out loud to the huddled confused group.

Disgruntled; Ffelin quickly grabbed the pistol from D'rasnah's grasp before he could use it again. The rest of his friends went sulkily quiet and reluctantly returned to haul the carts back to Ersatz's tower, refusing to discuss this awkward situation anymore.

Chapter 7

Awakening

The morning sun was warmer as it arose slowly above the horizon, melting the last of the snow that still lay in the darker, colder, isolated parts of Evermore. The season was drastically changing into spring after a long, hard, winter, bringing with it the expectancy of brighter days ahead.

The woodlands too were celebrating the revival of spring, in showing their natural beauty. Ferns, flowers and grasses both common and rare species forcing their way up through the leafy forest floor. Over the coming months - as if by magic - the majestic trees would slowly change the skyline, sprouting branches to display new lush leaves of green. The effect was varied and flourishing like a signature of joy, reaching out across the living landscape of Evermore. From their mountain retreat, the Oakmen could observe this mystical effect over Evermore, knowing that now, was the right time to return to Oak Village.

For some months now Brimen and his miners had been occupied in the mines at the far away region of Isolate with not even a hint of what had been happening in their absence. Their thoughts and fears from the previous threat to Evermore from the year before, was almost forgotten.

Likewise, some distance away Smarty and the rest of the miners led by Graff had been busy at the other location - Pewt hill. They too had been completely out of touch with the developments that had taken place back at Oakwood. Now; the end of their labour was in sight and everyone without reservation was beginning to feel optimistic at meeting up with Brimen and the other miners. To be returning home was a good antidote to deal with the depressing fact that had been relentless work - entombed throughout the long winter months.

Back at Isolate it was no surprise to find that everyone had been getting 'niggley' with each other. Especially with Brimen, who had been constantly going on throughout the long enduring term, about the escapade in the Marsh – Ankra; Gunpowder fairy; Elves. What was so irritating was his-own interpretation of the turn of events, giving to his-self all the credit for heroic deeds that no one else could relate to. Stubborn as he was he still clung on to the outrageous idea, that a statue should be erected in his honour. Ideally, it would be placed on a decorated plinth in the middle of the village square. "That is never going to happen," laughed Olan every time it was mentioned.

Brimen took a long last look at what had been comfortable living quarters dug deep in the mine. Somehow he would miss the warmth, cosiness and camaraderie that had been their home for the past months. He doused the candles and followed the last of the miners outside then shut and locked the iron grill door. "There! Now that's that and all about it," he said with satisfaction. "Let's tidy up and go home."

He halted for a moment in the stillness of the early morning air, listening! Sure that he heard the faint, howling cries of Wolfpack. He huffed dismissively yet, started to wonder why it carried a warning air about it.

Inside the little wooden hut that served as an office just outside the mine entrance, Brimen was removing the sprigs of holly that decorated the small window. The berries had shrivelled and the leaves had withered, although still spiky as one pierced his thumb. "You idiot!" he scorned at his own carelessness.

At that very moment, Wolfpack could be clearly heard howling again, a lot nearer this time. It was an eerily; haunting; warning call carried speedily on the wild chilly wind increasing the impact on Brimens' ears and fears. It was a clear distress signal that would hardly stop echoing around the ravine - of an encroaching danger.

Up until now Brimen had kept his feelings in a buoyant mood but all of this bought back instant memories of his damaged big toe and the events that followed on when returning from Big Oak with the gold. He took a close and fearful look at the swelling with the thorn imbedded deep. In his minds eye he could see the goblin D'rasnah,

79

laughing at him and pondered over problems he may face on his return home.

Iffy took no notice of the fuss and bother that preoccupied Brimen. He went about the chores of tidying the mess of dirty cups and plates, piled high from many unfinished meals, accumulated over a long period. In actual fact nothing had been washed or cleaned properly since the first day that they had arrived.

"If you want these plates and cups, put back into the canteen, then you will have to re-open the mine door," said Iffy vexed with the work load. He stepped outside to empty the leftovers onto the rocks and for a while, stood watching the wild cats scavenge the scraps before the mice or birds got near it. Brimens only reaction was to expresss a martyr like suffering for his injured thumb.

Smarty expressed a little sympathy at Brimen's plight and after cleaning and dressing the festered wound, carried on sifting the plans, papers and maps of the mines into the satchel. Then for the third time the sound of Wolf, enhanced by his pack echoed loudly through the mountain gorge.

"What is wrong with him?" said Brimen peering through the small cabin window trying to catch sight of him. "What is he trying to tell us?"

"Something is bothering him?" said Smarty. "I'll go and see what it is!"

"No! Don't concern your self," said Brimen. "If he won't come off the mountain and tell us then we can't help him."

In the drying hut next door, Pole, Lobe and Chip were finishing off the marathon task of sweeping the floor and sifting through the tangled mess of work clothes, dirty boots and general clutter that littered the floor. The heat from the iron stove that stood in the centre became unbearable. Mingled with the floating dust it became intolerable.

It was a nasty job, crushing and shaking the mud and dust from overalls, but everything had to be sorted and made ready for the wash. Laundered, ironed, and put back on the numbered pegs in perfect order, before the end of the day. The benches and boards also had to be scrubbed clean and left in spotless condition.

In the stores hut – the next one along - Gannon and Olan were accounting for all the tools as they were returned by the miners. They too were concerned with Wolfpacks unsettling cries, warning of trouble ahead. Their reaction to it was silence, looking at each other wondering and speculating the consequences in their own way.

Instead, the two chose to remain busy: rewinding yards of rope, grinding and sharpening axes, repairing broken pick handles, hammers, chisels, shovels and oiling the wheelbarrows. Cleaning and trimming the lanterns they then stacked them neatly in rows, chained and locked them away. All should be safe enough in their absence under the watchful guard of the Trolls they decided.

Smug and Stretch were outside working on the narrow gauge rails, organising the parking of the 'bogeys' into a locked position in the sidings. Others were in the wheel house, servicing the system of, wire cables and winches that were used to haul the heavy loads of mined rock to the surface. The pit ponies were now only used inside the mines for light duties and to transport the miners on their long underground journeys to the pit face.

Returning from the stables, after grooming and feeding the ponies, were the hill folk. Some of which were employed to glean through the dumped soil and rock waste searching for small treasure, for which they were duly rewarded. In the Oakmens absence they would care for the pit ponies.

It was now late in the day when Brimen, stepped cautiously out of the hut behind Smarty and Iffy. A strong, bitter, cold, wind was howling through the open clefts in the rocks that surrounded them, creating an ominous feel to their impending departure. The 'music' sounded almost like a mourning dirge.

Brimen, again paused while listening to the 'dirge'. He placed the key in the lock to secure the hut, almost expecting to hear an accompaniment from the Wolf-pack. Every-body else was staring at him, restless and impatient to get moving for home.

Feigning a pitiful stance, Brimen held up his bandaged thumb for all to see, offering a weak apology for being late. "You will have to carry the satchel for me," he said to Olan wincing. While one handed, he struggled too replace the key chain in his pocket. Iffy, offered over the weighty item, he was carrying, too Olan. Only to watch him burst out laughing.

"But you wear it over your shoulder?" he said to Brimen, who immediately responded with an angry, TUT! - He might have known he would get no sympathy from Olan:

"Don't be difficult or else…" came Brimen's embarrassed and irritating reply.

"There is no need for me to carry it!" said Olan still laughing at the absurdity.

"What is your problem?" said Brimen sharply. "You can see I am Injured?"

"NO, What is your problem?" retaliated Olan. "Getting awkward because you are going home?"

"I might not be able to defend myself if attacked," answered Brimen indignantly.

"Well, nor I too!" answered Olan.

"I'm sure you do this deliberately," said Brimen.

"Last time we had to endure the 'big toe' incident!" said Olan. "Remember that?" Everyone else started to laugh at the memory.

At that moment, Gannon stormed across to the pair of them demanding that they stop arguing and get the carts moving - there was a long way to go and he was eager to get home. "Put it on the first cart with Smug!" he demanded. "HERE! Hand it over!"

"Now look here!" stressed Brimen, looking very serious. "It is far too valuable. This holds all the plans – including Pewt Hill – of tunnels, pot holes, crevices and new seams, if 'IT' goes missing?"

"It won't if you put it in the toolbox and lock it," snapped Gannon.

"That's the last place you should put it!" chuckled Olan. "Look what happened the last time." Reminding himself of this terrible catastrophe caused Brimen to surrender the idea. He bent his head, indicating to Iffy to slip the bag carefully onto his shoulder. "Humph!" he stated. He then strode purposefully to take up his usual position at the front of the six cart caravan alongside Smarty, determined to remind Olan of his shortcomings at Big Oak. So; as Olan was making his way to the rear of the convoy Brimen shouted to him. "Has every wheel been checked and tightened! - Mister? We don't want any; 'Accidents' on the way home."

"They were tightened the last time!" sounded the quick retort from Olan without turning around to face his leader. "Checked and tightened!" he bellowed even louder, dismissing any doubts of that time - when the wheel come off - causing so many accusations. "And if you recall correctly? On that day it was sabotage!" finished Olan.

"Sabotage, Pah!" replied Brimen, having the last word. He used his hand to dismiss the contentious idea, whilst displaying a satisfactory smile at vexing Olan.

At least, the squabble made Brimen feel better. He finally slipped the satchel strap over his head and adjusted his clothing beaming an even bigger, contented smile. He then raised his arm and gave the robust command. "Jib up and pull, Jib up and pull!" and the convoy started to move.

Not expecting to return to Isolate, at least for sometime, they all looked affectionately back and waived good bye to the Trolls and hill folk. A final glance at the mine entrance and the carts slowly picked up the pace.

They had barely moved a hundred yards when Brimen's expression stiffened, becoming seriously concerned to hear Wolf pack again. A lot closer this time and Brimen could see the leader perched high up on the ledge. Smarty went over, to find out what his problem was!

"He's telling us that D'rasnah is back," said Smarty on his return. "And, threatening his pack, with the return of the Skelt Hound!"

"Mmmm! That is what those mad sisters predicted." said Brimen, sighing.

"Just a minute.," said Smarty, gripping Brimen's shoulder. "He also said that Fox was badly injured and suffered under D'rasnah when we first left for Isolate."

"You Mean, that nasty little goblin had returned while we have been occupied up here?" angered Brimen. "What was Sprite thinking of?"

"Yet, If hadn't been for Tether's interference, Fox would be dead!"

"That, huge beast! On the side of Fox?" questioned Brimen. "Oh! Let's get home first!" he snapped, trying not to get overwrought on the long journey ahead. "Tell Wolf, we will deal with it all when we get home."

The first part of the journey home was easy, mostly on level ground. It then gradually sloped away twisting and turning around the hill, leading into the gorge. Once across the narrow wood bridge that spanned high over the river they had to negotiate a twisting path, dipping steeply over loose shale. It eventually levelled out and they would pass through the slate quarry then rapidly descend with ease, onto the hogging path below.

It was a tough descent from Isolate, calling on all their strengths with expert handling of the heavily laden carts. With most of their time taken up in strenuous activity, they decided on a well earned rest, stopping off at a sheltered cave for the night.

The huge size of Isolate into which the Oakman and gnomes had bored their mines dominated the four craggy mountains that circled it. Looking up, at the surrounding snowy peaks, so early in the morning, inspired them to break into song:

> "We've worked the mines
> Longer this time
> And seen the sun
> Rise O'er the chine
> We've split the earth
> And found our treasure
> Made up lost time
> That seemed gone forever."

Soon they were about to cross the flat sandstone region of barren rock, that covered a vast area. To avoid being exposed to hostile elements and, would be attackers that hid in the Cricks, they took the sheltered option. This was a natural channel that had formed a pathway, skirting along the edge of the sandstone rock. It ran below the top surface approximately midway of its sizable depth.

The channel twisted and turned along its irregular rock face until it reached the region of Pewt Hill - some distance away - where they would eventually rendezvous with Smithy and the other miners.

As they were about to turn into a sharp left turn - the third bend of about twenty they would have to negotiate - Brimen could hear unsighted voices. Deep, rhythmic sounds echoing a distinctive chant, repeating over and over. "Hoo! Hoo! Hoo!"

The open side of the sandstone channel left them little option as there was no where for them to hide or to avoid whatever it was coming at them. To the left hand side, above them was shear rock to the top. On their right hand side below, a steep drop into bracken: Halting the carts they waited.

When the 'sound' eventually came into view, they caught the site of an angry group heading their way. At the front was Acktoo, leader of the Yewmen. Brimen held his hand up as a sign of peace and friendliness. Aktoo briefly exchanged the greeting before coming to a halt, looking wild and scary he went into a rant. Something in the Yewman's character that Brimen had never seen or heard of before

"Ix., Axle., Skelt! Yew., D'rasnah, Erasatz, Atch.., King...."

"Stop! Stop!" winced Brimen putting his hands to his ears. "I can't understand a word you're saying." Although he did register in his mind, the word 'Skelt!'

"Hoo! Hoo! Hoo!" continued the chant of the wild looking Yewmen, huddling closer together behind their leader. They were angrily raising and jabbing their staffs high above his head in rhythm to their demand.

"He's telling us that Cretin – the Hobgoblin - has raided the yew wood, chopping down trees to make weapons for his expanding tribe," answered Smarty. "Cretin has declared war on the Yewmen and is going to rule the yew wood."

"But, what is 'HE' doing so far from Yew wood?" said Brimen. "And where are 'THEY' off to now?" he asked looking perplexed and wincing at another rant set off by the Yewman.

"D'rasnah is back!" shouted out Aktoo. "He's back and we are going to get him!" A surge of anguish rushed down the Oakman's spine, making him shudder. He didn't expect, or want to accept this maddening situation, with so much of their journey left to cover.

"Now calm down, calm down," urged Brimen looking tired. "We need to think this thing through." He turned to look back at Gannon and Olan at the rear of the convoy, shrugging as if to say – here we go again. Sadly the combination of D'rasnah and the Skelt bought back painful memories for him.

"But he has bought Cretchin with him and his tribe will take over our land," Said Aktoo pressing his gnarled nose onto Brimen. "Together they will rule Evermore?"

"Cretchin's no challenge to me!" stated Brimen. "I've beat him many times in the past. Now go home and we will sort it out when we return."

The Yewmen's only reaction was another loud, "Hoo! Hoo! Hoo!" Aktoo raised his staff clumsily, nearly hitting the Oakman, blew a note into his rams horn and the tribe were motivated once again. Moving forcibly forward they pushed Brimen aside with an obvious contempt for his lack of respect.

Brimen scratched his head wondering as they all squeezed by. 'Where would they hope to find D'rasnah?' It was answered when Aktoo yelled out. "To the flint mines."

"Mmmm! It's just as well that we avoided that route," said Brimen to Smarty, smiling. He then saw them stop to talk to Gannon and Olan - at the rear - going through the same routine. Instantly annoyed he shouted out. "Come on! Leave them to it. Let's get moving," then bellowed the command. "Jib up and pull, Jib up and pull!" Olan nudged Gannon as the carts started rolling again, guessing the forlorn expression on Brimen's face, he whispered with a chuckle. "Let's see how he handles this one!"

They had left the narrow ridge channel at sandstone rock, crossed over the Heath land and had reached Pewt hill without saying a single cheerful word to each other. Possibly, it was because they were growing weary after being away for so long. Or, possibly fear and trepidation over what they must all face when they return to Oak village.

Even more assuredly it was because Brimen had taken the gruelling decision, to speed up the journey, ordering only short breaks between long speedy spurts of hard tough pulling. The punishing pace went right through the day, long into the night, until they arrived - exhausted - at their destination the following mid afternoon.

Meeting up with Graff and the other miners at Pewt hill was a welcome relief after all the dramas so far endured. The camaraderie, a welcome pleasure!

The rest of the day however, was spent strictly on business. Words and enthusiasm kept to a minimum as they organised the transport of another six carts, checking and comparing the quality of minerals mined, with a correct tally of the weights and amounts being transported back to Oakwood the following day. Grateful to finish the tasks early, the miners went to sleep thankful for their well earned rest.

The next day, as they were preparing to set off, Brimen, was turning over in his mind what he may have to face when he gets back to Oak village. He had had another disturbed night of sleep, caused by the suggestions of the previous day.

The unpleasant thoughts kept recurring, reminding him of what had taken place when they were returning with the gold from the Big Oak. He gripped hold of the satchel tightly, determined not to experience a repeat of those disastrous events.

Lightening his mood, to take attention away from worry, he decided to have some fun. "Olan!" he said on impulse. "You and Gannon must get a group together and check the wheels, on every cart, at regular intervals, on our return to the village." He waited for an objection. "We must not have any delays!" he stated firmly. "Not like the last time?"

Olan couldn't resist a considered reply. "WE," he said assuredly. "Have absolutely nothing to fear. WE are ahead of you and have already serviced the wheels on every cart. He too paused, waiting for a reaction; then said. "There are enough of us on this journey that we could handle any problem that may arise!" Then he added with a laugh. "Even, if your thumb swells to the size your head."

"Don't get Clever!" sniggered Brimen happy to be back in contention.

Olan winked at Gannon and said to Brimen. "Just concentrate on keeping the satchel safe!" Then moved away, intending to do what he was told.

"Jib up and pull! Jib up and Pull!" roared Brimen in high spirits.

It had been another long and weary haul from the cold and lonely mines of Pewt hill but at last the Abbey ruins were in sight. All twelve carts eased off their demanding pace. As the light faded the group decided to stop for the usual overnight rest and tensions began to fall away.

As always, this stop over gave them excellent shelter from the chilly winds, with the promise of a good nights sleep. The prospect of an early morning start meant they would return to Oak village at around midday. Fortunately - for Olan, there would be no 'short straw' to deal with or, 'waiting' cart to be hauled back with the harvest. Eagerly, they crossed over the bridge – to the ruins – and rubbed the lucky blue touchstone.

The group moved around silently attending to the mundane chores –lighting the camp fire, then preparing and cooking their supper. Meanwhile, Smarty cleaned and re-bandaged Brimen's throbbing thumb then remade a padded arm sling for extra comfort. It was all beginning to feel far too familiar with the summer of the year before.

And just as they always did, on such occasions, Olan took hold of his accordion and began playing and singing in harmony with Gannon. Several other miners also took there part and entertained, with reels, jigs and juggling. Again it was a special time, under the clear, star lit night, encouraging also the fairies of the forest to join in.

Brimen, of course, did not join in the reels and jigs but he did get up to give a fine solo rendition of a very sentimental song:

> "When I see the stars at night
> I think of home.
> Oak woods in the heart tonight
> I think of home.
> Loved ones calling
> Our tears are falling
> With the dawning
> We will head for home.

Fed and contented the two groups of miners began to relax, swopping stories of rock falls, near misses and disasters. Then came question time! Iffy had one or two burning questions to ask that had never been satisfactorily answered. "What was it that the sisters told you about, when we first set off from Oak village?" Everyone looked intently at Brimen, waiting for his answer. "We have a right to know?" pleaded Iffy.

"Oh! It was nothing to get alarmed about!" answered Brimen, holding up his mug to be refilled with tea. Smarty obliged and offered some buttered toast all round.

"Just one other question then," said Iffy. "Why did you go the long way round to Isolate?" He then postulated. "Is D'rasnah back in

Evermore - and hiding?" waiting patiently for an answer as Brimen gulped down his nettle tea.

"Well! I., er.!" flummoxed Brimen, not intent on wanting to commit him-self, before he had all the facts. "Mmmmm! perhaps he has paid a visit or two." He eventually confessed.

"So banishment hasn't worked," said Iffy defying the silence that often occurred when awkward reasoning presented itself. "We have a right to Know?"

"Rubbish!" responded Brimen coughing on his toast as he tried to swallow it. "Of course it has," he said taking in a sharp intake of breath, trying to dislodge the crumb. "Now, stop pressuring me!"

"We all heard Aktoo say that D'rasnah has returned to Darkwood, with Cretin."

"There's no such thing," said Brimen gulping down the crumb with tea. "No such thing!" he continued spluttering.

"He also said Cretin is cutting down the Yews! Then Drasnah must be helping him?"

"There's no such thing!" repeated an obstinate Brimen, hoping to push the idea out of existence.

"It must be true!" interrupted Olan, staring straight at Brimen in a challenging way.

"Ersatz is going to attack the King! It's only ever been the moment, WHEN! That we know for sure and the goblins will help him?"

"Rubbish!" mumbled Brimen half believing it. "We can't be sure that anything has happened yet!" He carried on coughing and spluttering for a while until he finally cleared his throat.

"But, what about Cretin?" said Iffy. "Aktoo was heading for the flint mines when he left us at sandstone ridge? We all heard him yell?" Iffy's constant questioning held everyones attention. "This is a very important fact that you have not thought of," he said to Brimen.

"Well, I did!" said Brimen looking annoyed. "We all know very well that the flint mines were mentioned - But let's get our cargo home first?"

Iffy carried on his penetrating questions. "Acktoo, also garbled something about, tunnel! Fox and the Skelt hound. Did he mean that the goblins are going to use our tunnels to escape after we have all been attacked by the Skelt hound – that you were sure had been banished?

"Well! I don't know! said Brimen, raising his voice angrily, tired of tolerating such insistant questioning. "No, one is going to get past Ughem and Seghi, that's for sure!" he snapped. "Now let's get some sleep and sort it out when we get home."

The mention of the Skelt hound, was disturbing Brimen more and more, although he was struggling to suppress its effect. As he lay there, he could not get the vision of his previous encounter out of his mind. It was to give him another unpleasant night. "None of this makes any sense!" he mumbled sleepily before finally getting some rest.

Brimen was first to rise in the early morning wih just a faint mist rising from the grounded leaf mould, the fresh smell permeating the air. It was a lot lighter now with the oncoming season of spring, he was eager to get home. He breathed in deeply, just as he did every morning when he exercised. He then set about waking the others.

"Come on Olan, wake up!" he shouted then gave a good shake. "Come on! We have the harvest to pick," he said fooling him.

"Oh! No," stirred Olan sleepily. "Not the short straw again," he yawned. Brimen laughed with joy, at the Oakmans confused reactions.

Gannon was soon on his feet waking Graff and the rest of the miners. "You won't be so 'problem' free when we get back to Oak Village," he said to the joyous Brimen.

'Problems!' grinned Brimen defiantly, as he clutched the satchel tightly to his body.

"Bah!" he said dismissively. "Nothing could be as challenging as last year."

"Yeh, well, don't get over confident, that's all," said Gannon. "I have the feeling that we are going to get a shock when we return, that's all."

Chapter 8

Brimen loses the Satchel

Arriving back in Oak village the carts divided. Nine of them, consisting of iron, coal, tin and other minerals were taken to the pier at Berber creek, where they were unloaded and sorted onto canal barges under the direction of Smithy and the Smelters. These would then be sent onto the merchants at various locations for general usage. The contents of which, would be split equally between the little folk and the industrial side, of Evermore. The three most valuable carts; of gold, silver, precious stones and gems would be taken to the vaults beneath the lodge, to be sorted for the King.

Brimen was eager to get away from all the formalities of trade, leaving the gruelling work for others to work out. He had this tremendous urge to take off on his own, but first he had to meet the Mayor and other Elders for a briefing at Oak Civic Hall.

Before he actually left, both Gannon and Olan pleaded with him to leave the satchel with them, locked in the toolbox on the cart for safety. Yet! He protested, ruefully. "You didn't care to relieve me of its burden before, any way we are in the village." He said confidently. "I'll be safe, what can possibly happen here?"

"Then don't take to lingering around the Chambers, expecting to discuss your Statue." said Gannon. "We have a lot of work to get through,"

"And remember!" said Olan. "We will have to have that meeting with Sprite."

Brimen went merrily on his way, stopping occassionally to chat to one or two old friends, who were pleased to have him back, to share their worries "Rumours abound..," they stated ominously. Others mentioned fearfully. "Things are changing..," Then what he didn't want to hear. "We've heard D'rasnah is back - with the Skelt!"

Brimen's anxiety increased with every meeting. He knew he would have to deal with these issues and decided that perhaps his friends were right maybe he shouldn't take things for granted. Maybe he should have left the satchel in their care. Perhaps now, he will secure the satchel in the lodge before he meets up with the others. That decided, while still retaining a buoyant mood and so happy to be home, he was about to climb the stone steps leading up to the lodge.

Speculation over his feelings was diverted for a moment when he caught a sight of young Tad and his bother, about to finish their grocery delivery round. "Mmm! I'll cadge some eggs and a spare, current loaf and scones - for free," he chuckled mischievously.

Calling out he gave Tad a wave, beckoning them both to come over and stop for a 'friendly' talk, while at the same time encouraging them to part with some 'spare' grocery's for free. "Don't tell Mr Gannon," he whispered to Tad as they parted.

By now, it was mid afternoon: the town hall clock chimed at three pm. "Spot on," he muttered checking on his timepiece. He would have expected Gannon and Olan to be returning to the lodge about now and considered that maybe they would leave their cargo in the vaults and finish the laborious work tomorrow. With that in mind he was thinking of spending a quiet evening with his love Eva. Perhaps the Mayor and the Elders could wait at least until tomorrow.

More amusing to Brimen, as he gained the top step to the lodge was the sight of a broken broom left laying on the porch. 'Oh! Oh,' he smirked. 'Prims has been at it again,' he thought. "Somethings never change!" Overloaded with arms full of buns, eggs and encumbered by his sore thumb, he fiddled for his keys. "Poor, old Rooney," he muttered affectionately, picturing Prims in full battle charge.

When he eventually opened the front door, Brimen chuckled, preoccupied with balancing the buns, scones and eggs that he awkwardly held onto. "That temper of hers," he mused as some of his 'spare' groceries fell to the floor. He then slipped – one handedly - the satchel over his head to rest it on his shoulder as he stooped down to retrieve the scattered food.

It was a strange welcome home and he hesitated in the stillness. There was no sign of activity, no smell of fresh bread baking, gooseberry pie, or sight of any food on the dining table. Not even a fire in the hearth to warm the place.

"Where are you?" shouted Brimen, while searching in and out the different rooms.

"Obviously you are not expecting me," he said to the silence then made for the large pantry intending to shelve his load of eggs, buns and scones.

On opening the door he got a massive shock; too see Rooney and Prims gagged and roped together, floundering around on the floor. Aghast, he dropped the load – smashing the eggs - and rushed in to help them, hearing the door slam shut behind him.

"Got you now!" said the jarred voice of Nescient, echoing in his ears as he fell helpless to the floor entangled in a net. Instantly Brimen was jumped on, by many feet and held captive on the ground.

"You'll never get away with this!" protested Brimen with his face held firmly, pressed to the floor. Feeling duped and weakened after his busy time in the mines he tried to rally all the fighting strength within him. "We'll track you down and..." he wrestled free a fist and let go a punch through the net, catching Nescient on the nose.

His protest was soon overcome when, held down by many hands, they pummelled him into submission, stuffed a gag into his mouth and bound his hands and feet. The net was then removed and he felt the wrench of the satchel torn from him.

Further stiffled cries of, 'You'll never get away with this! We will hunt you down and..,' were met with a sniggering objective fact. "We already have - got away with it!" snorted Nescient. "Look, what I have in my hand?" He gave off a loud raucous laugh left ringing, tormentingly in the captive's ears.

Further protests led to another heavy beating. The goblins then roped Brimen together with the other two captives. They all had to watch helplessly as these, enemies of Evermore, ravaged the shelves of cakes and buns, including Brimen's favourite – gooseberry pie.

The humiliation sent Brimen crazy as he watched them all racing out the door with Nescient gripping tight the satchel while all three victims – Brimen, Rooney, Primms – looked on in a state of extreme shock. Tied up, gagged, and hopelessly trying to wriggle free.

Suddenly! Nescient reappeared and threw back into the room the leather, carrying strap, saying. "Here! You will need this for the next satchel – we now have all we need," he said holding it high in triumph.

It was to be sometime before Gannon and Olan were able to release them. The two had decided to finish their heavy work load first and rest later, expecting Brimen to join them at anytime. Instead, they became extremely annoyed at having to do all the hard work in the vaults while their leader, as they understood, was socialising with the Elders. In fact they had become furious, thinking that perhaps Brimen was now resting, taking a crafty snooze.

Frustratingly, they began a search of the empty rooms. "Something is not right!" said Gannon. "There is no sign of Rooney?" He looked around the main room. "No fire in the grate? No lights on? No supper ready on the table?"

"I can only think that Brimens not back yet!" replied Olan perplexed. "Then, perhaps Rooney and Prims, are away visiting relatives?" They were about to give up the search and prepare their own food in the scullery, when they saw the traces of crushed bread and scones left laying on the floor. They appeared to come from the pantry, the trail continuing out of the back door that showed it wasn't closed properly. It was then they became aware of muffled cries, coming from inside the pantry.

Opening the door revealed a serious, yet amusing sight. Somehow - writhing and glowing red with temper – Brimen, in his attempt to get free had put himself into an impossible position, completely entangled in a web of rope, with Rooney and Prims. Straight away Olan burst into a fit of laughter at which Gannon couldn't help but join in - until he realised something was missing!

"Where's the satchel?" he screamed rushing over to untie the three entangled victims. "They've taken it!" yelled Brimen when the gag was removed. "It's robbery!" he raged wriggling out of his bondage, forgetting the pain of his ordeal.

While he was anxiously trying to explain how he was attacked, his voice was drowned out by the hysterical Prims, when her gag was removed. She began yelling and accusing Rooney of not protecting her. Sobbing that he 'didn't love her' and then deliberately shoved Brimen out of the way as she got to her feet.

"Hmmm!" thought Brimen frowning angrily at the overwrought Primms. "The huge, whack, THAT, that broken broom took. I wonder how the goblins ever managed to get inside the lodge…"

"The satchel, they've stolen it!" pressed Gannon. "What will they do with it now?"

"I don't know!" snapped Brimen, rubbing the rope burns on his wrists. "What can

'THEY' do with such information?" As usual Brimen was getting complacent and needed a jolt to be reminded.

"There you go again," said Olan. "Telling to your-self, that 'nothing is amiss'."

"Rubbish!" said Brimen dismissing the idea. "It's letting us know they're back."

"Olan may be right," defended Gannon. "They've obviously got something 'terrible' in mind – We've all heard the rumours?"

"I'm warning both of you," snarled Brimen. "Now that's that and all about it!"

"You always think you know best!" said Olan too the distraught Brimen. "If you had locked the satchel in the toolbox – when we asked you to – then this would never have happened."

"I'm warning you!" said Brimen again, waving his fist in Olans direction.

"Well!" responded Olan to the threat. "It would now be safe in the vaults! So it is YOUR! Fault. Don't blame others."

"I'm warning you!" said Brimen getting redder and redder with embarrassment.

"Well! Admit it!" said Olan. "Aktoo was right the goblins have returned to cause havoc." He was going to stop there but had the intuition to know how serious this was going to turn out. "You know that as a fact!" said Olan pointing his finger directly into Brimens face. "Folks, in the village know that!" he continued. "We all know that! NOW! What are we going to do about it?"

This was the last thing that Brimen was going accept from Olan. That somehow he was failing in his duty to protect Evermore. Gannon knew what was about to happen next and grabbed Brimen arms to his side, too stop him throwing a punch. As he did so, Prims glowered at Brimen, disapprovingly, and he relaxed his stance.

Brimen, calmed "I'm telling you now," he said firmly but friendly. "The goblins will not get away with it. So let's investigate just how D'rasnah, managed to get back here?"

"By what I could see and hear," said Rooney with a shudder while still holding Prims hand to soothe her. "They had bought back with them the SKELT! Hound," Prims let out an even louder cry, in sympathy over Brimen's previous encounter with the hound some time before. It was she who had dealt with the bites to his ankles.

"I saw D'rasnah hold onto him outside, before we were tied up," carried on Rooney. "It was, snarling, spitting, growling.., and bit into Prims broom, when she hit out at it!"

"That red eyed monster!" spat Brimen sounding tough for Prims attention. "If it comes any where near me, I will strangle it!" She looked appreciably back at him.

"We shouldn't act so surprised," reminded Olan. "We know it is back!" "Aktoo told us! He also told us that Monk has locked himself away!"

"Huh?" expressed Brimen.

"On the Ridge - remember?"

"Yes! yes! yes! Now let's investigate further," and turned to Rooney. "Didn't you see them come up the steps?

"No!"

"The booby traps! Were they set?"

"Yes! All the alarms were!" defended Rooney.

"Ah! Wait a minute," interrupted Gannon. "The window, It was wide open when we came through."

"But, that's a sheer drop outside, you would need a rope to climb up…," suddenly Brimen realised that before they left for Isolate, 'he' had been hauling up chunks of 'Special' white granite at the foot of the rock. "YOU, left the window open - again?" Yelled Brimen, "You know that Owl was suspiscious, last time?"

"I'm sorry," said Rooney feeling guilty. "YOU, left instructions for me to bring up some more rock when you were returning," he justified. "I only started it this morning"

"But, you left the window open?" shouted out Brimen, he then started to brood, pacing up and down the lodge floor.

"I'm doubly sorry!" sobbed Rooney. "I never thought of being attacked in daylight!"

"Now, that is enough!" said Gannon raising his voice. "Don't blame Rooney! There had to be another way they got here?" He insisted.

"So what do you have in mind?" grunted Brimen. "They sprouted wings and flew?"

"Just consider this!" said Gannon. "The 'Skelt' can't climb a rope! and D'rasnah doesn't have enough muscle on those skinny arms to lift his fat belly up a rope?"

"Exactly!" agreed Olan. "There must have been some other way?"

"Mmmmm!" pondered Brimen reaching the same conclusion. "We now need to find what that 'other' way was."

"The question is - how have they managed to move around so effectively," said Gannon. "Nobody has reported seeing them arrive and nobody has seen them leave?"

"Mmm! that is an interesting point," agreed Brimen getting calmer. "We need a rest to prepare our selves and then, get that satchel back." He then apologised for putting Rooney and Prims, through such a distressful time. Prims, 'huffed' her disapproval and left the room, to prepare their evening meal.

While they agonised over the injustice of being attacked on their first day back in Oak village, Smarty and Smug arrived as previously arranged and were shocked to hear of the events that had taken place. Then minutes before they were due to sit down to a hearty meal, a missile smashed through the window crashing into the trophy cabinet where, the medals and one of Brimens prize mugs - awarded for services rendered – was placed.

Concerned more about the damaged cup and how he would repair it, he totally ignored the rock laying on the floor. Olan picked it up and removed the message tied to it. The message read:

'I'm back with your favourite pet and his special taste for Oakmen's ankles. Hah! Hah!' signed D'rasnah

Almost immediately, another rock came hurtling through the window destroying one of Gannon's prize cups inside the same cabinet. This time, Brimen caught sight of the goblins arm as the rock smashed through. "He's on the roof," yelled Brimen.

Olan was quick to move and hurriedly went over to the cabinet to rescue his own awards before a third stone landed. The other message read:

'Thanks for giving me all the plans. I've got plans of my own'. signed D'rasnah Hah!

Furious! Brimen grabbed his club, shouting out for immediate revenge. Gannon and Olan automatically grabbed theirs with Smarty and Smug running ahead of the chase as they went after their tormentor.

Rooney was already outside armed with his catapult and fired several stones at the figure scrambling over the roof of the lodge making for higher ground. "Set the traps!" yelled Brimen and whacked a lever that would release a net flying through the air. But it didn't work. The mechanism had been tampered with.

The intruder had a good start over the steep rock as Brimen began his climb. Straight away he could see the culprit scrambling ahead of him. He also noticed a stout rope that the goblin was desperately heading for, hanging down from the higher rock face.

Reaching out for it, the goblin began to ascend. Brimen sprinted almost getting to within grabbing distance. Close behind, were Rooney, Smarty and Smug who held on to the rope to steady it for Brimen as he began his ascent. Gannon and Olan soon caught up and ready to climb close behind.

It was a tough climb, yet Brimen, was fit and resolute that the goblin would not escape. Looking above, he could see that the skinny legs of the goblin were about to disappear over the ledge and made a desperate grab for his swinging ankle. Gripping firmly onto the rope with one hand, his other hand held on to it.

Awkwardly, he battled the force trying to stop the goblin from getting over the top, which in turn set off an uncontrollable spinning motion - that the gnomes below found extremely hard to steady. The weight of three Oakmen was overload. Brimen, grimaced determinedly. "There's no escape up there!" he warned. "It doesn't lead anywhere."

Brimen then gasped in surprise, feeling the added weight of someone climbing on his back. Grabbing hold of Brimen's belt buckle, Gannon, was hauling himself up and had now reached out for the other swinging ankle. "Hold on!" he assured Brimen. "I'm nearly there." The struggle to hold onto the goblin and now his fellow Oakman, was exhausting. After two or three failed attempts, Gannon could not hold on any longer either and slipped.

In desperation he wildly grabbed hold of Brimen's tunic to steady himself, but that became a disaster as the stitching gave way, ripping the cloth off his back. Brimen, almost successful in capturing his attacker, would regrettably have to let go of the wriggling goblin too.

"We nearly got him!" lamented a disappointed Brimen as he let himself down. Looking at the other two laying prostrate on the floor exhausted, he lay down too. As they were recovering from their ordeal, Iffy came rushing over panting. "He's still up there," he said pointing to the top of granite rock. "You can still get him?"

"Are you sure?" said all three together ready to try again.

"Yes! He hasn't come down yet – even from the other side - because most of the folk from the village have the area surrounded!"

"Wasn't there a rope hanging down from the other side?"

"NO, so he can't escape!"

"How did he get up there?"

"He'll answer that, when we bring him down. Come on, let's try again."

Brimen had reached the top, his arms hot with the effort, struggling to get a good grip on the rock. Pulling him self up he balanced the top half of his body on the ledge just about to swing his 'shaking' leg up, when he saw the skinny legs of the intruder they had been chasing directly in front of him.

An even bigger and unbelievable shock was the sight of a hot air balloon - The type that Monk was sometimes seen to use – rising up behind him, waiting to take off.

The next moment - between the goblins legs bounding towards him, was the Skelt hound held on a long leash by D'rasnah. It growled menacingly, large paws gripping the rock to propel itself faster and faster toward the stunned face of Brimen.

Gannon and Olan – not aware of what was happening - were just below him hanging on the rope yelling at Brimen to move on up. Then - helpless and frozen to the spot – Brimen took the full blast of foul breath as the Skelt's jaw opened, bearing a vicious set of teeth with huge, sharp, fangs on blood red, gums.

The horrifying surprise forced Brimen to lose his grip, sending him falling past Gannon and Olan, who were still clinging tightly onto the rope. Luckily, for Brimen he fell on top of Rooney and only sustained a sprained wrist with scratches, Rooney was crushed and suffered bad bruising.

"How did that hound get up there?" said Gannon as they all lay on their backs panting, struggling to get their strength back. "It's just not possible!"

"Oh! It is," groaned Brimen. "They've got a hot air balloon?"

"Are you sure you didn't imagine it?" said Olan massaging his tired legs. At that moment the evening sky was that much darker as they watched the round shaped shadow of the balloon pass over head.

Focusing high above them, looking down on the distraught Oakmen, was D'rasnah, Nescient and the goblin, laughing out loud as they both held onto the snarling Skelt hound, its red eyes intently locked on to Brimen.

"What caused you to fall," mocked D'rasnah. "Don't you like my pet?" He then threw the rope down on top of them. "We have even more surprises coming your way!" The falling rope was followed by rocks and bags of sand as they ascended higher.

"I told you I had not imagined it!" raged Brimen jumping up on his feet to avoid being hit by the falling debris. He began to shake his fist angrily in the air as a dire warning to the goblins.

"How did they get hold of that balloon?" groaned Rooney getting help to be carried back to the Lodge.

"They stole it from Monk. That's how! It's his own fault for locking himself away!" Back inside the lodge Prims was dutifully nursing the wounded, giving Brimen more attention than her own injured Rooney. Olan showed disapproval when she took so much time fitting a sling for Brimen's arm. "It's only a sprain!" he said.

The late tea time chimes sounded as the heavily bandaged Rooney came into the room wincing and limping with every step he took. While pushing the trolley he was profusely apologising for not detecting or seeing the intruder before the rock was thrown through the window. Brimen showed no sign of sympathy at the confession and accused him:

"Things are getting lax," said Brimen frowning, intent on making his housekeeper feel guilty. "Your booby traps are not working."

"That's not fair! Who would have expected them to use a Balloon?"

"That is now twice in a very short time that the goblins have attacked the lodge!"

"I'm sorry!" replied Rooney still wincing with discomfort. "But I think we need extra look-out patrols, like we had before."

"He's right," said Olan "We have, ALL got complacent since our victory last year.

"Bah!" dismissed Brimen.

"Aktoo and the Yewmen are so angry they don't want a meeting. They want action!" said Gannon sharply. "I'll get Fisty, Knuckle and Bone to help us," he added turning to Brimen for agreement.

There was no real answer, just a grunt of displeasure. Then a low groan as he moved his bruised arm to a more comfortable position.

"NO! Need for that!" He eventually said. ""The goblins won't use that balloon up here again. They'll expect us to be ready for them!"

"They have just proved to us that they have an advantage!" said Gannon. "Then they could drop anything on us?" Brimen thought for awhile knowing that Gannon was right and said "Then, we must find it and destroy it on the ground. Preferably with that red eyed Skelt hound in it! "Meanwhile we need someone to tell us where Fox is hiding. Remember! Owl insisted that this challenge must take place."

Minutes later Prims returned with bandages and ointment to treat the rope burn marks on Brimen's wrists. She then began fussing over his sore thumb. Gannon and Olan looked at each other, half smiling, raising their eyebrows with surprise. The humoured look soon turned to dismay when the door swung open and in stepped Eva, May and Daisy

Eva's presence demanded immediate attention from Brimen, as did May and Daisy from Gannon and Olan respectfully. After all they hadn't seen their partners for many months. Prims quickly gathered her things together then hurriedly removed her-self to the scullery, while Eva took over the fussing of Brimen's wounds.

At the end of an exciting evening, recalling their latest adventures, the wives left in protest over the Oakmen's claim that they needed to stay at the lodge for a bit longer in order to heed off the latest threat to Evermore.

After an extremely late supper the three retired wearily to their beds. Prims briefly returned to remind them to behave or else! She was not prepared to tolerate the result of another pillow fight.

As he lay awake, Brimen, felt guilty about losing the satchel. His main concerns, were haunted by the image of the Skelt hound and the nasty bites he had received on that previous occasion. It was so long ago that he had almost forgotten the event. Now the vivid memory was almost as if it were yesterday.

Gannon, lay there wide awake working out a plan in his head to recapture the beast by luring D'rasnah into a trap. Olan lay there thinking about the comical sight of Brimen, tied up in the pantry, having to surrender the satchel.

Soon all three were snoring in harmony, chasing dreams in another world while searching for results in this one. It would turn out to be the most comforting sleep that they had enjoyed in months.

Chapter 9

A warning to all

The new day soon arrived and Brimen awoke to the comforting smell of freshly baked bread, accompanied with the pleasant strains of Gannon singing. Glancing at the empty bunk beds meant that Gannon and Olan had been up early to give Prims a rest from her daily routine, helping her to recover from the brutal treatment of the day before.

It was then that he realised his fears of the previous day had not been a bad dream.

"Oh!" he groaned turning over. "We should have stayed longer at Isolate." Brimen's snug reverie then sought comfort in the idea that someone else should lead Evermore,

Well - at least and until - after his statue was erected. He spent the next moments pressured while still agonising over the stolen satchel and how to destroy that, balloon.

Rooney put his head around the door to remind Brimen that it was breakfast time and not to forget that his guests would be arriving soon. Rooney also relayed a message from Eva, that she understood why he had to stay longer at the lodge. She missed him but enjoyed last night and looked forward to seeing him again soon.

The sentiment cheered Brimen, he had almost forgotten that some would never desert him - no matter what. An ugly mood now changed to one of optimism as he entered the lounge where another happy surprise awaited him: the trophy cabinet had been repaired. 'Or was it a bad dream'.

"Olan had it fixed early this morning," said Rooney entering the room to lay the breakfast table. "Dewey always does an excellent job, always cheap, always quick."

"Mmm! That was quick work," he muttered bending down to examine the repair.

With such a positive start to the day, the statue now became the focus of Brimen's thoughts as he heartily looked forward to all the attention he would receive from his friends after being away for so long. For now, he had conveniently put aside the challenging events of the previous day, eagerly awaiting his early morning guests. Brimen moved over to the open window to breathe in the fresh air, sipping his tea whilst looking at the view thinking, 'no more strenuous digging or loading of carts for a good while yet.'

While he lingered at the window, the contented frame of mind was soon jolted back to reality when he heard and felt a rumble. It was very slight yet strong enough to rattle his cup in its saucer. In the far distance he could then see a thin plume of smoke rising from the disused sand quarry. The effect was almost as familiar as experiencing the Gunpowder fairy's antics in the marsh – the previous summer.

Suddenly the front door burst open taking his attention away from the burning scene to more immediate matters, as Rooney welcomed in the morning guests: Smarty, Smug, the Mayor, Town Crier, and others. Brimen then became alive and preoccupied in his role as host as all were joyously received with lots of hand shakes, pats on the back and gifts on his homecoming. All accompanied by warm compliments for the successful and lucrative venture to Isolate.

The alarming events from the previous day were eagerly discussed and matched by their guest's rumours of any return of the goblins. "The villagers currently feared an impending doom," said the Mayor. This matter was then put firmly behind them and they eagerly tucked into a hearty breakfast. "No matter what may happen in the present," claimed Olan. "The Oakmen were entitled to one full day of relaxation - and err, merriment," he chuckled to a fine applause.

That said, Brimen decided not to mention the far away rumble that he heard or the rising smoke that he clearly saw. After all it wasn't that loud, he reasoned. 'Mmmm! perhaps it was Monk up to his usual 'tricks' when inventing something new, he convinced himself.

He continued to enjoy his meal whith the agreeable company, hoping to promote further his personal ideal. More than once the triumphal statue - to be erected in the square - was suggested and more than once the idea was laughed, politely out of existence.

Owl, who had not been around to advise or throw any light on current difficulties, suddenly arrived on the window ledge and Brimen would not get another chance to raise the issue, which made him moody.

"Where have you been?" said Brimen, scolding Owl as he let him in, whilst at the same time scanning the quarry for signs of more smoke. "And where is Sprite?" he said, half listening for another explosion. Something else then seemed to attract Brimen's attention but because he was distracted, chose to ignore it.

"Give me time to get warm," said Owl staring at Brimen oddly. "It's colder than I thought it would be." He spread his wings and moved inside hooting acknowledgement to the guests and landed on the tall pendulum clock.

"Huh!" grumbled Brimen. "Some of us have had to put up with this cold weather for months," he moved over to slam the window shut and saw another plume of smoke rising up from the quarry. 'That's what it was - a flash of light?' he realised.

Owl, made him-self comfortable while the guests were finishing their breakfast, complaining at the same time that his perch hadn't been dusted since they went away. Making a fuss, he flapped his wings to dispel the dust, nestled in then closed his eyes for a short nap. He eventually thawed, spread his wings then demanded that the satchel be ready, to take back with him for Monk the Elder.

Brimen became distant, not in the least interested in Owls request. The only thing his mind was responding to was worry over the increasing activity in the sand quarry. 'But that plume of smoke?' he thought. 'The flash of light," he kept thinking. 'Ah! The wood cutters!' he suggested to self. 'Mmmm! yes, that's who it is," he reasoned assuredly. Yet, he had to admit to reality, 'wood cutters burning in the sand quarry?'

There were too many questions that could not find any answers now racing through his mind and his distant mood showed. He continued to finish his meal wearing a heavy frown.

The fretting expression soon gave cause for concern. "Come on!" said Gannon. "Tell us, what is troubling you?"

Relieved at last to share his worry Brimen said. "It's the sand quarry!"

"What about it?" said Gannon. Getting out of his seat Brimen moved over to the window and looked out. "Something odd but serious is happening over there!" he said nodding in that direction.

"What do you mean by that?" said Gannon.

"It's the second time I've seen it," said Brimen. "Look! Come over here?" he said gawping. The guests, taken by surprise, looked on and gathered at the window too. "I also heard a rumble! Earlier," said Brimen watching another plume of smoke rise. They all stared in disbelief trying to work out a logical explanation. "THERE! Did you hear that? See that flash? They all nodded solemnly looking at each other feeling deeply worried. "Look there's more smoke?"

Olan, added to the remark as an after thought. "There's nothing to catch alight in there?" Then, concluded, whilst searching for another reason. "Or, perhaps it is Monk, he does some odd things at times. Or, charcoal burners?"

"WHAT, charcoal burners, in the sand quarry?" said Gannon, now as deeply concerned as Brimen. "There's no need for them to use that place. No! This is far more serious than that."

"Then it must be Ersatz and the Neanderthals," said Brimen. "I fear the worst?"

"It can only be Ersatz! Somehow he has got hold of gunpowder from the marsh."

"That means D'rasnah and the goblins are helping him,"

"You must be right!" said Owl gloomily. "It definitely isn't Monk because as you know - he has locked himself away, in the grotto."

"Why?" asked Brimen

"He told Sprite that he needs a rest."

"That explains then how the goblins managed to steal his air balloon."

"What did you say?" hooted Owl. "That thing that 'he' thinks is a 'bird'?"

"Bird of the air or not, D'rasnah flew above us yesterday after he had attacked the lodge, just hours before?" said Brimen.

"Oh! That!" hooted Owl ignoring the seriousness. "We heard all about THAT!" he continued to snigger until all of them were in a state of amusement over Brimen's predicament, tied up with Prims and Rooney.

"Enough! Enough!" shouted Brimen, tempted to see the funny side but raising an objectionable hand, said. "Let's decide how we are going to deal with THIS situation."

Meanwhile, Brimen's guests where looking flummoxed at Owls casual approach to matters of grave importance. "Is no-one interested in saving Evermore?" angered the Town crier moving everyone away from the window. "Where is Sprite?" he insisted. "She should be here?"

Bremen's guests all turned to look directly at Owl, shrugging their shoulders as if to say, 'If anyone should know, YOU should?' Owl, seeing the expression of expectation, caught their attention with an honest reply.

"Sprite, can not be here," he said slowly. "She has secured another part of Darkwood with the help of Fairy Sow thistle and Willow herb, but is battling an even greater threat from the Red witch!"

"WE," cut in Brimen doubtful of Owl's excuses said sternly. "..Did not know of this. WE have been working in the mines all winter," he shouted angrily. "Now, if you have something to say - Say it."

Owl gave a long, low, disapproving hoot at Brimens intolerant outburst. "Ersatz had bought the, Red Witch of Drone into his tower and it was that move that had made Merva and Derva jealous." He said with an indignate expression. "Desperate! The sisters left him. Now, before you ask, it was the Red Witch that turned Brock Badger and the pixies to stone - Not Merva and Derva."

"Why didn't we know this before?" said Brimen.

"We hadn't realised this fact until you had left for Isolate," replied Owl.

"Where is the red witch now?"

"We do not know! We do know that Cretin is back in Evermore too."

"But doesn't all this put Merva and Derva at risk?"

"Yes! But the sisters have promised Sprite that they would help in freeing Badger and the pixies from stone."

"Can she trust them?"

"She has to! There kind of magic could reverse anything Redwitch tries to do."

"Are you really sure of that!" said Gannon. "Because Monk will have nothing to do with either of them, he has lost control."

"That's because they can't trust Monk,"

"And where is he?" said Brimen. So intense had he become, that he was forgetting his room full of guests.

"As I said earlier," hooted Owl sternly. "For some reason he won't leave the grotto"

"Why hasn't he been seen. Is no one interested in saving Evermore?" blasted the Town Crier for the second time.

"Of course they are!" hooted Owl. "You must understand: Monk has got a lot to answer for." he admitted. "That is why Merva and Derva are helping Sprite to release Badger and the Pixies from their petrified state: They want to help."

"But Monk's sisters are in great danger. Doesn't he care?" said Olan.

"I'm not so sure he does," said Owl reflecting on their imprisonment in the Citadel.

"Then we should go into Darkwood and rescue them," said Brimen.

"NO, you must not go in there," said Owl. "It is what D'rasnah would expect us to do, now that the Skelt hound is back under his control. Besides, your ankles couldn't take another bite," added Owl hooting a laugh trying to lighten the mood.

"Don't start the sarcasm, we know what we have to do!" snapped Brimen.

"So you're ready for the Skelt?" contested Owl.

"Well!" paused Brimen. "We need to work at it."

"Don't forget what Sprite mentioned," said Owl. "Fox must do his bit."

"Enough! Enough!" cried Brimen feeling the pressure.

"Remember?" Owl reminded them. "Sprite said to trust Fox when he appears: He must do his bit too?" he repeated.

"Now hold on a minute," said an indignant Brimen. "I like Reynard, but!"

"No buts about it," snapped Owl. "You all know what Sprite said."

Brimen's stance changed. He thrust out his face with his hands held firmly on his hips. "Are you saying to us, that Fox will take on the hound?"

"It's the only way," hooted Owl. "It's the only way!"

"But if that happens - and he wins - Fox will be hunted for ever!"

"Yes! But it will break the control of D'rasnah."

"What if he loses, as I'm sure he will; will he still be hunted."

"Yes! But it will break the control of D'rasnah," Owl insisted.

"Are you absolutely sure of this?" questioned Brimen.

"It's the only way," hooted Owl. "It's the only way!" he lamented.

"But will it reclaim Darkwood?"

"Most definitely!" hooted Owl assuredly. "Now Brimen you must find him."

"Owl, first you are going to have to investigate the quarry," demanded Brimen.

"I can't go," said Owl. "I do not have the time!

"It won't take you long!

"NO!"

"You won't be seen at the height you fly," pleaded Brimen. "You have perfect EYE's from a great hieght."

"Impossible! I have got to help Sprite and you have to find Fox!"

"But we all know there is something strange going on," raged Brimen.

"Well, then YOU had better take a good look yourself," hooted Owl. "I, have other business to attend too and promptly winged his way out of the window. The town crier took this as a cue to join the exodus, politely agreeing with the other guests that it was now time to leave.

The guests, had enjoyed an entertaining morning, almost ecstatic with the way Brimen handled the whole complex situation, convinced that Evermore was secure and in safe hands.

Observing Brimen's genuine resolve, to put matters right, one of the Elders bent graciously forward to whisper in his ear. "When this is all over – and of course to a satisfactory conclusion – we will have an extra ordinary meeting to discuss, the statue. It would now seem likely that Brimen would eventually achieve his own, personal award.

Chapter 10

Discovery

Within minutes of Brimen's guests leaving the Lodge, Gannon and Olan were busily tidying up after their guests and hopefully looking forward to a restful day, as arranged. Prims needed and had demanded a rest after the events of the day before. In no time at all she set off to stay with an aunty for some peace and quiet.

Suddenly, another urgent knocking came upon the door. "Not again!" huffed Brimen, caught moving halfway between the lounge and the scullery with a pile of dirty plates. He too was helping Rooney because of his injuries, who at that moment was awkwardly attempting to sweep the floor - one handed - near the front door and opened it.

This time it was young Tad with some friends; here to report that they had found an old mine entrance leading on to a newly dug tunnel that Fairy Snoop had told them about. They also had reliable information that D'rasnah was using it, intending to drain the river Fastflow into the underground caverns.

"Rubbish!" shouted Brimen placing the plates firmly on the tea trolly. "How will they achieve that?" He said it realising that he had just answered his own question. At that enlightened moment it had become obvious why D'rasnah had dared to attack the lodge, making off with the satchel and its contents that showed detailed plans of every mine and shaft in Evermore.

Brimen, put his hands up to his tired eyes and rubbed them hard. "Sprite, where are you, I need help?" he uttered softly. Regaining his composure he asked wearily. "Now, Tad, whereabouts is this entrance?"

"One of them is down by the weir," answered Tad enthusiasticly while his friends nodded excitedly in agreement. "And another is..,"

"ONE OF THEM," shouted Brimen wringing his hands to prevent him-self hitting out at something. "How many more are there?" he said giving a heavy sigh thinking that D'rasnah had out-witted him again.

"Ffelin reckons D'rasnah has ideas for many! And they are going to use gunpowder this time, you know, what was used in the marsh."

"But they do not know anything about – gunpowder?" said Brimen consumed with trepidation. Events were now crowding in on him after encountering the balloon flying overhead and now the sight of smoke rising in the sand quarry, still puzzling him.

"Well! They do now," said Olan reminding Brimen that they were not dealing with simple matters. "They also knew where to find 'plans' for their purpose – HOW?"

"From Grindle - that's how," said Gannon. "Had you forgotten he deserted."

"Ffelin said they have a cannon barrel too." added Tad watching Brimen's stiffened reaction when he noticed the youngster's blackened fingers that he and his friends quickly tried to conceal. "HE, stole it from the marsh."

"Well they can't take that down there, it's too big for any tunnels?" said an exasperated Brimen. Reaching across he grabbed hold of Tad's hands. "Have you been in the marsh, playing with that black gritty powder?" said Brimen.

"Yes, Sir!" stammered Tad feeling guilty. "But we didn't go into the marsh."

"Where did you get it from, then?" asked Brimen.

"There are sacks of it, stacked up at that mine entrance, where I just told you that the goblins are busy tunnelling."

"Now listen to me! You must leave it alone. It is far too dangerous to play with."

"But it only burns brite, it doesn't explode like the ones they drop from the balloon."

"From the balloon?" yelled Brimen looking seriously at Gannon and Olan. "Now this is getting very, very serious!"

"Yes! They can fly high up in the Sky," marvelled Tad. "They did it this morning. We were watching them when they started to drop them in the sand quarry."

"Where is that balloon now?"

"They are still using it in the sand quarry that is where they drop them from."

"Where I keep seeing the smoke!" said Brimen to the others. "And the flashes and the rumbles, we need to find out exactly what is going on?"

"I think we should take a look at the Quarry, NOW!" said Gannon, immediately ready for action. "Before they decide, to drop those explosives on the lodge." Instinctively, Brimen reacted and went to get the key to open the armoury. "We need to be armed!" he said firmly. What took the emergency out of the situation was another frantic banging on the front door.

"Oh! No, not again," whined Brimen feeling stressed on hearing the murmuring sounds of Yewmen chanting. 'Hoo! Hoo! Hoo!'

"Calm down," said Olan. "There must be a reason why they are here," and went over to open the door. It was Aktoo and his tribe, all looking as if they had been in a fight. Shocked, bruised with blackened faces could be seen, underneath their normally snow white hair that was now matted with dirt and scorched. Their sparse clothing, ragged and ripped in shreds, most had only one sandal on their feet. All were still chanting, bizarrely. "Hoo! Hoo! Hoo!"

"The Yew wood!" flared Aktoo. "The Yew wood – it is fast, disappearing." He glared at Olan while tapping his staff on the step, in rhythm with what he was saying. "Cretchin is helping D'rasnah - to get rid of US!"

"Slow down, slow down," shouted Brimen bounding over to greet them. "Make sense of what you're trying to tell us!"

"The flint mines, that's where we attacked them," said Aktoo displaying bright eyes staring out from a blackened face. "They used that 'explosive' magic to stop us. You've got to do something? This will destroy us all!"

"We will, we will," confirmed a tired and anxious Brimen.

"Ersatz's men are in the Ash grove too, they are felling the trees," continued the distraught Aktoo. All the while his tribe still continued to mumble. "Hoo, hoo, hoo."

"Then we will have to stop him!" urged Gannon getting impatient to deal with them.

"Tell them to shut up first!" raged Brimen red faced and pressured. "I can't take anymore of that - Hoo! Hoo! Hoo! One thing at a time!" he yelled over their heads.

"One, thing at a time; we can't respond to every emergency at once."

The Yewmen suddenly stiffened - all at the same time and went sullen – staring disappointingly at the ground. Unhappy with complacency, Aktoo forced his way inside the lodge saying, as he pressed his nose firmly onto Brimens. "The sacred Yew – OUR meeting place - is under threat, if D'rasnah undermines THAT then the line of energy will be destroyed. He 'MUST' be stopped."

"I know! I know! Don't pressure me!" raged Brimen turning away, getting redder and redder trying to cope. 'Gunpowder, cannons, balloons, mines' All these things going round in his head, imagining in vivid detail the destruction of the Lodge and Oak village being blown apart.

Almost instantly, he reacted to a suggestion as it went flashing through his agitated mind. 'Anything!' he replied to the suggestion as it gained momentum. 'Anything!' that would send Aktoo and his tribe away.'

"And stop him we will," Brimen suddenly yelled in response to the voice seeking justice as it resounded through his head. "Rooney, go and fetch Trier, Flyer, Catch and Fall." Such an ingenious idea should please the Yewman thought Brimen.

"What do you have in mind?" said Gannon surprised at Brimens inspirational turn-around. He looked at Olan and shrugged his shoulders in the calm spirit that fell.

"You'll see," answered Brimen with a satisfied grin. "Tad, You and your friends come too! You can carry our weapons - come on all of you follow me."

Trier, Flyier, Catch and fall were a tumbling act that often performed at the village fete. They could do all manner of acrobats at an incredibly fast pace, including swinging on ropes - from trees. Now! Brimen considered, was the perfect time for them to get some practice in and so dissuade the wood cutters from wrecking the forest.

The Yew wood was a dense, dark, evergreen forest of knurled and twisted branches. It was an eerie, mysterious place of wild imaginings, haunting of spectres and strange sounding voices hushed in whispers. Where, ingrained into the wooden trunks tortured features of ugly faces changed with the shedding bark. Sometimes laughing, sometimes crying, sometimes starring, sometimes threatening, but always softly groaning. Many feared this hallowed place, where little sunshine entered in.

Fortunately, most of the wood cutters had ceased their heavy workload when the Oakmen arrived. Several of them lay around snoozing, taking a rest after eating and drinking. They felt safer in the broad daylight of the clearing they had made, although dusk was falling fast. A few others had stripped the bark and branches from the fallen trees and were removing the trunks, taking them back to Ersatz for his Long bows and war machines.

Not a single word was spoken as Trier, Flyer, Catch and Fall set to work. Using only hand signals and gestures to indicate their pre-planned operation, they silently moved about the wood taking up strategic positions in the high canopy. Two of them – Trier and Flier - then set a frantic pace to frighten and out wit the woodmen.

Silently and swiftly, swinging down trapeze style, each side of where the trees had been felled, they accurately picked up the tools – one by one - that the woodmen had left scattered all about the site.

When they had collected them all, Catch and Fall set to work in waking the sleepers by throwing things at them and making strange, eerie noises while staying concealed. When they eventually awoke the woodmen, now confused and alarmed, the two of them then went tumbling toward the cutters at a great speed before the wood cutters had the chance to get to their feet. Taking advantage of surprise, they propelled themselves over the prostrate bodies, before vanishing into the undergrowth, where Gannon and Olan were waiting to then entangle the retreating workers in nets as they ran – startled.

As the workers franticly tried to escape the nets and the scary sight of crazy looking Yewmen running at them with their sturdy staffs, hitting them they eventually fled deeper and deeper into the forest. It had sent the woodmen mad with fright, screaming and falling about in all directions until finally they left the site in a manic frenzy vowing never to return.

"That's our problem solved – for now?" said an exasperated Brimen as they saw the last one dissappear "They won't be coming back here, to soon!" he said laughing out loud with the rest.

"What a genius idea! What a genius idea! It was Perfect," lauded Gannon and Olan together while patting their leader on the back.

The excitement was such that Aktoo celebrated with the Yewmen by taking a frantic dash into a nearby pond, to cleanse themselves. For now the Yewmen were pacified and stopped their incessant chanting, leaving Brimen content to move on quickly.

"Come on, let's get to the Ash grove," yelled a victorious Brimen sounding like a warrior, eager to repeat the success. "We will soon move them from out of there!"

It wasn't to be: They arrived only to witness the woodmen leaving. By the time they had returned to the Oakwood it was to late. Unfortunately damage had been done and the woodcutters, gone. Lamenting the destruction, Brimen looked at his pocket watch. "We still have plenty of time to find this mine entrance!" Placing his large hand on young Tad's shoulder said. "Do you think you can find it for us?"

"Just follow me," said Taz feeling proud to be leading at the front with his friends.

"First though!" suggested Gannon. "Let's make for the sand quarry. It's nearer and we can see what is really happening over there."

"Of course!" agreed Brimen. "It is getting late and you youngsters should be at home. We will visit that mine tomorrow."

Brimen felt confident that they were able to move around virtually unspotted. Somehow, since the return from Isolate, he had heard that the sisters had held Lurker prisoner. Of course, at this point he was not taking into account that his every move was being monitored by the most cunning, treacherous, deceitful, yet! - Clever goblin of them all. Lurker was standing alone near the cleft in the rock that led into the quarry at jagged rock.

He was looking ragged without his smart clothes leaning on a crutch to support his weakened leg, the result of an accident? More likely a spell cast by Merva and Derva when escaping from the sisters clutches, freeing Bloogoku much to Cretins delight. He had the look of expectation on his face.

"Oh, it's you again," said Brimen holding himself erect with fists clenched. "Did the sisters do that to you? WELL, what, is it you want this time?"

"Well, Sir!" came the sarcastic response. "I wouldn't go any further, if I was you."

"And who is going to stop us?" said Brimen with a contemptuous chuckle in his voice. "You: and that crutch?"

"It can get very dangerous in there!" warned Lurker.

"Dangerous," huffed Brimen staring at him. "Dangerous for who?" he asked.

"You should know about the power," enthused Lurker shifting his eyes to the entrance. "They are firing explosives!"

"Bah! What do you know about explosives - It is all stolen property!"

"No! no, no. Not stolen! No! It was given. Given to us by the, 'Gunpowder fairy."

"Oh! So that's it, you think you have found a powerful, knew friend, EH!"

"But Oakman, listen to me! He shares something in common with D'rasnah."

"Mmmm!" said Brimen unconcerned with intrigue.

"The destruction of your friend, Monk the Elder," smirked Lurker.

"Bah!" said Brimen dismissing the idea. "Now get out of my way!" and pushed him hard against the wall.

Olan, being heavier, also barged into Lurker, kicking his crutch away. It sent the goblin sprawling across the floor causing the others to walk right over him. Gannon, offered his hand to help him get up – with the hidden intention of hitting him - drew back his arm to strike a blow but Lurker was too slippery and ran – the best he could – hobbling with great difficulty, without his crutch. Gannon picked it up, snapped it in two and through it at him.

"Let him go," said Brimen as Smarty went to give chase. "We don't know what we are going to face through there yet," he said flicking his head toward the crevice entrance.

The smell of burning got stronger as they eased their way through the gap, reminding them of their time in the marsh. To make the moment even more real a huge explosion shook the ground sending black smoke, billowing, getting thicker as the wind funnelled it toward the opening.

It took them all by surprise leaving them coughing and gasping for air. To escape the discomfort they made a desperate attempt to retreat, sneezing with their eyes watering as each jammed each other in the narrow space. Recovered they tried again.

"At least that rabid Skelt won't smell us," whispered Brimen wheezing, as he carefully peered through the haze, only to find himself staring at the red eyed hound.

Although at a fair distance away, its gaze locked on to Brimen, straining on its leash, yelping and whining. "I hope he doesn't break that chain," fretted Brimen. Thankfully D'rasnah was too preoccupied with impressing Ersatz, not seeing the significance of the hound's agitation.

"There's that Balloon!" said Brimen. "That is something we must definitely destroy."

Olan and Gannon, desperate for fresh air, were stretching their necks over Brimen's shoulder to get a view as young Tad squeezed between Brimen's legs. All were now more interested in the magnificent iron cannon, proudly mounted on two wheels that they could scrutinise from a distance.

A monstrous, decorative cast with a fierce looking, ornate face moulded on the end, its mouth open where the projectile came out. Brimen was adamant - with its prominent sculptured nose and full beard - it resembled Culjern. The others could not see the significance, which sparked a minor row. Brimen defended his argument with conviction.

"Well, they did steal it from the marsh!" he claimed, admiring the back half of the barrel resembling scales of a fish with a tail.

"Meaning?" asked Olan with a quizzical look.

"Well, THEY couldn't make such a thing! Where would they get inspiration from," claimed Brimen.

"Meaning?" said Olan cornering Brimen's assumption.

"They don't have the intelligence, THEY! Have to 'filch' others ideas." He said filch with such indignation that it encouraged Olan to keep on annoying him.

"Meaning what?" he insisted watching Brimen roll his eyes and clench his fist.

"Well," snapped Brimen. "Gunpowder is not THERE Invention," he said forcefully.

"Otherwise it would be Ersatz's face on the cannon."

"Ah!" slipped in Olan. "But they can still cause a lot of damage with it in order to get there own way."

Brimen was now furious. How Dare Olan, even think that Ersatz had the right to attack the security of Evermore with the King's own weapons. The suggestion, that some how Olan was sympathising with the enemies, strengths and deviousness, made him intensely mad.

"They should do what they are told!" said Brimen putting an end to the matter. "Now, that's that and all about it!"

"But they are not going to," said Olan with a simple logic that infuriated Brimen.

"I'm warning you!" come the gruff reply while grinding his teeth.

Gannon ever the peacemaker intervened. "Shut up! The pair of you," he said loudly, squeezing himself between the two to stop the argument. "We are here to observe: Nothing else!" he emphasised. It was such a narrow gap that the three of them were now stuck again, wedged between the jagged rocks, with Smarty, Tad and the others looking on bemused.

Suddenly, another deafening explosion took them all by surprise; halting there churlish differences. They watched the red hot iron ball leave the cannon, projecting away from them. It found its target in the sand a good distance away. The wind had thankfully changed direction this time so the effects of the huge, black cloud of smoke, dispelled itself away with minimal disruption.

Smarting from the residue of the gritty remains forced the Oakmen apart. As the smoke cleared in the distance, they could see Ersatz and his warlords jumping up and down excitedly with the goblins dancing on the cannon.

"Oh! Oh!" worried Brimen, seeing Lurker making his way limping across from the other side of the quarry. He was shouting and waiving franticly to get D'rasnah's attention while pointing at the crevice where the Oakmen stood. "We've seen enough," he said. "Let's go!"

As they squeezed themselves out of the narrow gap between the rocks, Ffelin was waiting for them. Wide eyed and agitated, His squat, heavy body looked immovable. "I have to be quick!" he said looking insecure. "I have to tell you that Ersatz and D'rasnah will be celebrating the success of the cannon tonight with the Warlords." His usual reticence in holding back information, while wondering whether or not he was doing the right thing, took over; staring intently at Brimen.

"AND," Shouted Brimen snapping him out of his restraint; waiting for the rest of the information. "Hurry up! We've got to move out of here too!"

"I will make sure that no one is around here," continued Ffelin moving his arms to indicate the quarry area. "Then YOU can destroy THAT Balloon," he said pointing in the general direction of where it stood. "It is far too dangerous! He will drop bombs. It is far too dangerous!" He frowned. "Now I must go!"

Chapter 11

Three Goes Well

Taking Ffelin at his word the Oakmen returned to the lodge to take the idea of destroying the balloon further. It didn't take them long to go on the offensive and decide to strike the first serious blow in the early hours of the following morning. That would be, to destroy the balloon at its resting place in the sand quarry.

"Then it has to be tonight," encouraged Gannon. "If D'rasnah gets the chance to use the 'bomb' that Ffelin told us about, then 'HE' will drop it on the lodge."

"We should ask Monk first!" said Olan. "He might not want it destroyed?"

"We can't wait around for him to tell us," replied Brimen angrily. "He hasn't been anywhere near us since our return! And anyway, Owl said that he has locked himself away in the grotto."

"Then we need to get in touch with Ankra," said Olan. "And learn how too fly it. After all gunpowder is his responsibility, it can only come from the marsh."

"Mmm! I think that he is too occupied with the troublesome 'Kordi'," considered Brimen. "It is he that has given secrets of the marsh away."

"We have two options then," said Gannon. "We could cut the line, that anchors it and let it float away or we can thoroughly destroy it with fire?"

"If we let it fly away then it just might come down again," responded Olan. "And that could give the goblins another advantage. Think of the problems that would bring if THEY managed to retrieve it and hide it somewhere else?"

"Then, we have another two good options!" said Brimen. "The first option: We could take control of it ourselves – and fly it? Or! The second option: We can thoroughly, destroy it by fire."

"But we don't know how to fly it?"

"So obliteration it is?" said Brimen appealing to all of them. "Now that's that! And all about it!" Tiredness was creeping in and an uncertain, slow reaction to his demand.

"It is final then!" said Brimen, to everybody present. "A Total obliteration of the balloon and then; any thing else that we find loitering inside the sand quarry: Agreed?"

"YES!!" came the unanimous reply after prompting.

"Now; we have to work out exactly how we are going to carry out this attack!"

"First things first!" said Gannon. "We are going to need some extra support if we are going to hit them hard and fast."

"Rooney!" shouted Brimen who had just bought tea and scones into the room. "Go and tell Smithy to meet us at the sand quarry and bring some of his gang with him and plenty of tar, oil and rag!" When Brimen had his mind concentrated on duty nothing could surpass him, even the statue was furthest from his mind.

"The best time to attack would be just before the early morning dawn," he reasoned. "It will give us more time to get everyone together and at that time, the whole of Evermore is fast asleep. So now we have to work out exactly what we need to do," he said without a pause. "I know Ffelin said that no one will be around but we shouldn't take any chances." Brimen moved across the room to get his slate, gripped a stick of chalk and drew a circular diagram of the sand quarry:

"Olan!" he said putting the slate on the table for all to see. "I think that you, with Fisty, knuckle and bone, should stay guarding the main entrance." He paused while putting a cross at the spot. "Aktoo and the Yewmen could spread out, as double security, hiding in the woods in front of you and the quarry entrance – here and here," he marked with two crosses. "In case there is a sudden attack from loitering goblins.

"Now!" he considered studying his plan on the slate. "Myself, Smarty, and Smithy will make our way into the quarry, down this sloping track," he indicated. "To the bottom; where the Balloon is anchored; and destroy it!"

"Gannon, take, Smug, Iffy and the rest of the Smelters and get to the other side." He marked the spot on the slate with another cross.

"Come in here; through that cleft where we observed the goblins and Ersatz getting excited at firing that cannon." He then had to assure the group that it wasn't as steep as they feared on that side of the quarry. "NO! no, no, the shale is built up. It is quiet a gentle slope," he guaranteed them. "Your job is to destroy the wooden wheels that support that cannon.

It was just before the dawn when they got within reach of the sand quarry. All was extremely quiet, cold and dark with a damp mist rising as each group took up their positions. Brimen checked his watch just as Gannon and his gang signalled their arrival from the other side.

"We have about thirty minutes to get in there, destroy the balloon and then get out," whispered Brimen, while watching Smithy prepare the tar/oil and rag arrow heads.

Brimen had the truest aim with a bow and arrow. He dipped the prepared missile into the tar and oil, Smarty lit it. Taking careful aim, Brimen fired off the first shot successfully penetrating the big yellow balloon, setting it aflame immediately.

The balloon dissolved in an instant as tremendous billows of flame seemed to extinguish the dark sky itself, brightening as if it were daylight breaking through. The ignited gas continued to leap and roll into balls of flame, higher and higher into the night sky.

From the other side of the quarry, Gannon had discovered that there were more than 'wheels' of the cannon to destroy. Just out of sight of where they had earlier observed the goblins firing off the cannon, several more balloons were being built - some of which were already inflated for immediate use - complete with wicker cradle.

Gannon sent a volley of faming arrows to puncture the first balloon, which alerted Brimen from the other side. Everything was clear for him to see as more balls of flame continued to brighten the night sky. The timing was perfect as more arrows moved swiftly and silently through the dark early morning air and found their target.

The next target was the cannon, in situ on its wooden wheels, poised and ready for destruction. Gannon Smug and Smithy hastily stacked up sacks of gunpowder and set it alight. A tremendous 'whoosh' of a force they were not expecting swept them off their feet. The blast fanned the flames high into the air.

Undeterred and within minutes Gannon and his gang were racing back across the quarry floor to join up with the others. With all this excitement the Oakmen couldn't resist a victorious yell! "That will wake them up!" shouted Brimen. "We've done what we came here for, let's get going!"

Gannon had other ideas "Fracture that pipe," he said pointing to a contraption that had attachments and pipes to supply the gas into the balloons. He held out his bow with another arrow tipped with oil and rag. "Light it!" he said to Smug as the others were making there way up the track.

The fist arrow imbedded in its wooden frame, catching it alight. "Hurry up!" urged Olan shouting back at them. "I can hear those yelping hounds. The second arrow found the container and for a moment nothing happened. "Fracture that pipe again," he demanded of Smug.

Their attention was then taken up by noisy goblins getting nearer and nearer, rushing frantically back to the scene. Nervously, Gannon hurriedly sent another flaming shot and this time it struck perfectly, igniting the contents and the whole contraption went up in a huge blast of blue flame. He and Smug – for the second time - felt the powerful force flatten them to the ground.

In the brief illumination, the Yewmen were seen halting and battering the goblins advance while Olan and the rest surrounded them so that they couldn't escape further punishment. D'rasnah held the Skelt on a lead with Cretin looking cautiously over his shoulder staying just out of reach of the trouble and thankful that the canine would not go any further. The hounds too were huddled close together whimpering, refusing to advance into the smell and smoke of burning.

Acktoo set his eyes on the main target – Cretin. Fearlessly the Yewman ran at a lightening pace with the sole intention of destroying his enemy. Cretin made a run for it as D'rasnah turned the Skelt on Aktoo, which bit into him fiercely. D'rasnah then whipped into the prostrate Yewman as he squirmed on the floor.

"You can see..," said a cheerful Brimen not realising what was taking place. "No hounds will come anywhere near here, they don't like fire and smoke," he chuckled. "Let's join Olan and batter the rest of those goblins into submission!"

It was only then that they come across Aktoo and realised what punishment he took while defending his right to secure Yew wood. They found him crawling, hopelessly on his knees. Every now and then he would lash out with his staff in a delirious manner while muttering threats in a language that not many could understand. The rest of his tribe soon gathered to rescue their leader then carried him away chanting – Hoo! Hoo! Hoo! Defiant yet determined to rid the wood of D'rasnah.

After the big fight the Oakmen returned to the lodge totally exhausted, reeking of gas, oil and tar, battered and blackened with soot but feeling satisfied. They had only been back in the village for a few days - with very little rest - Yet, had already put a serious halt to D'rasnah and the goblins destructive advance. They fell into their bunk-beds and slept and slept without disturbance throughout the remaining morning hours.

It was around mid-day when the Oakmen awoke from their slumbers to welcome Smarty, Smug, Smithy and others to yet another discussion of what to do next. After last nights successful out come, all of them felt more relaxed and eager to devise a better strategy to defeat the goblins - once and for all.

Before they had the chance to put together their ideas, young Tad was soon knocking frantically on the door. He had come to remind Brimen that he never had the chance to show him where the goblins were tunnelling.

"Ffelin said to inform you: you had better get over there quick!" said Tad sounding out of breath after he and his friends had run all the way. "D'rasnah is placing more hounds around the pathways of our village."

"He can't do that!" shouted Brimen. "Who does he think he is?"

"Ffelin said; that he might do the same at the mine, because Ersatz is furious over what happened to his balloons." Tad took another deep breath while his friends joined in. "Ersatz warned D'rasnah to destroy the Oakmen – or ELSE!

"This is OUR Village; not theirs!" boomed Brimen. "Tad, take us to this mine?"

The mine that Brimen was now staring at was an old working now extinct, cut by the Kings men to supply fossil fuel for their industries. Brimen could recall that the huge caverns, so high and so deep, made the place unsafe and that is why it was abandoned. Details showed that tunnels went for miles underground, spreading out in many directions and would be a key link for anyone who wanted to destroy Evermore. He also had to admit that there were detailed plans of this mine, in the lost satchel.

There was one tunnel in particular that run too close to the river Fastflow, the plans of which were also in the satchel, making this knowledge dangerously available for D'rasnah with his evil intent to destroy Evermore.

Confident that D'rasnah and most of his goblins were now preoccupied with trying to repair the destruction at the sand quarry, the Oakmen had arrived at their destination undetected.

Before them hung the ivy, cascading over the steep rock face, concealing the long forgotten entrance - just as Fairy Snoop had said. Stacked up outside the entrance to the mine were even more sacks of 'gunpowder' that had been stolen from the marsh.

"How is it that they have so much gunpowder available?" questioned Brimen.

"The last time that we saw Ankra!" said Smithy. "He was smirking, acting strange – talking hysterically about....Not needing gunpowder anymore....We have something better, he said."

"Mmmm! that is a mystery," answered Brimen frowning with concentrated effort.

From their hidden vantage point they could observe the goblins movements - whilst employed in frantic activity - pushing the overloaded wheelbarrows full of the sacks of gunpowder, into the concealed entrance beneath the ivy. The wheels were squeaking under the pressure of heavy loads often getting stuck in the soft ground.

"Hah!" said Gannon enthused, softly with a pleasant grin. "I've just had a wonderful, clear thought; do they know gunpowder has to remain dry because they are taking it into a very damp place?"

"Possibly not!" responded Smarty adding an infectious snigger but he then voiced reservations as to there expected, easy entrance. "We don't know who else we may have to encounter yet!"

Noticing that the ivy was parting at regular intervals, Brimen elected two of them to make a cautious advance. "Gannon," he whispered. "There must be another side door near that entrance, leading to the wheel house. "Go ahead and find it. Olan: give him support, when you think the time is right signal to let us know."

Olan, made a dash across the open ground thinking that there was no one about but was caught completely off guard when suddenly challenged by Trypannon. The monster appeared without a warning, club in hand, as if from out of nowhere. The purple eyed gaze penetrated into Olan - momentarily freezing him to the spot.

Olan's first reaction, was dread at the thought of being suddenly overpowered by hoards of others coming to support the goblin. Then total commitment to overpower what confronted him. Next, the real fight began. Instinctively, Olan used his weight to unbalance the lanky goblin but it didn't work. Trypannon resisted, hit him with the club and pushed Olan to the floor kicking him when he was down. Olan rolled tightly into a ball to protect himself from the goblins hefty boots and repeated blows.

For Gannon, who was looking on; hesitation meant failure. It was all or nothing as he rushed up from behind the distracted goblin to defend his friend. Raising his staff high in the air, Gannon circled it round his head, let out a yell, and whacked Trypannon with such a force that it doubled him up. Olan revived, got up and rammed his head into the monsters side with such a force that it sent him reeling, knocking him out cold as he fell through the door and lay across the open threshold, jamming it open.

"Wonderful!" said Brimen, watching the action closely from his hide. He patted Smarty on the shoulder. "Come on let's get inside and take a look." Turning to the others he said. "Wait here! "Only attack if you see the goblins carrying on as normal, then, don't hesitate - come and get us out."

Gannon and Olan had Trypannon tied up and gagged by the time Brimen got to them. "Well done!" he said excitedly. "That'll keep the rest of them scared and out of our way for a time."

In the dark recess - to the left hand side of the main entrance - was the wheel house where the main winch mechanism was operated. This hauled the bogeys, filled with mined material up down the steep incline. They could clearly hear that it was still intact and working as through the dirty, cabin windows a soft candle light was glowing, where they could see a shadowy figure moving about operating the large wheel.

On closer inspection they discovered it was Turncoat, chained to an anchor bolt set in the wall. His movements restricted to just about be able, to operate the wheel. Quick to seize him to find out why he was here, it didn't take much enforcement by the Oakmen for Turncoat to reveal all:

"What have you told D'rasnah?"

"Nothing."

"Then what are you doing here helping the goblins?"

"D'rasnah, found me and forced me here! It was because of Fox! He hid me from that wolfhound Tether," he cried.

"Fox?" quizzed Brimen. "It's not like him to get involved?"

"I swear to you, I was running scared from Ersatz: Find Fox, ask him?" said Turncoat. "Set me free - Please. I'm on your side!"

Smarty objected straight away to his fellow gnomes plea with a forcefull. "NO!"

"I'm on you're side," begged Turncoat pleading to Brimen. "Free me!"

"What have you told D'rasnah?" pressured Brimen. "Have you betrayed the oath?"

"NO!" squirmed Turncoat.

Turncoat was made to repeat his oath again and swore that he had not told D'rasnah where the Big Oak stood. "You can see?" he pleaded. "He has me chained up all the time. He'll only free me if I tell him!"

"Why did you not tell him?"

"I bluffed him, I said to him – When you have control of Evermore, there will be plenty of time to find 'Big Oak'.

"What else is there to tell ME?"

"First he wants to drain Fastflow and then the marsh, then he wants the gold. I've told him I can't remember and anyway it would be another five years before the yield."

"He wants to drain Fastflow and the marsh, that's impossible!" said Brimen unbelievably repeating his words. Yet, sure he had heard of this idea before.

"Now get me out of here," demanded Turncoat. Smarty was still enraged with the distrusted fellow gnome and wanted to leave him there as payback for all the times he chose to change sides. "Fox took a beating for you and still didn't tell where you were hid. I think you should stay and suffer."

"You've got to free me?" begged Turncoat. "Otherwise I WILL be telling D'rasnah where the gold is and anyway I've learnt more than you lot know," he said edgily.   "What's that?" demanded Brimen reacting violently, grabbing him by the throat and squeezing hard.

"Cut me free and I'll tell!" squealed Turncoat chocking on the grip.

"Do you really think that you can bargain with the Oakmen?" raged Brimen increasing his grip even tighter. Gannon trapped Turncoats arms from behind and Olan rammed a heavy fist into his weary body

"YOU don't bargain with us! We'll agree only if it's important enough!"

"Oh! This is.," gasped Turncoat, doubled up in pain. "Now, please! set me free."

"If it's not good," said Brimen loosening his grip. "Then you stay here! Tell us and you will have your freedom. But remember we want proof."

"Drasnah intends to mine through to the Grotto," claimed Turncoat gasping and panting with fear over Brimens viscious attack. "...and then explode Monk into pieces! That is why he wanted the plans and I know where it is."

"But we need proof?"

"You'll get your proof! Take these chains off!"

"Then tell us?"

"He's working from the Abbey ruins. Monks old escape route."

"Is he in there now?"

"I don't know! But you should not risk it! D'rasnah has several other escape routes."

"How did D'rasnah know the plans were in the satchel?"

"It was Grindle our fellow gnome!" he said looking at Smarty. "He told him, not me! He and 'his' miners are still supporting the goblins – remember?"

"Of course they are," agreed Brimen, dissapointedly. "Of course they are."

"While you Oakmen were working at Isolate," answered Turncoat. "D'rasnah was locked up in Ersatz dungeon and Grindle was mining esape routes."

On there way out they watched Trypannon trying to wriggle free of his bondage.

"I've got an idea said Brimen. "Let's send him down to meet his friends. I'm sure they all miss him, he said laughing.

It took all of them to lift the struggling goblin into one of the bogeys. When they were ready they unhooked the restraining chain, took off the break and gave the truck a hefty push down the steep incline.

As they were leaving the mine Gannon had the idea to destroy the entrance with the remaining sacks of gunpowder that were left scattered about.

"I'm not so sure I know enough about it," pondered Brimen at such a good idea.

"We know enough to do damage," answered Smarty, with everyone agreeing. "And it will completely seal them in and take them days to get out.

Brimen considered the option, confident that it would take sometime for the goblins to respond to Trypannons misfortune. "Tad!" he said. "You have been playing around with this stuff, show us what you can do?"

All of them knew the risk they were taking, it was now a race against time as Brimen grabbed the first sack and placed it at the entrance. "Let's use those tin cans," said Tad. "Pack it in tight!" They loaded large heavy rocks on top to give it greater compression.

Olan lit the fuse, rushing back to where the others were sheltering. With great joy they looked on to see a massive explosion seal up the entrance. Yelling and cheering at their success bought a feeling of invincibility. In their minds eye they had now become a colossal force to be reckoned with.

"Well! Done, young Tad! It will take them some time to dig their way out of that pile," laughed Brimen feeling powerful. "It will now give us time to concentrate on our next plan."

"What is that?" said Gannon.

"Fox!" Replied Brimen. "It's clear now what Sprite meant. Fox must take on the Skelt, who else could clear the pathways and byways of Evermore?

Chapter 12

Alarm at Never Halt

At first there was total alarm in the den at Never Halt:

"You want me to do, WHAT?" said Fox unbelievably. "Take on the Skelt hound?" He felt trapped by the dependant look on others faces as they circled him. "How did HE get back into Evermore?" said Fox feeling vulnerable over impossible demands.

"D'rasnah has bought him back under his control!" said Brimen.

"Why, Me?" said Fox. "Why am I expected to fight him?"

"Because Sprite said so!" snapped Brimen getting edgy. "You are about the only one who could have helped – when we battled in the marsh – but you did'nt?"

"That is because I had other commitments!" replied Fox.

"But now it is your turn – you must lead from the front," said Brimen forcefully. Then, correcting his hasty remark in case it was misunderstood, rather quickly added. "Well, at least for the 'animals' benefit, – NOT ours!" he stressed pursing his lips.

"You're the only one who can enter Darkwood without suspicion!" said Gannon stating the obvious. "You are crafty! a loner, with enough cunning and stealth, to fool the likes of D'rasnah." Fox appeared quiet pleased with such accusing compliments causing a smirk to spread across his face.

"HAH!" said Fox dismissively. "Don't you realise what D'rasnah tried to do to me when you went off to Isolate?" he then shook his head at the thought of the Skelts return. "YOU, have seen the 'TEETH' on that thing," he said to Brimen. Then, added with a terrified whine. "You, also felt his bite!"

"Take no notice of that," said Brimen with total disregard. "Er! Yes," he then agreed while swallowing hard as he was now imagining the wicked scene again and shuddering. His hand automatically reached down to his ankle feeling for the deep bite marks that he had received when he had encountered the hound for the first time.

"Take NO, notice..?" yelped Fox. "If it hadn't been for Tether..,"

"Take no notice of that!" quipped Brimen not letting him finish. "We will be behind you! To protect you," he said assuredly. "Now that's that and all about it!"

"Look!" said Fox about to leave before he commits to something he may regret. "I've been hunted enough!"

"Take no notice of that," repeated Brimen for the third time. He then glanced at Gannon and Olan as if to say, 'This will be harder than we thought.'

Fox, searching for an excuse, took his time to answer. "This will only make matters worse. Win or lose, packs of hounds will rise up against me!" he said.

"Not if you beat him!" insisted Brimen. "Sprite has said so!"

"Oh! Sprite has said so., WHY?"

"For the good of everyone, that is why!!"

"I have an even better idea!" replied Fox. "Ask Tether, he's bigger than me, I'm sure he will oblige you - on second thoughts - What about Wolf and his pack?"

"No! It has to be you! Wolf is too far away, it HAS too be you!" retorted Brimen sounding impatient and demanding. "Now, that's that and all about it!"

"Well at least I should have their support," demanded Fox.

"Ehem!" coughed Brimen hedging as he turned to the others nodding 'yes' agreeing to the request. "Of course, of course!" he bluffed. "We can arrange that. First, we need you to do a bit of, spying."

"Spying..?" was the curious response. Yet, Reynard Fox wasn't so easily convinced. 'What am I getting myself into?' he thought. "Mmm! Then perhaps it's not such a bad option and if I don't like it?" Fox decided there and then on an alternative course of action. 'There could be only one way out of this predicament - an agreement. "Yes I'll do it," he said convincingly.

"Good!" said Brimen joyfully, with Gannon and Olan joining in the excitement.

"What is it you want me to do?" said Fox.

"Ah! Now.., Darkwood, that is where the real spying takes place." He looked at Gannon and Olan as if to say 'At last we've got what we wanted'. "You must enter that dismal place," he continued. "Find out exactly where Badger and the pixies are! Then report back to Merva and Derva the exact location!"

"But, they are Mad!" said Fox raising his voice. "They only want to cut my tail off., for there 'magic' practises," he made clear.

"NO! NO! No!" stressed Brimen you are mistaken. ER..! They are not mad now," he said yet still uncertain as to their sanity.

Fox felt the uncomfortable pull of persuasion from the Oakmen, asking submissively.

"Are you sure this will work?"

"Of course it will work!" smiled Brimen convincingly. "All you have to do is guide the sisters back into Darkwood to where Badger is trapped!"

Reynard gave the idea a bit more thought and came to the conclusion that this would even up his debt to all in Evermore. After this he would at last be free, so perhaps he should see this mission through.

"Yes!" he said enthused by the idea. "When do I start?"

"Straight away," said Brimen.

Every thing went well for Fox. He guided the sisters safely to the spot in Darkwood and promptly left the scene to report back to Brimen. His only complaint was the Sisters strange fascination with his tail – as he had previously feared.

"But, I had to let them have some hairs – it was scary!"

"Don't worry about that!" said Brimen dismissing his worries. "There are more important things to concern our selves over."

"But, the scissors were huge – it was scary!"

"Don't worry about that!" said Brimen. Fox had the look of disappointment on his face. A bit of appreciation for his speedy response in agreeing to take part would have been welcome.

"D'rasnah is now using the hounds to guard the pathways and mine entrances." Said Brimen determined to use Fox again. "We need to get them away, so that we can gain entry and put a stop to whatever the goblins are planning."

"What has that got to do with me?" said Fox. "I've just done what you wanted?"

"WELL! Coupled with a little chase – to lure them away - you can get all your friends together, to give you support?" Brimen's tone of voice made it all sound so easy.

"I thought you just said it was only, spying?"

"Well, it is, in a different way! Your next part in all this is distraction - draw them away from the mines: OH! That includes the paths that they are guarding".

"Then you, trap the goblins in the tunnels?" confirmed Fox seeing the pattern of a well thought out strategy emerging. "Is that the idea?

"Yes, Exactly!" stressed Brimen. "You and your fellow 'hunted' can lure them into the deep Chasm, where we can keep them hemmed in! – the Trolls will help us!"

"But that won't get all of them," said Fox.

"NO!" said Brimen huffing. "We know that, But! That is when YOU actually challenge the Skelt. He will then have to take up the challenge, virtually on his own, with only his own pack in support."

"OH! Simple!" said Fox sarcastically, glaring hard at Brimen.

"By doing it, that way…," replied Brimen totally ignoring Fox's misgivings.

"What about Badger?" interrupted Fox. "When will HE be freed?"

Brimen, huffed and tutted impatiently. "That I do not know. You have done what is important. Now we have to wait – it is up to the Sisters, it could take days? As you know they are at this moment working to free them." He turned to nod agreement with the others and carried on forcefully. "First! You must challenge the viscous cur to a duel on windy plateau." And! ER! Of course, you will then have the help of Wolf and Tether" said Brimen assuredly. "Why, this time we might even encourage Hog to help you," and he laughed. "Too take care of any strays – of course."

"WELL, I… Well, I..!" flummoxed Reynard.

"And - of course, you will have the support of the Oakmen."

"Well I..?" said a defeated Fox.

"Now, we will meet you at Jagged rock, in the morning! – first light." arranged Brimen without further consultation.

Momentarily, Reynard felt assured in agreeing to the Oakman's enforced plan, because it seemed the right thing to do. However, during the long sleepless night that Fox endured, he had a change of heart and did not feel confident to face the day ahead.

As Fox sneaked out of his lair in the early morning light, he looked behind him and saw Graff arriving with a long line of miners, all equipped for the job in hand, ready to move into the tunnels when the hounds had been routed.

"Thats a relief," he said to himself. "I've got myself out of that little trap! Things should be in safe hands now while I'm away." Smirking with satisfaction he kept reflecting on Brimen's earlier comment. "Crafty indeed: A bit reluctant, yes! But CRAFTY?" he sniggered as he hurried on his way.

Running and leaping with relief, he soon made a good pace on his intended long journey of escape. "Hah!" he answered to his nagging thoughts. "They don't need me, I'm sure they'll save Evermore," he decided. "What can I do? – crafty indeed." He then bounded joyfully on his way, to the Beeches. "HAH! Anyway, it's a job for the Oakmen," his troubled mind told him. "They'll find another way to lure those hounds away from the mines"

Reynard Fox eventually left Oakwood about to enter unfamiliar territory. Dropping down to the lower level at the lea he took the precaution of using the long grass tunnels that ran on into the braken. Slowing down to a steadier pace, too ease his heavy breathing, he rested, taking a short nap, knowing that he would need his wits about him when he came out onto the higher rocky landscape. It was important to take this exposed route in order to get as far away, as quickly as possible and he thought - the start of a new life.

It was gently raining when Fox attempted the narrow gully climb to the top of Limestone Rock. The loose stones and slippery earth made his steep climb to the top awkward. Grabbing hold of an old tree root, growing through a crack in the rock face, he pulled himself up to look out across the vast expanse of bare, undulating, virtually treeless landscape, offering no natural cover just stunted growth of grass in patches here and there. In the hazy, far, distance stood the tall, majestic beeches.

"That's where I'm heading," he said to himself assuredly. "They'll never find me over there. Distracted, he looked to the sky in response to crows accusing rasp. Crow, then swooped furiously at him. "Caw, Caw," he screamed. "Turn back, Caw! Caw! Coward!" It aroused the other crows, bringing attention to Fox's whereabouts.

As Fox lowered his head – dismissing the shame that he felt - he heard a sneering, snapping voice challenge him. "What do you want - Mut?" It was one of Nescient's Scallywags sitting on a rotten stump. Skinny little thing he was, one whole tooth, struggling to exist on poisoned gums, the rest broken and blackened. His long, red narrow nose, covered with spots to match his huge pointed ears. From the 'cracks' others popped their heads up. Each goblin held in their hand a catapult and fired off a stone just missing Fox.

"D'rasnah's looking for you, Mut!" he shouted as a second then a third stone in quick succession, bounced on the rock flying over his head. Fox moved to avoid the stones and lost his grip on the tree root. Caught off balance he slipped, falling all the way back down into the bracken.

"You will never make it Mut!" shouted out the goblin as he leapt into the fern with his staff and catapult. The next minute Fox could hear others all around him, jeering, mocking, hysterical laughter and the constant threshing of bracken, followed by death threats and snarling sounds. "Mut is on the run! Where are you?" they kept repeating.

Fox was up and running for all he was worth, staying as tight as he could between the fern and the bottom of the rock face, where there was enough space to move freely and speedily on.

All around taunts and shrill whistles, continued coming to his ears from all directions, as stone after stone was being hurled at random into the fern, some bouncing off the rock, just missing him. "Is this it?" thought Fox. "Am I never going to have any, peace." He remembered witnessing Squirrels adventure the previous summer. "Will I get what he got?"

The next moment, Fox felt the sharp pull from strong hands around his throat. It was a powerful yank pulling him into a crevice of the rock. "Calm down! Calm down! Said a sympathetic voice as

Fox resisted the restraining force. "Here this way, quick," came the command. It was Gannon, Smug and Iffy acting under strict orders to shadow the runaway Fox. Brimen was aware that Fox may just decide to change his mind and flee.

"Let them go by," whispered Gannon calming fox down.

It wasn't long before the goblins got bored and gave up their hunt, they returned to the high ground to laze around until something else turned up to entertain them.

"Where were you going?" said Gannon scratching his head inquisitively. "Didn't you know the little tormentors hang around on Rocky landscape?" he waited for an answer. "Soon they will have hounds with them!"

"Oh! I er! um!" whined Fox, caught in the act of desertion. "I'm going to meet Brimen, he's waiting at Pewt hill," gasped Fox carelessly. "I mean, Jagged rock," he blundered knowing that that was the agreed meeting place.

"Crafty Fox!" sneered Gannon. "You should have been there at first light and this is not the way to Jagged rock! And Brimen is not at Pewt hill?" he pointed out.

"I., I., must have lost my way," stuttered Fox.

"None of us would have thought that?" said Gannon glaring at the others with a false expression of surprise. "You have backed down, haven't you, running away from your responsibility, eh!" He gave Fox a moment to confess his weakness.

"No! I just need more time, that's all!" he whined. Reynard Fox was now feeling ashamed. He could see by the look on the other's faces that he was letting a lot of people down.

"Time, you haven't got!" Gannon reminded him. "Think your self lucky that we came along to rescue you, but, if you want to go it alone? Then the Skelt and his hounds will find YOU!"

"Do you think that they knew where I was heading?" panicked Fox worrying about the goblins and the rest of his cowardly journey.

"Of course!" said Gannon. "It would only be a matter of time before D'rasnah finds out that you don't want our protection?" he paused awhile then added. "The goblins are becoming more and more, cocky with the support of more and more hounds," added Gannon. "Now, where will you hide after the beeches?" he asked making a move as if to leave. "The Skelt will be sent to - sniff you out?" he warned.

"You can't leave me!" said Fox devastated by the thought.

"I'm sure you will feel safe at the beeches," replied Gannon, stopping to adjust his bow and quiver. "You are a master at going to ground!" He then followed the rest of his group, who was waiting out side of the crevice. "After all you are nearly there," he said looking across, pointing in the direction of the Beeches. Fox couldn't reply he was stunned with fear at being left without protection

"Be warned!" said Gannon. "The paths over there are already guarded by hounds?"

"You can't leave me unprotected," cried Fox. He begged and pleaded calling them all back. "I., I., I'll do as you say, honest."

"Well..! Prove it?" said Gannon turning round sharply. "NOW.!"

"What do you want me to do?" replied Fox, his voice shaking, his body trembling.

"You could start and rebuild your reputation by taking on those nasty little goblins that chased you here," he said determinedly. "Get back up there and make yourself seen, they will give chase and we can all teach them a lesson." They all sniggered at the thought of catching the goblins by surprise and giving out punishment to these spiteful little creatures. "There is one other provision," warned Gannon underlining his option with force. "On your way to jagged rock you must stop and encounter the goblin with a hound defending a pathway – AGREED?

"YES! Yes! Yes!" said Fox relieved of his burden.

"Also!" emphasised Gannon, loud and stern. "You, MUST win the fight!"

Gannon could be cold and calculating enjoying nothing more than surprising his enemies in combat. His group were well armed with winder, sling-shot and clubs.

"Come on then you 'one toothed' wonder," shouted Fox, as he climbed back up onto the high ground to engage the goblin. He then started to run towards the appointed place. Stones soon came crashing all around as he turned this way and that to avoid them. Fox's new found confidence - bravely stopping now and then to let the goblins think they would catch him - was becoming unstoppable.

The goblins became furious at being tormented and gave immediate chase, but just as they were closing in on Fox one tooth fell to the ground, then another goblin fell, then another. Gannon and his gangs aim was perfect as they let fly the winder and sling shot from behind, felling them one by one. The others scattered in all directions chased by Gannon, Smithy and Iffy.

Fox made for Jagged rock, pleased with himself and thankful that Gannon had been around to help. He determined not to let anyone down and made sure to follow the pathway as planned eager to secure another victory. As he turned into the bend he came face to face with the young goblin and small hound that was guarding the pathway.

To Reynards surprise they both looked lost and scared in this lonely, isolated place. Without strong leadership the naïve pair, were useless. Instinctively, the young hound was braver and ready to make a stand

Fox took advantage of his surprise appearance and immediately went on the attack. In no mood to be intimidated after his previous humiliation he fought a glorious dog fight. Victorious, he drew first blood, not once, not twice, but three times punishing and hurting the small, young hound, sending it whimpering off. Undeterred, Fox then went for the small goblin. Although the young goblin came at him with a lengthy branch, hurting him, Fox again drew the first taste of blood, sending the young, nervous goblin, running off in despair.

Safely out of reach from further attacks Fox suddenly felt invincible and briefly returned to watch Gannon and his gang, unmercifully finishing off the bludgeoning of the remaining goblins. As two others were running away he could hear Gannon shout. "Let them go. It will be a strong warning to the others."

Hearing this made Fox feel even stronger and more determined to take on the Skelt. This pre-determined victory would also be a warning to others. At last he had gained his self respect back realising he could take on the challenge of Darkwood. "Crafty indeed?" he said to himself with a smirk of pleasure and made his way on to Jagged Rock. Although it was now late in the day Fox was hoping that Brimen would still be waiting for him as planned.

Chapter 13

Fox faces the Skelt

When Fox at last arrived at the agreed meeting point it was past mid-day and he decided to rest. It was obvious that Brimen, or any of the Oakmen, would not still be waiting there; he was now on his own. What ever it was, that the Oakman had in his mind, would now have to wait until they meet at the plateau.

The experiences of being constantly hunted gave Fox an advantage over his enemy, cunning. This was a valuable asset when being pursued. His favourite hideout was always Brock Badgers Sett – one of many when he was not at home – having four or five exits was an ideal advantage in the fight for survival and the mixture of scents would always confuse a rabid hound.

This location was where Fox had gone to ground. In this security he lay, breathless, weary and waiting. Waiting! Waiting! Waiting! With the anxious feeling of dread, that the Oakmen would not be ready to play their part, as they had promised him. He licked and cleaned his wounds, trying to slow his pounding heartbeat.

After he had taken his rest, Fox slunk silently out of the rear entrance of the sett making for the plateau edge. The sun had broken through the grey afternoon giving a clear view of the forest floor and the open spaces that lay beyond. He hadn't got that far, when he felt the awareness of someone following him.

Twice he stopped to look around. No one was there? Fox picked up his pace on the track, turned into a bend and concealed his-self behind a holly bush then waited. When the suspect came into view: It was Tether, keeping a cautious distance between them.

This was always a difficult moment and they stood apart, staring at each other, Fox wanting to run but knew that he must'nt give in to fear, trusting that the Oakmans promise of help was here. It would be some time before they eventually moved on down the track to a clearing. What then broke the tension of uncertainty - as to Tethers motives - was the unexpected shouting and screaming, resounding throughout the still forest.

The disturbing noise that captured and held their attention began to get louder and louder as it appeared to be heading in their direction. It was at this point that the two canines now felt a firm bond of interest and decided to openly support each other.

Fox's whole life had been lived in fear and although he stood alongside his new found friend, could he trust him? When, either one get the taste of blood they could turn unpredictably against him.

There was no other option at this moment in time the thought of battling with the Skelt, all on his own, was even more terrifying. "You now have a reputation to defend!" said Tether to Fox in response to the noise coming right at them. "And I am here to help," he offered.

Suddenly; one fearful, hairy looking goblin broke free from the cover of the wood and ran out onto the clearing, limping while holding onto chains but moving fast. He went speedily past, panting and whinging. "It's not my fault, it's not my fault," the hairy body screamed. He was running away from something that was obviously and noisily pursuing him.

The runaway was immediately followed by Lurker; huffing, puffing and gasping for air, limping as he struggled with his bad foot while not being able to use his crutch for support.

Moments later they were all followed by the Red Witch of Drone, howling and screeching threats while trying to escape from who ever, or whatever was out to get her. The long, red cape she was wearing was flowing in the wind restricting her advance as she in turn was lashing out wildly at anything, with her ebony stick. Chasing her and bearing down fast were the frenzied sisters; Merva and Derva, screaming out threats and curses at the Red Witch, while with eager, outstretched hands were trying to reach out and grab hold of the cape:

> "Gaping hole,
> Where are you?
> Open the ground!
> Redwitch - fall through!"

The sisters began to tire as they were crossing the open ground, with Derva losing a shoe. Spotting Fox and Tether nearby, Merva yelled, while pointing a bony finger. "Stop them! Chop them! Drop them!"

"Now the real challenge begins!" said Tether to Fox, excited at the prospect of a good hunt. Both felt inclined to help out the sisters. "Are you sure you are ready for it?" Fox nodded approval then joined in pursuit of a different quarry.

"Bight her ankles!" gasped Merva at the two of them as they caught up alongside Red Witch, who then began cursing and swinging her stick at Tether - the larger target.

The first strike missed, the second strike was a lot closer. Before she got the chance of another lunge Tether's faster pace moved him on ahead. He decided to run down Lurker and the two goblins and leave her to Fox.

At this point, Red Witch couldn't see Fox at her feet but then soon felt his sharp teeth dig into her ankle and it sent them both sprawling to the ground with Fox being kicked into the distance by her hefty boot as that too went flying through the air. As she fell, the momentum of the sisters – who couldn't stop - overshot their target and followed Fox tumbling into the prickly gorse bushes, getting all tangled up together.

In no time at all, Red Witch had time to compose herself. Quick to see an advantage she then wrapped the cape tightly around herself and rolled down a steep slope to escape. Moments later Tether returned looking pleased with his chase for Lurker. "That's one goblin that won't return in a hurry," he said.

The cause for all this current excitement was because of Merva and Derva's attempt to rid Evermore of unwelcome 'guests'. The previous day, the sisters had fought a decisive battle and had also defeated Red Witch in Darkwood. They had been amazingly successful in protecting Sprite and freeing Brock Badger and the Pixies from their stone incarceration. Then earlier this morning after Lurker had informed Redwitch that they held onto Cretins scout; Blugoko, she tried to free him and was succesful. Now the sisters wanted to re-establish themselves as the only 'Witch' force in Evermore.

"We will help you Fox
And give you courage
To fight the Skelt today
You helped us halt the chase
Of the Red witch pace
How can we turn away?"

Merva and Derva slipped quietly away, disappearing into the darkness of the forest to keep their promise to Fox. The spell that they would now cast would be applied to the hounds that had turned up to support the Skelt. The sisters played on the fact that hounds could only be effective as a pack. All though Skelt was a dangerous exception they would confuse it enough to give Fox an added advantage.

As the rest of the evening passed on into the night, the moon cast its long bright beams giving off a cold light of dread. It created shadows in the forest as black as coal. Fox's sharp eyes could penetrate this darkness. His ears could pick up every sound. His panting tongue tasted every movement in the damp night air. The only give away to his whereabouts was his musky odour and for this reason he could never escape the boisterous hound's attention.

"How am I going to deal with that?" replied Fox as his frightened eyes absorbed more fear and intimidation at the thought of the hound's powerful bulk. Fox looked at it and weakened. 'What am I doing here' he thought to himself, instinctively ready to run. Even Tether was having serious doubts.

If Fox was to continue to backslide, the odds of success were against him.Tether saw this weakness and reminded him. "Anything smaller and you would feel confident to destroy it!" Fox grunted an obstinate reply in agreement.

"Think of the mouse," said Merva arriving to support him. Her face pushed close to his, the warts on her face bouncing on his wet nose. She then recited;

Take its tail,
Make it spin.
Giddy heads
Can never win.
Underneath,
Cling on tight.
Now you know
You have too bite!

"Don't dwell on the moment! Think! Of that 'mouse'," hissed Derva echoing Merva's idea. Brock Badger, now freed from his stone prison, butted in snorting heavily. "Let me take him on!" he growled with a concentrated defiance. "Move over Fox, he said. "The Skelt doesn't frighten me," he reassured everyone. "My 'bite' would never let go!"

Tether felt the same. He knew that his size – as a Wolfhound – would intimidate the Skelt. But! Sprite had insisted that Reynard Fox must defeat this; enemy of Evermore.

And still others were turning up to support Fox: Hog, Stag, Bruin, all equally wanted to take on the Skelt and between themselves were debating a strategy to silence the yelping hounds, after the major event had taken place.

Fox, confident that he was assessing the situation correctly, could now realise exactly where his enemy was. He watched the Skelt take his position at the center, displaying agitation at the waiting.

Daunted, he looked out across the wide open space at the many eyes, caught in the moons glow, bathing this vast arena. "Mmm!" worried Fox. "Not finding me at Badgers Sett, has really got him angry." The hound instinctively turned his head in Fox's direction, knew where he was and growled. A chill ran down Fox's spine at the realisation of facing such a force.

Distracted with fear he never noticed that his greatest supporter had turned up. Of all the animals in Evermore Reynard Fox was favoured more than the others by this Oakman.

"Don't run away now!" whispered a voice in his ear. It was Brimen, returned to help as promised. Fox, felt instantly strengthened by his presence. Everything now seemed reassuring and falling into place – except his inner fear.

"How am I going to beat that!" answered Fox. "Look! He is terrifying."

"Use the Skelt's anger, do not let him use your fear," said Brimen. "And that is all the more reason to face him – he will worry about you and distract himself."

Fox's tail drooped low. His whole demeanor slunk into submission, about to scurry away. "Resist the urge to run!" said Brimen. "Stay focused! As you approach the hound, think only of what you are going to do!"

"And what is th..that?" stammered Fox shaking with fear while watching the hound; its muscled bulk, red eyes, huge jaw, massive fangs, magnifing a colossal power.

"Go for his underbelly, straight away!" said Brimen. "Bite hard and claw him, hang on so that he can't get at you. Then when he is really yelping, squealing and tiring, release your grip and go for the throat – do the same thing and don't let go."

"You make it sound so simple," shuddered Fox.

"Yes! Well.., er! Just stay focused," replied Brimen sternly. "That is all I'm saying, Now, That's that! And all about it"

"I must stay focused – I must stay focused," said Fox anxiously. "Do as Brimen said, do as Brimen said." He kept repeating.

At that moment Wolverine arrived with his wolf pack - howling. He blocked Fox's expected retreat with encouraging words of support. "Act the fool! Yell!! Taunt him! Only, do not run away - Face him!" he said. "There is a point when the hound weakens. And you can use that to your advantage. It's when he realises that his master is not around to tell him what to do."

"Supposing he turns up?" said Fox fearing another obstacle in his way.

"That's right Reynard," said Squirell jumping to the ground to give more support. "At least you won't take a beating from the goblins – like I had too." Fox looked sympathetic at Squirrels experience and ashamed of his own weakness, knowing exactly what Squirell had, had to endure. "Remember! They were much bigger than me and there were more of them," he said. "And just remember too, we are hopelessly out numbered if you lose this fight.

At that, three young Fox cubs broke through the gathering to greet Reynard and started to playfully spa with him. It was his siblings – the very reason that had made him appear so aloof - from the year before.

Fox couldn't back down now, show fear, or run away, so finally made his commitment to cross the Plateau to face this major foe. Turning to Brimen, he said. "Thanks! For being here, I only wish Sprite had turned up too!"

Brimen huffed, repeating firmly but with an understanding. "Stay concentrated on what you have to do - Now, That's that! And all about it!" then briskly walked away.

To his left, Fox could see lines of hounds, red eyed, sharp teethed, killers that had escaped the round up of his earlier efforts. There restless, whimpering and yelping for action, waiting the command for slaughter. Opposite them, to Fox's right side; Tether, Wolverine and his wolves.

"I wish Sprite was here," thought Fox a second time, about to reach the centre of the Plateau. Another quick glance to his left and the line of hounds, supporting the Skelt began to cease their yelping, further he could see them slowly dispersing. Fleetingly, he caught a glimpse of the sisters encouraging them away. "What kind of magic is that?"

As he reached the center the Skelt's stance looked unmovable. Long, low, growling sent shivers through fox's body each red hair of his coat stood out stiffly as the terrifying sound was gradually getting louder and louder.

The Skelt's large, square jaw opened to reveal massive, white fangs, dripping excitedly with saliva. The whites of his eyes, shone so vivid, it ringed the darker centre giving a mesmeric effect, penetrating and magnifying, Fox's fears of destruction. Even with these doubts threatening, Fox was now examining the Skelt closely, looking for a weakness to exploit.

He looked at the black eyed monster, now appearing to magnify itself into even greater proportions and shuddered, wanting to run away again, at the same time he realised that he had got this far only because of Brimen's faith in him. Yet, Fractions of time ago he felt more confident - Now..?

The sisters, after removing the Skelts support, remained concealed from a distance. They chanted a spell onto an Oakleaf and blew it onto the Plateau. It moved silently and swiftly toward the center, gently brushing against Fox's fur.

"Tizzy, Tizzy!
Fox get busy.
Dizzy, Dizzy!
Grab his tail."

A surge of confidence and invincibility, swept through Fox's body while at the same time another oak leaf touched the hound with a warning:

"You can't resist
The neck we twist
Or falling on
Your back.
A Jaw that's tight
Can't win the fight
This is something
That you lack."

The spell began to have an effect on the Skelt, causing his head to rotate under the mesmeric influence of suggestion.

Fox bravely and immediately took his chance and grabbed the hound's tail in his teeth. The Skelt was helpless to resist as round and round in circles he was pulled, choking in the dust. The Sisters urged Fox on:

"Dizzy! Dizzy!
Fox get busy
Dizzy! Dizzy!
Turn him round."

Suddenly, Red witch was back on the scene screaming out spells of her own at the luckless Skelt. She whipped up a wild frenzy on the wind, sending a whirlwind of dust and grit blasting the sisters from concealment. Boosting the Skelt's confidence – she said.

"Don't let us down
You wear the crown.
As leader of the pack
It is your right,
Take the final bite
Rip the pelt from his back."

Just as suddenly, the Skelt found an instinctive surge of energy. His rigid body with its colossal strength went into attack and pinned Fox to the floor ready to bite the bite of death in Fox's neck.

As the Skelt opened its wide jaw to administer the final blow, another spell was sent by the sisters - confusing and arresting the fatal action:

"Jaw that's large
Is only small.
A hound alone
Cannot take all."

At first the hound was bemused when he realised that he had lost the support of his pack. But the spell that the sisters had sent, had short life with no real power enabling him to raise his anger again. Redwitch countered, screaming back with another threat:

"Send the whirlwind
Cause displeasure,
Part the Sisters
For good measure."

Derva was immediately sent flying into the distance, while Merva – ready for anything - clung on to a sturdy Oak branch.

The Hound was now, nano moments from the 'final bite' salivating all over the finer features of Fox. He held back only because he wanted to enjoy this victory. Red witch entered the arena with a lightening flash of her presence to claim Evermore for D'rasnah, but she hadn't reckoned with the sisters secret power.

The sisters too had been experimenting with the black gritty powder and used it at their destructive best. Merva dropped to the ground, challenging the Red witch with her own lightening strikes. Cautiously she moved toward the center, buying herself valuable time screetching:

"Your Master D'rasnah
Is not here
You cannot deny
The blood to smear."

This gave enough time for Derva to return. It was then that the sisters moved onto the arena together fireing powerful lightening bolts to make Red witch retreat. The Skelt, was now confused and halted its final attack on Fox while looking around for his master D'rasnah, who needed to be there to take this trophy; the hound hesitated. Reynard Fox took advantage of the distraction.

Fox, being smaller could get to the underneath of the Skelt and savage him. He held on tight manouvering himself onto his back digging his claws into the generous flesh, shredding it to pieces. Fox's jaw opened exposing small but sharp teeth as the lips curled back. The whites of Fox's eyes displayed a horrific concentration not seen before and he sank his fangs, ripping wildly and deeply into the flesh of this once aggressive hound. Clinging on to Badgers advice; he would not let go.

The Skelt was beaten. Screaming and writhing in pain, it laid helpless, defenceless, shuddering in shock - defeated. Feeling the lasting effect of the sister's spells, the Skelt weakened and rolled over in submission. Proud Fox stood over the prostrate body, in his ears echoed the sound of victory as Fox's friends all rushed onto the Plateau to enjoy the moment. Tether then let out a victorious howl as Redwitch vanished into the dark night.

D'rasnah, Nescient, Trypannon and Cretin had arrived too late to save the Skelt. Infuriated that they knew nothing about this challenge on Fox, they let go another pack of hounds alongside the Hob goblins, onto the victors. Tether still had the taste for goblin blood and went for them, first sinking his fangs into Cretin, who led the charge.

This signalled the start of a riot as Wolf - his wolverines, Hog and his pack, Stag, Badger, Bruin and Fox's friends all joined in the riotous slaughter. At the end of it all, the Skelt was left where it lay – whining for help.

Fox and his friends had achieved the ultimate victory as the defeated goblins scurried back to recoup their last chance of an offensive – the mines and draining of Fastflow. The Oakmen had not interfered in the events that had taken place but had looked on with interest from a concealed vantage point.

Chapter 14

Prisoners at the Grotto

It was reassuring to have seen the Skelt and so many of the goblins punished by the animals of Evermore. In discovering the whereabouts of the goblins 'key' tunnel entrance too, the Oakmen would now have to act fast if they were to achieve the ultimate victory. The Oakmen and gnomes decided that they could prepare and plan their attack with utmost precision now that the goblins had retreated to the tunnels for the final offensive. If the operation to save Fastflow was to be a success then right equipment and correct procedure had to be followed.

"Tunnelling?" fumed Brimen. "What, do THEY know about tunnelling?" He said opening the door to the equipment hut situated at the foot of the lodge. Ugham and Seghi grunted a greeting as they passed by while Brimen was lighting the oil lamp.

"Enough to know that they can drain Fastflow!" said Olan moving swiftly across the floor to check and count everything that they needed. "Remember, they have Grindles knowledge of mining to depend on."

"AH! Grindle the traitor, Yes," mused Brimen. "But we have Grondo, and Graff."

"Everything here is accounted for." said Olan "So they never got the chance to rob us while we were away."

"Where did the goblins get their tools from then?" said Brimen following him closely, examining the locked and chained implements still intact.

"I knew you would say that!" muttered Olan feeling guilty at what he knew would soon follow. He started to unlock the chained tools that they would need, aware that Brimen was staring curiously at him. "Grindle," said Olan hoping to distract him. "Remember? He has joined them and taken all HIS tools with him so there would be no need for him to look else where."

"Mmmm! But, that would be for his-own miners. What about D'rasnah's goblins?" asked Brimen dismissing the fact of Grindle changing sides. He paused awhile then added. "When did YOU last check the spare, service tool boxes on the carts?"

"Oh!" said Olan trying to sound unruffled. "It was when we left for Isolate."

"That long ago?" roared Brimen, making a show of rushing outside to search the carts in the compound. "You were supposed to check them immediately we returned," he ranted. Brimen then forcefully unlocked the padlock, pushing back the wired gate in disgust at his perception of Olans neglect.

"How could I?" snapped back Olan loudly in his ear. "We had been so busy, I have never had the chance and anyway, I thought that they would be safe enough locked away behind a fence."

"That's not good enough!" raged Brimen.

"It should all have been safe with Ughem and Seghi guarding them," said Olan as the two came trundling back grunting at the remark. Now the Trolls always guarded areas for the Oakmen and always operated in two's. Subsequently, they were all called by the same names, although they were powerfully built and strong they were not intelligent.

"It is now obvious! They were not safe," growled Brimen holding open a toolbox lid with a broken fastener. Ughem and Seghi looked bemused and started to examine the damage closely. Brimen looked at the pair and grunted at their ignorance.

Gannon, Smarty and Smug were busy loading some more timbers onto the cart, listening and laughing at the amusing banter that was a surety between the two. Gannon couldn't resist the urge to keep it going.

"I think you should have got someone else to do the job!" he said out loud to Brimen, whilst winking his eye at Olan. "At least that way, we would not have a problem on our hands," he added provoking a response.

"That's got nothing at all to do with it!" retorted Brimen, not wanting to upset the trolls. He fumbled in his pocket to feel for his watch. "Smarty, Smug, take this cart over to Grondo." He turned to Gannon. "I think the goblins would have retreated much deeper into the mine by now, Grondo knows this mine, he can backfill their tunnel and mine a new one so they can't escape." He threw more wooden supports onto the cart. Puffing out his cheeks, he blew hard into the chilled air sounding exhausted. "This next cart Olan, can go to the Abbey ruins when we are ready. Meanwhile we had better get over to the Grotto and get in touch with Monk and ask for new plans of the mines: There! Now that's that and all about it!"

While Brimen, was tapping impatiently on the knocker of the Grotto door - for the third time before he got a response - he reflected on how long it had been since he last saw Monk the Elder or Sage. There had been little or no contact with him since the previous summer. Even though the Oakmen had been away for some months, they would still have expected to hear of, or from both of them together, as soon as they had returned. More so because, of Brimen losing the satchel to the goblins.

The fact was that Monk's involvement out on the marsh was taking up more and more of his time. Ankra's report to the Boffins over Monk's mistreatment of Kordi, had a serious effect on him, causing the Boffins to keep a close watch on his every move.

Sage opened the door slowly, whispering nervously through the narrow gap. "What do you want?" he said defensively.

"It's me! - Brimen. C'mon let us in?" he said gritting his teeth and pushing determinedly at the door while staring at a single eye through the gap peering nervously back at him.

"Who have you got with you?" sounded the muffled, suspicious reply.

"It is the Oakmen," shouted out Gannon above the noise from the water fall, whilst gradually getting soaking wet. "Who do you think it is?" he said leaning over Brimens shoulder attempting to push the door.

"Is Ankra with you?" whispered Sage opening the door a fraction more.

"No!" snapped Brimen, irritated by the mysterious behaviour.

"Have you seen him loitering, anywhere near here?" Come the next question.

"How many more times shall I say it? NO!" said Brimen pushing forcefully at the door. "NOW, let us in?"

"Sorry! But I must make sure!" replied Sage, becoming slightly more visible.

"NO! NO.! NO..!" Shouted! Brimen angrily. "He is not here! Now tell Monk WE ARE here!" At that moment a larger hand appeared just above Sage's head gripping the door, pulling it back slowly. The other hand shoved Sage brutally out of the way.

Monk appeared unusually edgy, greeting them cautiously. "Are there any others with you?" he asked while the eyes in his head darted about outside searching over their heads for other visitors.

"NO," was the impatient, yet, weary reply.

After ushering them inside, Monk stuck his head out the door again to glance nervously around. They all watched as he frantically shut and bolted the door, double checking the locks to make sure it was secure.

The bizarre interval gave Sage the chance to whisper to Brimen about Monk's fears.

"His problem is with Ankra!" whispered Sage. "He is still trying to get Monk to surrender Kordi and the naughty imps."

"Surrender the Gunpowder fairies?" said Brimen perplexed. "What do you mean?"

"Monk had another altercation with Kordi and kidnapped him!"

"Again, what is the reason this time?"

"Treason!" answered Sage softly.

Monk turned round from the door sharply acting terse and looking doubtful at the whispering of Sage and Brimen. "To what do I owe the pleasure of this call?" he said in a suspicious, enquiring tone.

"Evermore is being seriously threatened again by D'rasnah." replied Brimen, soon to realise that Monk was temporary, if not conveniently hard of hearing. He had large amounts of cotton wool stuffed in his ears.

"Eh! Speak up!" came the sharp reply cupping his hand behind his ear.

Brimen took a deep breath and raised his voice. "Evermore is under threat!"

"Debt?" He queried. "No, no, no, I paid him," said Monk waiving his hand to dismiss the idea.

"THREAT, not debt," shouted Brimen getting angry. Sage began signalling at Monk, pointing to his ears. "Take it out," he said then glanced at Brimen, sighing. Monk just huffed, waived his hand again dismissively and hobbled into another room. Sage beckoned them all to follow.

Expecting this to be the meeting room of their last visit - which was spotlessly clean and bright - they were led into a dirty, miserable, cold, damp and lifeless hovel. It seemed to reflect the deteriation of Monks moods and habits. "Sage, get some chairs for our guests," ordered Monk placing a dirty hankerchief to his runny nose.

Gannon and Olan did not feel comfortable with the way things were going. Choosing instead to get Brimen's attention, who was also feeling the same as them, they began making discreet signs on deciding whether to leave even suggesting and wondering if it would be such a good idea to mention that the plans in the satchel had now fallen into the wrong hands. They had come to the conclusion that they should have given the grotto a miss.

Confident that they had some knowledge in the use of gunpowder, they could easily put into action their own plans - with great effect. But! Sprite would not allow its unsupervised usage on such a large scale. Also; judging the tone of Sprite and Owls last visit at the Lodge, it may just make matters worse. If it wasn't for the fact that Monk had made such a drama the last time they went their own way, then Brimen may have taken the chance and responded to the moment. The other most important fact was that Brimen had to replace the maps that were stolen and it was only Monk that could do this. Then they would have to stay and be patient.

Momentarily, everything was in order with Monk humbly apologising, blaming his odd behaviour on feeling unwell. "I haven't had visitors for a while," he said self pityingly – my hearing? Compliments were then exchanged and worries listened too leaving the Oaken feeling a lot more comfortable with this bizarre situation.

Moments later, Sage appeared with a chalk and slate, signalling Brimen to use it.

"Ah! That's a good idea," he thought and started to write down – in his limited capacity - questions that needed an answer. Yet, this 'idea' proved to be just as problematic as Monk's poor eye-sight with out his glasses was abysmal, he couldn't see clearly, to read or write an answer to what it said. Sage came to his rescue, yet again, with a large horn for hearing and a pair of spectacles.

"So that's where they went," said Monk, looking relieved. He placed the glasses on his nose and placed the horn to his ear then sat down to relax.

Brimen was just about to explain the missing plans and the current problems threatening Evermore, when Monk's nervous reaction in response to another knock on the door confirmed what Sage had whispered earlier - He had something serious to hide.

"If it's Ankra, tell him I'm not in," said Monk jumping nervously out from his chair. He went bounding around the room seeking out a place to hide. "SH! Stay quiet!" ordered Monk in hushed tones. "Pretend we are not in."

The knocking became persistent, getting louder and louder; an urgency that would not go away. "I will have to answer it?" said Sage worriedly.

"I know you are in there, Monk!" shouted out Ankra through the letter box. We saw you let the Oakmen in," he said convincingly.

"Tell him I'm ill! – staying with Merva and Derva," said Monk quavering.

"Well, he heard that all right," said Brimen indignantly to the others. "Hearing horn? – Bah! There is nothing wrong with him, only guilt over something?"

Sage eventually opened the door to face a stern reprimand.

"What have you done with him?" demanded Ankra standing to attention with his baton firmly tucked under one arm, the other arm held in a sling. His eyes, still showed faded, puffy, bruising from being attacked that night in the marsh, by Ffelin. He then pushed Sage aside and forced his way into the Grotto completely ignoring the Oakmen's prescence. Monk, with his shameful secret remained hidden.

"WELL?" shouted Ankra looking all around the room for the concealed Monk. "Where is he?" More elves crammed inside the room all looking extremely angry.

"Calm down!" begged Brimen beginning to feel threatened. "We are your friends!"

Ankra lifted himself up on his toes, with a tight lip look on his face, stuttering. "It's., it's., n, n, not you, Oakmen. It's him!" he said pointing his baton at the invisible Monk.

"HE., he., he., has done it again!" Ankra slowly set himself down again, nervously twitching his moustached lip.

"Done what?" said Brimen bemused by all the excitement.

"He has soaked, our Kordi!" confirmed Ankra, removing his monocle to clean it. "He's reacted exactly as he had done before. Only this time he's holding him prisoner."

"You don't understand," whined the pathetic Monk from his hideaway. "He's given top secrets away!"

Just then Sage appeared holding a large glass jar. Inside, standing in water was the downcast looking gunpowder fairy. He handed the jar over to Ankra who quickly emptied the watery contents onto the floor whilst uttering a quote - in an assured, yet! matter of fact way - from the rules and regulation handbook. "Sec: 10 para 1. Gunpowder must always remain dry and kept in a safe and sec..,"

"I'll go and get the Imps," said Sage before he could finish the instuction, then went rushing away with Tono to rescue them. They promptly returned with two more jars and placed them on the table.

Ankra glanced at the Oakmen while placing his finger to his lips - too indicate quiet. He then jabbed his finger at the 'chase longe' where Monk had concealed himself. Craftily, after he had freed the Imps he poured the watery contents into one jar. He then passed it over to Tono who crept over and emptied the contents of the jar all over Monk, giving him a thorough, good soaking.

"HAH! HAH! HAH!" thrilled Ankra with joyful satisfaction, encouraging his elves to join in the humiliation. "That will teach you a lesson," he boomed. The Oakmen couldn't help but enjoy the charade too.

Monk, surfaced with his wet, embarrassed face covered by his hands, peering out through his fingers, only to see Kordi grinning menacingly back at him.

"Look, see!" he said indicating. "It's not fair, he taunts me so!"

"Oh! Don't be so childish," fumed Ankra removing his note book from his top pocket. "I'll have to report this you know." He said licking the top of his pencil. "This will be more serious than the last time," he warned, furiously writing down every misdemeanour. The Oakmen looked at each other sadly, thinking they had seen all this before.

"Well, just be sure to write this down," screeched Monk whilst drying himself with a towel that Sage had bought in. "Gunpowder and a CANNON, have gone missing from hut E132 and THAT! Traitor.," he said pointing at the smirking Kordi. "Stole it!"

"If that is true – and you can prove it! - then he will face a tribunal," said Ankra.

"Of course I can," scoffed Monk. "He's given secrets away to Ffelin and D'rasnah."

"WE..!" interrupted Brimen, getting everybody's attention while indicating with his hand to include both Gannon and Olan. "Saw smoke rising from the quarry. When we got there we definitely saw Erzsatz firing the cannon – and the goblin's were there stacking up sacks of gunpowder!"

"You see?" Gloated Monk. "That means Ersatz will now use it against the King!"

"No! no, no, it couldn't be a cannon," said Ankra looking shifty. "Nothing is missing from the marsh," he stated with a certainty.

"How do you know?" said Monk. "Can you be sure?" he challenged. "You just heard what was said." All eyes turned to Ankra, who was now getting extremely tense.

"Ho., ho., how could he?" he stuttered uncertainly. "Even a hundred kordis could never lift a cannon," answered Ankra thinking he had won the argument.

Monk saw the flicker of doubt in his eyes as he prepared his next question. "Have you checked the - burning ground?" he said with an over stated, enquiring tone.

"Burning gr.,gr.,ground?" stammered Ankra.

"YES!" you know! Where we burn and bury, to hide the old, unused, inventions."

"Well! er., er.," was the uncertain response.

"Have you also checked the disused powder and fuse mill?" asked Monk smugly.

"No, no, no, you can't fool me Monk, I.., I.," at this point Ankra was caught on a very long stutter.

"Kordi!" said Monk over riding the long reply by tapping on the glass jar that held the drying out fairy captive. "Tell our, 'Head' of security exactly what you did. Explain exactly, how all the lights got smashed by Ffelin and his gang." He waited for a reply.

"Go on! Tell him!" urged Monk. "Tell him where the 'pistol' went?" He waited even longer while Ankra was still stuck on his stutter. "Then remind your leader where he got his bruises from? Go on! Tell them! Tell them how my 'balloon' was stolen."

"AH!" Interrupted Brimen, making himself accountable. "We've already taken care of that!" he said proudly. The others all nodded approval looking pleased with themselves. Monks response was to scowl heavily but he didn't say anything.

Ankra, at long last took a long, deep breath and halted his stammer but was exhausted and frustrated by the continual barrage of accusations. Kordi remained quiet intent on giving nothing away and would not respond to anything. All the while Monk continued to cajole and insinuate the gunpowder fairy's treacherous role in the whole mismanaged affair.

Ankra, extremely annoyed with Monks knowledge at what had occurred that night, was satisfied that his own involvement was utterly professional. He had now calmed and got full control of his speech back. He winked at Tono then jerked his head, signalling him to check out the other sites that Monk had mentioned.

Regaining his command of the situation, Ankra blurted out with great authority: "Section 7, sub section 21, states.," "Anyone who gives away secrets can only be questioned inside the marsh bounderies. First and foremost by the Head of Security," he said puffing out his chest. Secondly, by the Boffins: Third and finally, by Sprite." Pausing briefly while at the same time snatching back the glass jar from Monks grasp, Ankra stood to attention with the remaining elves then prodded his baton at Monk stating. "Nobody else has any authority – whatever!" with that said he and the elves turned about and stormed out the grotto with military discipline.

"Clear off! Go on!" taunted Monk chasing after him. "Clear off! We all know you've lost control of the marsh." Brimen too chased after him pleading:

"Ankra, wait!" he said. "Come back! We need your help!"

"Talk to Monk the Elder," replied Ankra marching his troop away.

"Take no notice of Monk. He's guessing. He 'THINKS' he has all the answers!"

"Then talk with Sprite. Tell her!"

"But we did see a cannon!" yelled Brimen above the noise of the waterfall, to the disappearing Ankra, who was more intent on keeping his troop in line. "Hup! Hup! Hup!" he blasted out in rhythm, as they mounted the steps.

Downcast, Brimen became angry. No one was going to admit to mistakes being made. No one was going to admit to divided loyalties. No one it appeared was going to put the safety of Evermore first. 'Enough's enough' he thought. 'Now that's that and all about it.' He stepped back into the grotto fuming, demanding that Monk stops being secretive and contentious.

"Right!" said Brimen when everything had calmed down. "This is exactly what we had come here for. To tell you that Ersatz does have a huge iron cannon."

"Yes! Yes! Yes!" confirmed an increasingly, tetchy Monk. "I know! I know! I know! You do not have to keep reminding me."

"AH!" said Brimen. "But there is something that you don't know."

"EH!" answered a bemused Monk. "What is that?" The three Oakmen showed a quiet unity and wouldn't give an answer straight away. At least and until he realised his failings and vowed to listen to others; at what they had to say, they were not going to give in to him. It would be better when Monk tried to out guess them they thought.

"Yes! Well; tell me what it is?" said Monk impatiently.

"No! You are too contentious!"

"I'm not a contentious person; I just have a better grasp, of things,"

"You think you know everything, why should we bother?" answered Brimen being deliberately obstructive.

"But it's all Ankra's fault. He thinks he knows the marsh better than me - Now tell me?"

"Not until you realise how cruel you are to Ankra!"

"I, shan't; so tell me, tell me, tell me?"

"You are going to lose control of Evermore if you carry on being contentious."

"I AM NOT CONTENTIOUS!" shouted out Monk frustrated with the days events. I am telling you. Kordi did help them to steal a cannon and gunpowder."

"Yes! But who encouraged him too?"

"I order you!" demanded Monk "Stop your accusations."

"Not until we get an apology!" By now Monk was in an extreme mood of agitation that he found difficult to come out of. Selfishly; his tantrums always got the better of him and he started to rant on about his own life of sacrifice. How he always protected the Oakmen. How he was always made to consider Merva and Derva. How Ankra was always reporting him to the Boffins. The final insult, he admitted, was too be always over ruled by the prettiest of Fairies; Sprite.

To halt the pathetic charge of self pitying nonsense coming out of Monk's mouth, Brimen raised his voice, defending Sprite. "Any decision she makes is in the best interests of the king," he stated.

"I know! I know! I know! But I have to deal with it all; I have to find ways to outwit our enemies, yet all I get is mistrust!" Brimen, Gannon and Olan, decided not to persue the self pitying, demoralised, pleas of Monk's angst. They were paying more attention to a welcome break of tea and scones, bought to them by Sage and his helpers.

After refreshments and a lengthy interval, when things had finally calmed down, Brimen decided to inform Monk of his latest discoveries:

"D'rasnah also intends to drain the river Fastflow and the marsh!" he said looking at Monk for a positive reaction.

"That is ridiculous!" said Monk startled by such a claim.

"Well you certainly won't like the next part," said Brimen. "He is using the ruins of the Abbey to do it."

"That is ridiculous!" he repeated; again completely startled.

"It's not so ridiculous, he is using the old escape tunnel," replied Brimen knowingly.

"And he is going to tunnel through to the Grotto."

"Bah!" said Monk dismissing the impossible idea. "It was sealed up with explosives when I had to flee. It will take them forever to clear the debris or even find another way to here."

"Not with Grindle the deserter?" said Brimen. "He knows it's there and is an expert miner in doing what he's got to do. It means Evermore is under a greater threat.... which leads me to another request?"

"What is it you want?" snapped Monk with a sneer now speading across his face.

"We've come to ask for plans of the tunnels!" said Brimen tactfully.

"But you already have them," replied Monk his eyes penetrating into Brimen.

"Well, er!" puffed Brimen. "We did have, until I was er! robbed!"

"ROBBED!" shouted Monk; then descended into mocking laughter.

"Yes!" replied Brimen, feeling small and embarrassed, waiting for a serious reprimand.

"So who has them?" said Monk sniggering. "D'rasnah?" he pondered.

"Yes!" nodded Brimen "The goblins attacked me in the lodge."

"You mean; he has 'EVERYTHING' from the satchel," said Monk laughing at the thought. He made his way over to the door to make sure it was locked securely.

"That can only mean that he now has plans of the cannon he stole and a deeper knowledge of gunpowder." Monk's pondering over this gave cause for concern. "But you did destroy the Balloon?" he asked.

Brimen somehow had the horrible feeling that all of this had been set up. He could tell by the look on the others faces that they too felt the same.

"D'rasnah's intention to tunnel through to the Grotto means he will flood it as well," added Brimen. This statement shocked Monk and had him going from, the extreme of misunderstanding, too one of vicious intent to put paid to D'rasnah.

"He can't do that to me?" he screeched as his legs began kicking the air with his fists wildly flung about in a remonstration of his darkened mood.

"There is one other thing!" said Brimen. "He had bought the Skelt hound with him!"

"The SKELT!" yelled Monk horrified. The instant recall came up with an image of sharp fangs, biting deep into his leg. "If it comes near me, I'll kill it!" he screamed losing control of his emotions. "SAGE!" he ordered. "Sharpen my sword!"

"What NOW!" came the unprepared response while gaping at the Oakmen.

"Yes! hurry, hurry and get the snares ready – sharpen my axe!"

"SLOW DOWN!" shouted Brimen. "Fox has defeated him!"

"Defeated him?" asked Monk perplexed with the idea.

"YES! OH; But you wouldn't know? YOU have hidden yourself away?

Olan could not remain calm; becoming enraged at Monks stupidity. "Why would you put plans of the cannon, in the satchel amongst plans of the tunnels?" This enquiry forced Monk to take a defensive stand.

"OH; it was a mistake, a mistake, a BIG mistake," said Monk unconvincingly turning to hide an absurd grin of satisfaction, almost as if everything was going to plan.

"Well! We demand to see Sprite," ordered Olan.

"You don't trust me, EH!"

"Should we, after what happened in the Marsh?"

"I know, I know," said Monk.

"Should we; after what has just happened with Ankra?"

"YES; yes, yes, I know, but you three need my help now don't you?"

Suddenly, from out of nowhere Sprite and her entourage made a timely appearance, after watching and listening in to everything that had been said and done. She insisted that Monk should apologise to Ankra.

"You are not doing the right thing!" she said to Monk. "Your attitude is unfair."

"He is responsible for the security in the marsh," replied Monk indignantly. "And it was his duty to discipline the gunpowder fairy – not me".

"Then let Ankra deal with it, you had no right to kidnap him."

"I was only trying to …,"

"Silence!" said Sprite then turned to Brimen. "Your plans and ideas to defeat D'rasnah are good: Since the retun from Isolate you have stalled major advances that may well have destroyed Evermore. Now; you must go back with the plans you need and organise what you have set in place. "You must then return here, with a selected group to prepare for; 'what is about to come your way.' Ankra will also join you." She then instructed Monk to consult the Red and Blue Annals and was gone.

Chapter 15

Secrets at the Grotto

Monk's refusal to apologise to Ankra – whose help he depended upon – was totally unnacceptable. Yet Sprite, demanded and got what she had requested, a truce between the two of them. The very idea of D'rasnah returning to drain Fastflow, destroy the Marshland and attack the Grotto was an intolerable situation and more than enough reason for them to work together harmoniously.

This whole affair prompted Monk to consult the oracle – as Sprite had instructed. Special books of this magnitude must only be consulted and acted on, when all other options had failed and only with the sole permission of Sprite, which she had given. The prophecies were contained in several, large, red and green volumes to be read together with the Chronicles of Evermore.

Clutching the door keys off the hook while Sage held onto boxes of candles, Monk immediately set off for the library with Sage and the Oakmen in eager pursuit; leaving Ankra – whose eye would not stop twitching with indignation - and his elves sulkily dragging behind. The troop were still very much annoyed with Monk's grovelling apology and irritated over Sprites demand to 'work together'.

Down a long narrow corridor they all sped to an annexe that was reached by a spiralling iron stair, at the top of which was a large double oak wood door. The door frame was ornately carved with oak leaves, burnished with golden acorns. The door itself had two large iron ring handles and a large iron keyhole into which Monk inserted a large iron key that took both his hands to turn. When it opened the door creaked on hinges that had not been oiled for years.

Monk entered the room, stepping carefully over many scattered books lying on the floor. He then leapt to avoid others, sidestepping and hopping his way as he crossed the room to avoid the clutter. Standing on the top of his desk he then threw back the wooden shutters to let in some daylight. It then took him some time as he struggled to force open a small window; to let fresh air circulate amongst the dingy, dusty atmosphere of ancient manuscripts, decaying leather and mildew.

Meanwhile, all of them had stayed obediently quiet waiting at the library door for permission to enter. Ankra was particularly motivated at what he saw. He anxiously stretched his neck to peer over Brimens shoulder, keen to notice that the library was in a state of extreme disarray.

In Brimens ear he whispered. "Sec; 66 states: ….All Ledgers; Files; Records; Indexes; Catalogues; Scroll….

"Come in., Come in.," said Monk halting Ankras hushed tirade of rules. He beckoned them forward. "Come in, Come in," he repeated. On entering; all that was before them were piles and piles of precariously stacked large volumes of books that Monk had dodged, many littering the floor; many of which needed immediate repair. More books were crammed tightly into the shelves, on top of others.

As Brimen was 'tutting' his disapproval, at such a messy, disorganised room of neglect. Smarty answered him with a chuckle. "What does this remind you of?" and gave a playful nudge on his arm. Meanwhile, Ankra was sniggering and whispering in Brimen's ear again. "Looks like I have another report to submit - Sec, 54: sub sec 3 para 1," he said removing his notebook and pen from his top pocket.

In an adjoining room untold amounts of scrolls and parchments were randomly racked to the ceiling. Maps, of all areas in Evermore were spilling out of there half closed draws. Loose papers and pages were strewn all over the place. There were also dirty plates, cups, and cutlery strewn across the floor. Ink, from inkwells, had leaked out on the chairs leaving a dried stain. On the main desk, candles in there holders had burnt down to nothing, the residue of wax hardened on it's once polished top.

Smarty couldn't let the moment pass and whispered into Brimen's ear. "It looks like the office at the mines?"

"I should not have let them in here!" bemoaned Monk about his sisters. "Soft! That's what I am – soft and too considerate," he continued to groan while attempting to replace the scattered collection of books and manuscripts.

There were times before all of this when this precious collection was meticulously cared for. An industrious elf called Thingummey – employed by Monk - used to be the keeper of the Library until Monk took the responsibility away from him and put his sisters in charge. That was when they ran away from Ersatz. That was until Monk disowned them again.

Monk had snce decided against letting Thingummy have the keys to the library anymore due to his extra demands in order to sort out the chaos caused by the sister's neglect. Thingummy had demanded to have help with tidying it up and expected rewards to repair the damaged books.

Yet this was an emergency; authorised by Sprite. Not being able to find the books he was looking for and frustrated by his efforts, Monk was forced into a sudden change of heart: "Sage!! Go and fetch that annoying elf, Thingummy."

"What.., Now?" said a startled Sage. "But he won't come if you don't pay him!"

"YES!! Yes! Yes! I know that: Then tell him I will!"

In the interval that followed; whilst patiently waiting for Sage to return with Thingummy. Brimen, Smarty, Ankra and others were helping to reshelve and tidy up the mess. In between all the action, Ankra was still sniggering and scribbling in his notebook every so often, trying hard to provoke Monk. He knew full well that he had the advantage with Sprite on his side.

Suddenly Monk screamed out. "There it is…" he pointed shaking a finger. "There it is…" he became animated, gleefully staring at a large, red bound volume, bearing, strong, brass locks. Displacing clouds of dust he removed one of the heavy items from the shelf. "Clear me a space!" he screeched at Sage nodding at the cluttered desk top.

After clearing a space he eagerly sought the other volumes. "Now, where are they?" he said puzzled. Before he could work out their location, Sage had returned with Thingummy.

"What are the new terms?" demanded the elf.

"Well I.., er.., better conditions?" said Monk dithering.

"Helpers, that I choose?" replied the elf.

"Yes! Yes!" agreed Monk, smiling begrudgingly.

"No more sisters meddling?"

"Yes! Yes!" grinned Monk. "No more, no more."

"Rewards:" Monk hesitated. "For all my hard work;" claimed the elf.

"Well, small rewards?" replied Monk sheepishly.

"Rewards?" asked the elf uncompromisingly.

"OH! Yes! Yes! Yes!" fumed Monk compelled to give in. "Just find them?"

Immediately, Thingummy then went straight to the other books that Monk was looking for and in addition produced the runic stones of destiny and the large, thick, dark green bound volume that accompanied it. He slammed it down on the desk then held his hand out for a cash reward: Monk handed over a small sum but never said thank you or even acknowledged the elfs usefulness. Instead he pushed Sage out of the way, demanding: "Get some more candles." After fumbling about with several smaller keys that he kept on his person he unlocked and opened up the two red volumes.

Reading the two books together were anxious moments. "Now let's see what it reveals," he said scrutinising the verse for accuracy. Monk then began to read out loud:

> "The Kingdom will crash
> When intruders do bash
> On the Walls Of this sacred place,
> They would look on in anger
> And bring about danger
> To a truly; hallowed place!"

"Does it mean that if the goblins succeed in penetrating the walls of the Grotto, that we will have to surrender Evermore?" asked Brimen.

"Yes! But the thing to consider most of all is the wall to the Sanctuary. If they break into that too, then there will be no return for any of us," said Monk gloomily. "More seriously, there would be no more King: He would concede power!"

"That is it!" said Brimen excitedly. "By using your old escape tunnel – from the Abbey - they ARE going to tunnel through to here; just like Turncoat had said."

"Yes!" said Monk. "And the plans that were stolen will show a mine shaft running close to this Grotto. Now, Graff; our rengrade gnome, will know exactly whereabouts it is and the angle to mine into it!" He then rushed across the room to a tall stack of wide draws that held detailed maps of that area. "We must beat him to it!"

Monk was the only one who had access to the Secret Inner Sanctuary which the verse referred to so they had to believe he was telling the truth about its existence. In fact, it was true, the Inner Sanctuary was so protected that it generated a magnetic force. But if, D'rasnah was successful in taking the Grotto then he could gain access to it and Evermore would fall under total control of dark forces. For the first time ever the Oakmen; Gnomes; Elves and Fairies would be enslaved or banished.

"They must never succeed," raged Monk. "Never; Never; Never; and it is at this junction that we must stop them." His finger indicated a place in the book without letting them see it. "This place is secret..," he said, staring an accusing glance at Brimen: insinuating his carelessness over losing the satchel. "How would they know it ever existed?" he teased. There, were no plans inside your satchel to tell them so!" An awkward moment of doubt had arrived for the Oakmen, resulting in a shuffling taking place with Brimen wincing at Monks 'Tomfoolery'.

"Only, I know this secret escape route," continued Monk acting dramatically. "This is not recorded on any map." He then broke out in a manic laugh that had a disturbing effect on everyone.

"Read on Monk," interrupted Ankra unperturbed; trying to keep the momentum going. "What else does the oracle mention?" Monk took his time with a smug look of contentment on his face before he finally moved onto the next verse:

> "But when quick as a flash
> The response is to bash
> The intruders, deep into disgrace,
> Then the Realm is assured
> To exist unexplored
> Denying the strangers face"

"Unless we can get at them first," said Brimen. "But where shall we start...? They're probably close already."

"Then we should destroy the Citadel first" stated Ankra. Turncoat said they were tunnelling from there: We all know they are hiding in there"

"Not so hasty! Ankra," said Monk putting him down. "Now hear this all of you," he warned and recited another verse:

"The Citadel can only lead to Hell,
For those that would pursue it,
But I'm telling you, of a cautious route,
Where THEY will just fall through it!"

Monk went silent for a time searching his mind for the correct interpretation of another line. Seeking an alternative option to find the answer, he took hold of the Runic stones that were tenderly wrapped in linen and squatted; crossed leg on the floor. After muttering a ritual prayer he began to cast them across the illustrated board.

They all stood in silence feeling strange to watch Monk, who appeared to go into a deep, trance like state; now absorbed with a deeper thought. He stayed like that for some considerable time. When he eventually came to, he started to read the rest of the script slowly using a magnifying glass to decipher the tiny hieroglyphs that accompanied each line. This time however he would not disclose the verse but pondered on a very important option which was contained in the lines.

This ancient script could only be deciphered by the Monk Elders so its message could only be interpreted by them, that way the true meaning would stay concealed.

"What does it say?" said Brimen, impatiently attempting to look over his shoulder.

Monk then offered the open book to the Oakmen with a smirk on his face knowing full well that they could not read properly. And then offered the; Runic stones for Brimen to decipher. "I need a good reason to take action!" he said. "That is all."

"But you have the best reason of all," said Brimen. "We must save Evermore!"

Monk further scoured the oracle for what seemed like ages, he had just scoured another volume when: "YIPPEE!" was the sudden outcry. "I do have a reason!" Then he infuriatingly added: "Brimen, Smarty - Look!"

His finger energetically followed the line that excited him. "I can now disclose what to do: First you must take an oath never to discuss this with anybody; that means even to each other. What you are about to discover must never be confessed; even under the hardest trial," he said dramaticly. There would come a time when all the folk of Evermore must learn of these mysteries, but that time was not yet. Follow me we have no time to lose," then closed the book with a purposeful thud!

Monk suddenly took off faster than any flying armament he had invented; disappearing into yet another chamber leaving Sage to direct them through the maze of darkened corridors. Here Monk instructed them on strategy, signs to look out for, about the Chamber of lights, and the 'V' shaped seal that would determine their fate. He then told them of the plan that would defeat D'rasnah and the Goblins forever.

Ankra meanwhile was getting excited at the thought of getting some real action at last. Nodding eagerly to his elves - anticipating his role in the matter - he dipped into his pocket and removed what looked like a small stick, black in colour about six inches long and started tapping it in his hand while displaying a smirk of self satisfaction, with his elves looking eagerly on.

Nudging Brimen he winked casually. "We'll give them what for, EH!" he said while tossing it in the air. He then twitched his moustache mischievously; nodded playfully; winked again; then offered it to the Oakman to inspect.

"What is it?" said Brimen taking hold of the offering.

Ankra sniggered. "Wait and see! This will do the trick!" he assured him. Taking the 'stick' back from Brimen; Ankra tossed it even higher into the air.

"No! no, no," shrieked Monk. "You can't play with that: In here," he panicked.

"What is it?" said Brimen alarmed at the suddern outburst.

"It is explosives!" continued the screeching Monk. "Our latest invention, that does away with Kordi: NOW! Put it away."

"But, but, but, Is D'rasnah going to use it against us?" said Brimen.

"No! no! no! "This is Dynamite, more powerful than gunpowder," stated Monk.

"It's safe enough without a detonator," smirked Ankra. Defying Monk he again tossed it high in the air; catching it he did it again; then again. "Hah! Hah!" he laughed as everyone dived for cover.

"Put it away and let me finish," demanded Monk. "The idea is to stop the goblin before he gets the chance to stop us. Not for us to destroy ourselves."

Chapter 16

Goblins Challenged in the Tunnels

Everyone present swore the Oath of secrecy; read and memorised from an ancient parchment scroll that bore the Oakleaf seal of Evermore. Blinfolded; they heard the words echo off the walls as if a higher force was listening to them. When they had finished they listened to Monk - who was stood facing one of the walls - letting out a strange vibration in his voice. It startled the blindfolded attendants when his forced breath caused his lips to move rapidly as the air passed between them.

The weird effect activated the entrance of a concealed doorway and the grating sound of moving granite could be heard as it slid open. "Through hear..." directed Monk guiding them in. "Now remember!" he said. "Follow my instructions and only remove the blindfolds when you hear this door shut... Good Luck!" then promptly stepped back.

The heavy door slid slowly against the rock, settling back into place. It finally locked into position concealing the entrance beyond recognition. When they removed their blindfolds they were now on their own in pitch black darkness, listening to the silence.

It took several more minutes for their eyes to adjust, to a gradually increasing effect of an orange, low light. It took a few more minutes for their sensitives to adapt to the momentous task that lay before them.

The chamber that they now found themselves in was pristine. No evidence of dust or fallen rocks, no draught, no sounds, just emptiness. Encouraged by this cool stillness they began to survey their new surroundings noticing the surface of the walls. Although uneven and irregular they were smooth, of varying colours like beautiful polished agate stones. Brimen unrolled the chart to read the instructions he must follow.

Somehow, the room was now giving off a different shade of light; a bright orange glow. Warming, embracing, encouraging, urging a confidence to explore even further. Where this energetic light came from they were not sure, it was to remain a complete mystery. The effect certainly had a cheering result on the group, their next move though, through a slim, crevice in the rock would not be so pleasant.

Brimen was not amused at the first attempt to pass through this natural opening. Yet! It was the only option for them to continue. Commenting on the 'secret' path in the marsh he said frustratingly. "Why! Does Monk always send us into tight spaces to face impossible tasks?" he groaned as he got wedged and retreated to start again. There was no other alternative they must go through as Monk had instructed.

Huffing with objection Brimen forced his body – with his backpack - through the tight gap, closely followed by Smarty, who was smaller and not so encumbered. Progress was slow as Brimen had to move sideways, shuffle, turn this way, that way, while each time trying to haul the boxes of essential equipment that each of them following on, would also have to haul.

Meanwhile, Ankra had his troop around him debating a better approach; offering a different strategy. "What we., we., should do!" stuttered Ankra, watching and hearing Brimen continue to huff and puff. "Is to send 'me' th., th., through first, with a rope! Then To., To., Tono and I might say, my organised troop, can pull all the equipment through, then they could all fo., fo., follow on!"

At his third attempt; Brimen reluctantly gave up his struggle and agreed. But, he then ordered, that 'they' would have to pull everything through, 'after' everybody else. Brimen took off his own encumbered equipment then led the way determined to be first through. Movement was still slow and extremely awkward but they got there. Sage would be the last one through after checking that nothing got left behind.

When they had finally squeezed their way through these narrowest of gaps, they found themselves in a larger chamber with three tunnel entrances taking off in different directions. Water was seeping from the rocks gently running down, through the cracks in the stone floor.

While they waited for Ankra and his elves to bring everything else through, Brimen looked at the chart again to consider which one, out of the three options he should take.

The one, Brimen had to focus on, had a descending path stepped at lengthy intervals, bathed with a green light. At the bottom it levelled out joined by a riverlet of water steadily flowing alongside, gradually getting wider and deeper.

Just ahead of them three boats and a raft were moored. Again: It bought back memories of their battle in the marsh – at the moorings. Ankra was particularly interested in there existence and began jotting down details in his notebook. Once they had loaded their equipment, they then continued to paddle along a small, tight tunnel of smooth stone walls embedded with crystals. These clusters of crystals, set at intervals, acted like beacons when torch light caught them.

Further ahead they would come to the small Hexagon shaped opening that would lead into the Chamber of lights. When they had alighted from the boats, Sage halted them all to tell them that next they will enter into a much larger area and would behold a wondrous sight yet must only speak in hushed respectful tones; at the effect it would have on them. This was the holy of holies, a mysterious place where long, glistening, stalactites hung from a great height, streaked with bright colours. From the floor arose huge stalagmites, ringed with rich dark colours alternating with lighter shades.

At the centre of this magnificent spectacle, seven beautiful colours of the rainbow were harmoniously swirling, creating and forming endless circular movements enclosed in an area ringed by large, white, pristine marbled stones; at the middle of which was a golden column placed on a Jet black plinth.

This was beyond anything they had yet experienced causing them to stand in awe for what seemed like an eternity. Mesmerised by the movement of this soothing effect   Brimen had to be strong to resist its hypnotic state. "Come on," whispered Sage reluctantly. "Remember! We can only pass through; we have got to locate the 'v' shaped entrance that sits on the sand of time. Feeling in buoyant mood they were now ready and eager to press on to the next 'reward'.

Passing through another hexagon shaped doorway led out into a smaller cave bathed with a soft, yellow light. The walls in here were rough and irregular but the area felt peaceful. They continued to follow their course into another space. This cave was very similar but the light was now of a soft, green tone. In front of them was another door opening, just wide enough to take the entry into a shorter passage.

Again the chart was checked and down they all went. Around and around following the crystal beacons until, at the bottom, they entered into another cave, this time the whole area lit by a brighter light showing the many shades of blue, indigo, and purple streaks in the layers of rich, smooth granite.

Up until now the journey had been pretty straight forward, with only one sure direction leading to the objective. The hardest part – they anticipated - would be when the 'V' shaped entrance cut them off from returning; they would then have to rely on destroying the room that they would then find themselves in - which, according to Monk would also reveal the escape route.

This 'v' shaped entrance signified an exit from the light and entry into the dark. A foreboding errand that they had trustingly, come to fulfil. It would automatically seal up once the group had passed through, leaving no trace of its location.

The group now found themselves at journeys end, standing in cold damp emptiness, completely the opposite effect too what they had just witnessed and their confidence began to subside into melancholy. Sadly, they all turned to watch the 'V' shaped rock slide gently into its saddle, completely sealing their fate. "No turning back now," said Brimen, feeling his heart sinking fast as he lamented the closing of the door.

Sage was an adept of Monk but not such a recluse. He lived among and moved about with the little folk looking after their welfare. With his knowledge and self belief at this critical time, he would add an enchantment to their well-being. It was a privilege for him to pass on learned teachings that would reassure them in times of need. He got them all together into a circle then began instructing them in the Grand Elder philosophy.

This was a very simple and uncomplicated ideal but it appealed to their logic and trusting nature. Part of it was - that the Sun is always shining even on a Cloudy day, and that the colours that gave them such a lift in the Holy of Holy's are always in operation even when surrounded by the dark impregnable rock - It creates it's own light is always there and can never be extinguished. Lecture over and feeling refreshed the group began to survey this 'huge' cavern.

A big surprise to them all was the obvious fact that this place had once been a working mine, plundered for its precious 'mineral' over a long period of time. This was evidenced by the fact, that mining tools, oil lamps, ropes, timber, supports, rail tracks, bogies, lay rusting, scattered all about them.

Right in the centre of this huge space, rising up to support the high ceiling, stood a single column of rock. All around it was a void.., an opening to a bottomless pit.

"Ideal for our purpose," said Brimen rushing over to survey the single column with intensity. He cast an eager eye up to the high 'Cathederal' roof of the Cavern.

Ankra, who was standing close behind - looking over Brimens shoulder - peered nervously over the edge of the pit into the abyss. "Many of these will do the trick," he whispered, patting the stick of Dyno in his palm. "Six holes drilled in the middle of 'that' column, will move a mountain!" He nudged Brimen playfully in the ribs while letting out a manic laugh, then he was off, chasing across to the other side, with his troop to find where the narrow rail tracks led. "This must be our escape route?" he said optimistically then hopped onto the hand propelled trolley to explore.

On the other side of the void was a wheel house with a winch; almost a replica of the one that Turncoat was operating when they freed him. The wheels and cogs were jammed but it still had attached to it a crane jib with a powerful wire cable and hook.

Brimen took control and began to organise the unloading of their equipment for the job in hand. He ordered the use of the oil lamps and too light as many as they could find then to make use of the wood from a crumbling shed. "It will make an excellent bridge to cross to the center column," he said

"Lobe?" said Brimen, glad to be rid of Ankra for a while. "We need to know how far the goblins are away from this point," he stressed. "If you climb up, move over onto the left side of the void, you can also fix some anchor bolts: to attach the pulleys that we will need, when we span the void to get to the column. "While you are up there listen out for any sounds of there approach.

"Lobe was an excellent Rock climber, totally unnerved by any crevice, overhang or sheer Face. He made for the high ceiling to listen for the chipping of rock or any movement of goblin activity. "Nothing yet!" he reported and started to secure the bolts for the pullies to secure the rope bridge across the void.

At the same time, Smithy, Chip and Tug started to unpack the block and tackle and the many yards of rope that would be used to put the bridge across. Then set to work in were hammering into the ground anchor posts that would support it.

Meanwhile, echoing from across the other side, Ankra was giving his 'troops' the necessary pre-talk – while standing on his box of dyno – giving orders and instructions to operate and carry out the 'final reply' to the goblns when they were passing directly overhead.

"Lobe," shouted Brimen, "Are the bolts fixed and ready?"

"YES!" came the positive reply and began scaling down the central column.

"Are the brakes, 'Off' the pully?"

"YES!" came the reply.

"Right!" said Brimen, calculating the distance with a meaningful eye. "Chip, get your equipment ready. Tug! You too! You have both got to swing across to that ledge and establish a platform; to work from. Lobe will catch you when you land."

With a victorious expectation of what was about to take place, Brimen repeated what Ankra had said earlier – 'many of these will do the trick.' He stared down into the unfathomable depth. "We are literally going to bring the roof down and plug that hole."

Underlining this aggressive objective he added a comment, all of his own. "When push and pull meet stress and strain, only the goblins will feel the pain." Then, nudged the nearest to him for agreement. "EH!" he encouraged - chuckling.

Chip and Tug were not amused. They were too concentrated with what they had to do. They clicked the hook onto their body harness and uncoiled the rope. Chisels, Hammers and Wood Props were strapped and attached to them. As they looked across the void, they realised just how far they had to swing carrying such extra weight, and just how troubled they felt at the depth of the bottomless pit.

"Are you ready..?" said Brimen. "Chip, you go first!" Chip looked up to see Lobe clinging like a 'Limpit' to the central column of rock. "I hope you have done your job properly," he shouted to him. He took in a deep breath then felt a huge shove from behind as Brimen sent him flying over the void. He dipped quite low at one point with the weight he was carrying then rose with perfect timing to be caught by Lobe on the ledge who then secured his harness firmly to the column.

"Your turn now!" ordered, Brimen to Tug!" He too was then sent flying across the void weighted down with equipment to land perfectly on the same ledge.

"Excellent!" said Ankra arriving just in time to admire the feat. Brimen puffed his chest out with pride. "Such, excellent organisation!" added Ankra. "We need you in the Marsh," he said with a laugh. Brimen just smiled with authority and smug satisfaction, thinking to himself, 'Mmmmm! Only; 'I' would be in charge.' Ankra twitched his moustache as if he knew there would be a struggle for power and discreetly moved away to get his troop ready to cross the bridge that was about to be built.

Chip and Tug eventually returned across the bridge that was now firmly held in place; to report that the bridge was now safe and sound. "Excellent! Excellent!" praised Ankra waiting to go after carrying out last minute checks on his troop's equipment:

"You four will go across first," said Ankra using his baton to indicate. "Everything is accounted for in the tool box. Now! You know what to do – drill seven holes only around the circumference at equal centers - Be quick! Be careful! Be thorough!" he underlined while patting his baton in the palm of his hand. He turned to look briefly at Brimen with a self assured look as if to imply; discipline is the only way to handle things correctly.

"When you report back," he said shouting to his troop as they were crossing. "That 'all is correct'. Myself and Tono will bring across the 'Dyno' for insertion."

Everything went correctly and efficiently; it was then Ankra and Tono's turn. Tentatively they began to cross with the weighty box of Dyno. When they got to about a quarter of the way, the bridge slipped from its anchor point under the strain of the heavier load. Ankra wobbled as one foot lost contact with the walkway. Balancing on one leg while gripping the rope rail; he shouted out to those watching from the edge. "HOLD ON TO THAT POST!" whilst still keeping a tight grip of the box. Another sudden jerk put Tono off balance too. Yet! He managed to hold on firmly, his body moving rhythmically to counter the awkward wobble.

When it had eventually steadied the two attempted the rest of the way very carefully and had reached about halfway when it slipped again. This time it was the roof bolt that came away falling into the void with the rope still attached. The violent movement bent Ankra sharply over and he now found himself hanging from the rope bridge, by one leg. "I'm., I'm., s s.,s.,slipping." He screamed desperately clinging onto the handle of the Dyno box while Tono still held on to the other. Ankra wriggled trying to pull himself up with his free hand.

Tono; on the now violently, swinging bridge, soon lost his balance and fell completely off the bridge, sailing over Ankras head yet still gripping tightly onto the other handle.

"The box!" yelled Ankra dangling upside down, his breath heaving as his chest tightened with fear. "I., I., can't hold onto it." The combined weight of Tono and the box stretched Ankras arms to the limit. Suddenly his fingers had to submit to the force. Then Tono and the Box fell like a stone into the void.

The release of the combined weight had a catapult effect on bridge. It sent Ankra high up in the air, with the velocity of a rocket. He reached its zenith then also dropped into the terrible void.

Brimen and the others were horrified, watching helplessly from above gasping in disbelief as they had just witnessed the two of them disappear into the darkness.

"HELP!" yelled Brimen. "Everybody, get the torches; fast." Calamity had now befallen the group as everybody's hopes fell apart on realising what has happened.

This being the first real setback; Brimen questioned his approach. How could it happen? Have we been pushing our luck? Have we been careless? Have we thought victory too soon? All these questions raced through Brimen's head, as he felt victory for Sprite and Evermore slip away. "We can't fail NOW!" he wailed in desperation.

Brimen's mind continued swimming with doubts and fears. If it all goes wrong what chance would THEY have? All of them would be trapped, swallowed up, finding only our bones at sometime in the future. Gloomy and fearful thoughts of letting down Gannon and Olan, knowing full well, that they would now be chasing the goblins through the other tunnels above them. Niether had any contact with the other only trust and perfect timing in seeing the mission through.

Circling the pit they all peered nervously, over the edge, into the blackness of the unfathomable void. "Ankra! Where are you?" screamed Brimen into the blackness. "Are you alright?" there was no answer only the echo of his voice coming back to torment him. "Torch light; Torch light;" he yelled. "Quickly, more Torches."

The added mass of light eventually picked out Ankra and Tono laying unconscious, prostrate on a ledge. Miraculously the pair had landed safely; even more Incredible, the box of Dyno had settled between the two of them. "Phew!" they all sighed at once.

"We can reach them," said Brimen joyfully. "That ledge is certainly in the right place," Undaunted by the ordeal and showing a fearless disregard for the pit, Ankra and Tono began to stir.

"Don't move!" yelled Brimen. "You have both landed on a narrow ledge." He looked all around him for inspiration to rescue them. "Smarty, swing that winch over, it only needs a drop of oil," said Brimen enthused. Smithy, Chip and Tug started working hard to free the seized up mechanism. Thankfully there was enough grease and oil left in abandoned tubs. "Smarty!" shouted Brimen. "Grab that wheel and guide me down when we've hooked up that skip," he said leaping into it without a moment's hesitation.

"Hurry up!" screamed Brimen. "Send me down to them." Smarty gently released the brake sending Brimen on his way into the pit. "STOP, he yelled when he finally reached them.

"What took you so long," said Ankra looking dazed, battered and bruised. His shaking hands attempted to clean and replace his monocle. "Don't look down," said Brimen stretching across to take his hand. Ankra gripped it tightly and made the short leap onto the skip forcing it to sway and dip. "Come on Tono," encouraged Brimen when it had settled. "We can just squeeze you in."

"Dyno first!" ordered Ankra.

"There's none left! It's all rolled out," said Tono lifting up the shattered remnants of the explosives box.

"Are you sure?" doubted Ankra. "There must be? – check it again!" he insisted.

Tono did so then leapt onto the skip. "It's empty he said."

"What are we going to do?" fretted Ankra, obsessed with losing the explosive.

"We will have to think of something!" said Brimen, angrily.

"What are we going to do?" fretted Ankra again. A phrase he repeated endlessly, until they got out of the skip.

"I don't know, YET!" snapped Brimen as they regrouped to think things through.

"What are we going to do?" sobbed Ankra. "We can't blast the column away!"

"Then; we will have to 'CHIP' it away," stressed Smithy offering a brilliant glimmer of hope..., and then pull it down by block and tackle!" he said.

"That's a good solution!" agreed Brimen. "Is it possible, Sage?" he asked.

Sage set about doing some immediate calculations: Stress and strain times (x) ultimate destruction equal (eq) to success: "Mmm!" he muttered taking hold of a lump of chalk then starting to scribble a formula on the wall: Density of rock x height of column, divided by 1lbs per square inch. (dr x hc : 1bs-sq inch) bearing down on the smallest center possible. Supported and spaced at equal centers by wooden props multiplied by time (equaled) by effort. (s&s = ec = wp: x t = eq x E). Four pullies at 10 foot, angled at 45%, stress of weight will Multiply splitting the molecule particles forcing the kinetic energy (4p @ 10f ^ 45% sw x <> mp fk) of the whole load; into the void x = (mpf - ke) + (wl + v) then YES! We can do it!" he said with delight.

After some considerable time everything was meticulously made ready and the new bridge now put in place. Smithy, Chip, and Tug had worked really hard to make up the lost time and done a good Job cutting into the rock of the column reducing it's width down to about an inch at the centre, they had it propped with wooden posts linked to ropes and pulleys designed to destabilise the rock as soon as the signal to pull was given.

Lobe was still hanging up on the ceiling with his large ear tuned in listening for the slightest tremor that would indicate the goblins tunnelling, then he heard it; the urgent chipping away of rock and frantic activity above him. So preoccupied were the miners

from above that they paid no heed to any impending danger from below.

Meanwhile Gannon and his gang really had to fight hard every step of the way through the many tunnels and now found the one that Lobe was now listening into - the entrance of the tunnel leading to the Grotto. But the goblins, realising that the Oakmen would soon come upon them had now started to refill behind them. This barrier in turn spurred an even greater threat as Cretin and his hobgoblins had moved into position now coming up behind, trapping the Oakmen.

At the other location and with great co-ordination, Olan and his gang were pushing up hard in the main tunnel that was intended to drain Fastflow. Although the goblins had discovered that the gunpowder was of no use to them in the damp environment; they had made great speedy advances; getting dangerously close to achieving their objective. The tell tale signs of slow yet continuous seepage of water from the river made it hazardous as the Oakmen advanced.

Back in the cavern the Oakmen, gnomes and elves were gritting their teeth, as they pulled, and strained, heaving with all their strength putting the pulley's under a tremendous strain. Suddenly their strenuous effort was worth while. The first prop gave away, then the second collapsed then the rest gave way in quick succession.

Evidence of the effect was soon apparent when cracks appeared, running in all directions snapping, and grating sounding like firecrackers, leaving clouds of ground down rock. The cracks shot up the column with a thunderous rumble and shuddering; threatening to destabalise the roof of the cavern.

Unfortunately, the 'piece' in the middle of the column reduced to about an inch, didn't break cleanly away. The column had destabalised but, jammed only dust and small particles fell. Just as suddenly everything had settled and all went eerily silent. "It hasn't worked!" feared Brimen. "What do we do now?"

At the same time the devastating effects of movement were felt by the goblins above them. The sudden and eerie sounds of ground shifting and rocks splitting perplexed Grindle, his vast experience of mining had never encountered such a situation as this before. Drawing on his underground instincts, it told him to evacuate as soon as possible. His miners already in retreat.

The idea that the ground had now settled and all was well had D'rasnah ordering. "Get back to work, we are nearly there!"

Grindle, was adamant about leaving and challenged D'rasnah's judgements. "If you had listened to me earlier and took the other route that 'I' suggested," he said. "Then this would have been avoided."

"I told you that it was the wrong route," screamed Nescient at D'rasnah, siding with Grindle who was now attempting to dig himself free from the backfill.

"It was the Bungles fault, they always let me down," screamed back D'rasnah.

"Don't blame the Bungles. I will not stand IT!" threatened Nescient.

"Insolence! Insolence! Keep your place.., or else..." challenged an angry D'rasnah.

"Or else what....." come the snide reply. And so it went on until Atropine reminded them that they should all get back rather quick to the Citadel. If they lose that..., then? The ongoing disagreement was a sudden and devastating blow to their dishonest plans and signalled clearly to them that they were now facing a defeat of unknown preportions. Neither of them could bear the thought of their evil master plan being ruined and continued with instant rages of blame and counter blame. Atropine secretly enjoyed the spectacle; of poisonous words of blame, but could not show it.

Ankra, who had been up to now been subdued; preoccupied with his failure of not carrying out successfully what he should have done, now came enthusiastically back to life with an inspirational effort:

He now realised that earlier, when he was preparing to cross the bridge he put the stick of dyno that he carried, to one side. Now finding it was a matter of great fortitude.

His eyes lit up with an unstoppable certainty of what to do next. "I have one stick of dyno left," he said to Brimen excitedly. He put his hand inside his back pack that was on the ground with all the others and produced the piece that was often 'tossed' in the air playfully - like a toy. "I had almost forgotten it?" he said. "I bet that; one is all we are going to need." He looked across with eyes like a hawk sighting a deep gap at the base of the column. "That 'crack' should do it," he said. The next moment he was 'Off' post haste to redeem him-self. "Come on!" he said encouraging Brimen. They both made for the bridge without question, dimissing the destabilised column.

Tono and others immediately followed to give them support. "We will have to take a chance that the bridge will not collapse again?" said Brimen as it was still swinging wildly about. When they landed on the ledge, dust and grit was still falling away from the cracks in the rock as the slow momentum rubbed together. "We need to speed things up," said Ankra with a manic grin.

Brimen placed Tono on his shoulders then Ankra climbed onto his to make the height needed to be able to place the Dyno into the crack of the grating rock. Ankra wired the fuse and jumped down. "We've got to be quick," he said holding on to a reel of wire. "Here Tono take it across and tell everrimen. "I only hope we are not too late."

Swiftly they made their way to safety back across the rope bridge. Ankra took the reel of wire from Tono and making a point of showing the Oakman; wired the ends to a plunger. Ankra then gave out a nervous snigger and pressed it down to make contact with the charge to detonate the Dyno. Even on the far side of the cavern the blast forced the three of them off their feet, followed by the unbelievable, shock and tremor, dislodging the column completely. The noise that followed was horrendous; as the roof fell, pouring itself into the bottomless pit. Among the falling rock and the swirling mass of dust and debris, bodies were seen falling, screaming into the pit.

Meanwhile, Gannon and his gang, responding to the explosion pushed determinedly up from the rear and were not going to take prisoners. Brutally they chased and encouraged all the remaining goblins that were desperate to escape, sending them over the edge, into the oblivion of the bottomless pit.

"What a stroke of luck" He said to his pals realising that it was Ankras handy work. "If we had been - that much closer.., well!" Brimen and his gang had long since departed the scene of destruction, using the escape route that Monk the Elder had told them of. Gannon and his gang looked down into the endless void.

"It just goes to show!" said Gannon. "That they knew nothing about Tunnelling."

"They got themselves into a right old hole." Joked Wedge.

Chapter 17

The Final Battle

"It's over! It's over!" Ersatz kept repeating, when he had learned that D'rasnah and his goblins had been blasted into eternity. "At last, at last, I am free," he yelled with relief. "Free from the selfish, scheming, lying, treacherous, goblin." Tether whimpered at his feet, wagging his tail with delight at his master's joyful reaction.

Ersatz boomed on as everything in his head became clearer. "If he had succeeded in his dangerous plan to drain the marsh - then he would have wrecked us all." He said with a realisation that he hadn't quite seen before. "My tower would be flooded; my Citadel, my tunnels, my dungeons – all gone."

Cretin who had survived through his own cunning methods wanted to reassure Ersatz that he was here to take over from the loser – D'rasnah. "He got what he deserved," he said. Then went on too reinforce the sly comment with. "For far too long he had fooled you, wanting the power over Evermore all to himself - I would never drain the marsh."

Red Witch cackled her support. "We can all start again," she insisted. Looking encouragingly at Ersatz, she then said. "This time, 'YOU' will be in total control."

"I am no fool," stressed Ersatz "Why were you helping the goblin to tunnel under the marsh – Why did YOU not stop him?"

"But, we are from the land of Drone. We did not understand what was going on," said Cretin speaking up to support her. He then gave a convincing whine to his plea. "I came here because D'rasnah promised me the Yewmens territory."

"The Yewmens territory?" Ersatz had to think for a while doubtful whether he had heard of them or not. This was yet another tribe of little men that he had never heard of. He remained perplexed. "Did you get it?" he said.

"No!" replied Cretin "The Yewmen are proving very hard to remove We must first destroy their supporters."

Cretin, cast a shifty, sideways look at Red Witch. Who in turn glanced back exchanging the evil bond that dwelt between them.

"Then I, Ersatz the great will get it for you!" promised the Neandthal displaying a rare glint of pleasure on his face.

Cretin was thoughtful in considering the sudden promise and said. "AH! But you do not have the gold?"

"When I've defeated the king," said Ersatz looking surprised at the doubtful reply. "I will have enough of everything!"

"Remember too," coaxed Cretin. "The Oakmen are still powerful." He took his time for the next suggestion. "I can still look for Turncoat to find the golden acorn?"

"I will be the new power in Evermore," growled Ersatz. "Nobody else!"

"Yes! That is understood," answered Cretin. "You just need a little help."

Red Witch was quick to intervene in the possible stale mate. "You should rest now," she said fondly to Ersatz. "Tomorrow is a new day for victory!" She then took hold of Cretins arm to leave the room.

When they were out of earshot Red Witch said. "You must find Turncoat and force this secret from him. The little folk's world in Evermore is yours if you do this. Round up the strays and take control – We will next bring into Evermore the 'Dune' goblins from Drone."

From his balcony Ersatz stood in a commanding stance, his flintlock pistol set firmly in his wide leather belt. Looking out across the vast expanse of woodland Ersatz demanded ultimate success of his allies standing along side him:

"Spare nothing! Prepare for me the steed that will carry me to glory," enthused Ersatz to his groom as he surveyed the swelling armies camped nearby. Admiring his latest weapons of war gave Ersatz a feeling of superiority and expected victory. The major piece of artillery – Culjerns cannon – set proudly on new wooden wheels, dominated the other two either side of it. Ersatz watched with pride as it was now being harnessed to large drey horses ready to be hauled toward the castle.

In the stables, at the base of the tower, the leaderless Scallywags, Trundles, and Bungles had been rounded up by Cretin and put to work preparing the warriors for battle. Waxing the leather harnesses that held brasses, listing numerous victories of past battles, polishing buckles, saddles, grooming the horses, platting the manes and the long tails, shining the hoofs and combing the long feathery hairs of the shires legs.

"Put these little men to use, and work them even harder," instructed Tansga to Ffelin. "Use your whips as a punishment. First! For retreating from the marsh! Second! For retreating from the mines" Tansga wanted the Goblins punished as some kind of rough justice for Ersatz, to avoid them running free and possibly back to Drone.

Belter and Welter, Ersatz's two Shire horses were coming out to exercise in the crisp early morning air. The heat from their nostrils condensed in the coldness, as they were about to be put through their arduous paces. The intense training was cruel but necessary, for these large, heavy and immensely strong horses. They responded to the challenge with an, awareness and enthusiasm at the prospect of carrying their warrior mounts into battle. The two flicked their long platted tails as they proudly bore the heavy weight of armour that would protect them from the weapons of battle.

In another stable within the castle grounds, two other proud Shires - Trouncer and Pouncer - seated Culjern and Miljern. In many ways like their opposites - Belter and Welter - they too had an awareness and enthusiasm. With courage and boldness they too anticipated victory for their riders. Both seemed equally determined and much better equipped to deal with battle, Culjern's side having a higher standard of discipline with a greater feeling that right is on their side.

Ersatzs side clinging to the notion that might is right, relied on total brute force outnumbering the Kings men three to one. They also had their 'powerful' new weapon.

Lining the battlements at the castle, bowmen waited for orders as crossbows were wound to full force ready to fire a volley over the lea into the distant woodland, where Ersatz was assembling his army. The King also had a powerful, yet untested in battle, secret weapon in his armoury.

The Sergeant at arms snapped his orders - FIRE - as the King approached to inspect his troops. The arrows cut through the uncanny stillness showing the King's mighty destructive power.

High up in the keep, Culjern was scouring the distant hills and fields for any signs of movement. Removing the spy glass from its leather case Culjern scanned the high ground further on, focusing clearly on two figures running away from someone.

"Who is that dancing about on the top of the hill?" he said, surprised to see them in such a dangerous position. He took his eyes away, rubbed them; adjusted and cleaned the lens then took another look.

"It looks like two old hags, with white hair," he laughed. "They must be the two witches - Monk's sisters?" he said bewildered.

"Witches – hah, there are no witches in Evermore," said Miljern. "That's Merva and Derva!"

"Yes, there is!" added Culjern. "And Monk is chasing them.., what is he going to do?" he said curiously. "Do you think he is helping the enemy?" Culjern passed the spy-glass over for Miljern to take a look. "He seems to be pleading with them," said Culjern. "Doesn't he realise that it's about to get very dangerous out there?"

"But, why are they there?" said Miljern, handing back the glass. Culjern continued to follow their antics, trying to make sense of it all. His attention suddenly diverted by a ribbon floating on the breeze. "There! Over there! Look, banners just below the brow of that hill," he shouted. Culjern pointed to the spot where he could see them, then handed back the spy glass to Miljern.

"So that's his plan," said Miljern. "He's going to try and outflank us when we engage him out in the open."

"Over there too," said Culjern sighting another significant movement while pointing in the other direction. Looking out across the battlefield at the advancing forces build up, a wall of siege weapons and war machines were slowly inching forward, getting closer and closer, almost within destructive range

As the attacking forces divided too take there stand each side of the field, the line opened in the middle to reveal the biggest threat; Five cannons, the one in the middle the largest.

"It's that cannon?" shouted Culjern. "The one they made in my honour. How did they get hold of that?" Although Monk had informed the King that Ersatz now had access to gunpowder Culjern wondered why the Oakmen hadn't informed him not knowing that they had thought it was destroyed on the night they destroyed the Balloons. Normally the Oakmen would have spied on such a build up of arms and kept him informed, but Culjern's slow recovery after imprisonment and now estrangement with Brimen - because he had to spend so much time far away in the mines, meant that events had overtaken him.

"They must have stolen it from the marsh," said Miljern.

"Where has he got all those Warriors from?" asked Runjern an officer of the new Artillery. "They must out number us three to one," he said fearfully.

"It has to be Rager," said Culjern spotting his banner flying alongside Ersatz's. Rager was a powerful force that had subdued many others in the past, he was to be feared. At one time he had wanted to join forces with Culjern and the King but was proved to be treacherous.

"Take a look at that iron battering ram it's got a monstrous skull on its end," said Runjern as the wrecking machine began to move toward the castle doors. He then gave the immediate order to fire the Mortars to destroy it.

Just then a huge blast in reply, shattered the air sending a red hot iron ball hurtling at them. It landed on the keep destroying a corner stone. What followed immediately after was a hail of boulders, fired from tranchards. This was then accompanied by a second volley peppering the front walls of the castle.

The boulders split apart on landing, sending sharp shards of masonry in all directions, mortally wounding and injuring many archers. Two other massive boulders followed and landed on the fortified walls severely damaging the casement.

"Many more of those and we will be forced to surrender," said Culjern harbouring resentment for the enemies weapons. "They are now about to scale the walls on those platforms." He then shook his head in shame, knowing that he had clearly under estimated Ersatz's potent revival. He was wanting more than revenge against Ersatz for all those wasted years in the dungeon.

"Many more or not, let's use our 'surprise' and send them a shock," said Runjern touching the launching frame of a new invention; waiting to be used.

"But we haven't used it in battle, yet," said Miljern. "Will it work?" All three looked at each other worriedly. "Our 'shock' will have to work!" they said in unison. A hail of flaming arrows followed their snap decision coming at them, whistling on the wind, many landed on the battlements and in the courtyard, setting alight stores and striking dangerously near the gunpowder mill where the king was preparing for an infantry charge.

"Bring up the 'Grieving' rocket." ordered Runjern to the officer in charge. He then spun the crane hoist round, opened the wooden, floor door then released the ratchet, sending the hook on its chain racing through the pully to those below. The large armament was soon attached. "Haul away," someone shouted from below.

The great weight was winched up followed by Kegs of gunpowder; cannon balls attached with iron chains soon followed. A dozen pair of hands gripped the armament, swung it round and placed it into position on its iron frame. The Rocket stood proudly pointing out across the battlefield primed and ready. "We will take out his troops behind the hill first," said Culjern. "At the same time; prepare the other mortars, then the King can make his charge!"

Runjern aligned the monstrous projectile, set the distance and measured the trajectory. "Now we will see if Monk's latest invention really works?" he said with great menace. In the tenseness that followed, Runjern carried out the drill order, giving command to his gunners to fire off the rockets. Landing at random among the assembled enemy it had a devastating effect on Ersatz's allied force, mutilating and unseating riders from horse.

"Prepare... load... aim..." before he had chance to continue sending another round of rockets; a huge explosion, then another, and another in quick succession released its punishing load of shot and shell causing maximum damage to the fortified walls. Ersatz's armies were now moving swiftly to scour the walls, threatening to over run the castle.

"Our next target," shouted Runjern to his gunners. "Are those canons and tranchards The gunners had immediately primed the larger mortars, ramming the powder into the bore then fed into it the most viscous contraption of three iron balls, attached by chain, It was a testing moment, nobody was sure if these new improved destructive weapons were reliable. In the past, the trials to perfect it showed many faults with the design of this particular misile. Sometimes the barrel would split or the cannon ball jamb.

"Prepare…load…aim…FIRE!" shouted Runjern again; his eyes concentrating fiercely on the tranchards. From the battlements, red hot iron balls, linked by chains spun at great speed until they reached their target, wrapping around the stout wooden frames of the enemies siege weapons shattering them into match-wood. "Aim… Fire!" shouted Runjern using the second launch of rockets to destoy the cannons.

"What is that?" shrieked Ersatz. "Wizardry?" he squealed watching his war machines laid waste and his cannons destroyed. "Is that the wizardry that Lurker talked of?" he questioned. Ersatz was watching the scene from some distance back with his warlords while waiting to charge the drawbridge, hoping to achieve a resounding victory.

"What has happened?" stormed Rager standing up on his saddle. "My siege weapons are destroyed, what kind of power is this?" Tansga who had felt uneasy, ever since Brumma's skull had fallen from the panelled wall, ranted. "The omens were true, we should have listened. I will withdraw my men."

"Stay where you are," snarled Ersatz. "This is not over yet, we will annihilate them when they come out to face us," he said convincingly. "Now get into line!"

"We are no match for this kind of wizardry," said Tansga terrified by such a devastating show of strength. "I think we should all retreat and rethink our plans," he looked at Ersatz desperately pleading, hoping that he would see sense, like re-grouping to devise a better strategy.

Crazed with the events of seeing everything going against him Ersatz would not listen to reason, "Yet again I have been deceived," he yelled as he watched the systematic destruction of his army led by the first charge from the castle.

Ersatz was the undisputed leader and he had committed his troops to battle. There was to be no retreat; to go against him would reap dire consequences. He knew only one course of action and that was direct and brutal force.

Tansga tried hard to restrain him but it was no use, Ersatz's hateful energy for Culjern gave him super human strength to go on to the end.

"Never," he shouted. "I will take that 'thing' from them and this time, take HIS head!" Immediately the beast that lived in Ersatz was released and roared its defiance.

The drawbridge to the castle was lowered and the large heavy oak gates thrown open to display the King's mighty force. Leading his men out to face Ersatz's rabble was Culjern seated on trouncer, next to him seated on pouncer was Miljern holding the King's banner. The King was advised not to risk the first charge in battle and persuaded to take the second charge.

"Culjern," screamed Ersatz. "I want your skull." Lifting his broadsword high into the air; the sunlight caught the glint of steel. It signalled the charge from behind the brow of the hill of those that had not been anhialated by the rockets and led those of his warriors that were left into close combat against the Kings forces.

Total mayhem and bloodshed of the hand-to-hand vicious fighting took place, as axe cut into shield, mace and ball destroyed features, axes dismembered limbs, sword and pikes penetrated bodies and arrows struck their targets.

The massacre of the Culjerns advance had become perilous as they were outflanked on all sides. The shear weight of numbers thrusting forward; accompanying the incredible speed of Ersatz, was alarming. This first charge from the castle was immediately overpowered. The second charge put the King and the colours under real threat.

Trouncer, Culjerns faithful steed had fallen from under him a lance had pierced the armour and gone straight through his heart. The horse was dead. Injured and without his sword or other weapon to defend himself, Culjern, standing alone feared death from his enemy.

"Your head is mine now," screamed Ersatz as he closed in on him brandishing the heavy broad sword. Belter sensed victory for his master and reared up on his hind legs to gain an advantage for Ersatz when he would bring his sword down on Culjern's head.

From the battlements Runjern had his attention fixed on Culjern. The whole field of action was covered with the option of using, either, rocket, cannon or mortar. Aiming straight and true he fired off a rocket, his eyes tracing its effect until it penetrated the soft underbelly of Belter. The missile sank deep as the horse exposed himself, rearing up on hind legs for Ersatz final thrust. It threw Ersatz to the floor as he too lost his sword. The sickening thud had destroyed Belter ruining the one chance Ersatz had of killing Culjern.

While the Battle continued to rage all around them Ersatz stood defiant, alone, dazed and shaken. Although not seriously injured he now stood face to face with Culjern. Looking at him he wondered - 'So near yet so far away.' Like an invisible barrier Ersatz could not reach him. "What is it? What is it that protects him?" he asked himself. "Why is it? Why is it that he always wins?" He began to say it out loud and to his surprise and wonderment, as if to answer him Sprite appeared hovering over Culjern.

Mesmerised by such a beautiful light, Ersatz sank to his knees his evil influence was fading fast. Braving the carnage, the two sisters also appeared among the fighting hoardes; as if from out of nowhere. Merva and Derva were still fond of Ersatz and in their madness had rushed onto the battlefield and now stood alongside Culjern, beggng him to surrender; cross over, join us they begged. They were soon followed by Monk trying to stop them. The whole effect saw the fighting stop.

Fearing for Ersatz safety the sisters tried to shield him as best they could then tried to help him up, his only reaction to the both of them was to shout abuse and push them away. Merva and Derva suffered great distress they both knew that Ersatz was doomed and begged him with another rhyme:

> "Oh, come away,
> And save the day,
> Don't take this to the limit,
> The light is strong,
> And you'd be wrong,
> To fight another minute."

Amongst the din of battle, truth; searching for a better way ahead had been upheld and for the first time Ersatz felt another side to his nature develop. It was as if a door in his mind had been opened and a deeper and calmer thought had awakened something new in him. Then a strange realisation took over. It all became very clear to him, that although the gold gave special power to the wearer of the crown, there was something else. The golden crown was the reward given from something higher yet the two were linked together. The unseen laws of influence that served the good and noble heart could never fail but these values Ersatz had never cultivated.

"But I will learn?" he answered softly to this silent vision. "First let me have the gold to make a crown," he begged this silent voice. He would now have to make the choice; either one thing or the other. Bewildered, he sank to his knees again and Sprite disappeared as quietly as she had appeared.

There was no further contact only disappointment and heaviness in his heart at getting so near to the answer and yet feeling so far away from a solution. Culjern was quick to see the anguish in Ersatz and was ready to talk and end the battle. "Surrender your arms now," he pleaded. "You have seen the truth? Let us, look to a new beginning."

The response was a scream of mental torment coming from Ersatz's deranged mind that could still not admit defeat. He knew that he would never reach the ideals of Culjern. Still convinced that if he could find the gold - capture the power of this mysterious truth and make a crown - he would rule Evermore. With that conviction resounding in his head he made a frantic dash to escape.

Fleeing from the battlefield on a riderless horse Ersatz made off in the direction of the marshland with some of his faithful warlords following. Although wounded Culjern mounted another horse and his men also followed in hot pursuit. With Ersatz and the warlords fleeing from the scene all the warriors lay down their arms. Both leaders it would seem; deciding by their actions to claim their victory off the battlefield. The remaining warriors would have to wait until the victor returned.

"Come back, don't go in there," shouted Culjern trying to warn Ersatz off. "Stay out of the marsh... we can make peace," Both the warlords and Culjerns men were briefly united and held back. In a desperate last minute bid they tried to stop Ersatz but even Culjern would not go into the marsh uninvited. They could do nothing but watch as Ersatz disappeared into the reed beds, only to face the danger of Gunpowder fairy and the Naughty imps. His fate was sealed there was no way back.

The suicidal mission, to enter the marsh while fighting raged within his heart, was a selfish act of greed not an honourable defeat - with sword in hand - on the battlefield.

Some days later they recovered Ersatz's body from the river fastflow his body washed up not very far from his tower and citadel at Ersatz hollow. Essentialy, it lost him the respect of his warlords and nobody would claim the body.

Tansga was now the new leader of the renegade Neanderthals and willing to move forward in a new direction. He and the Warlords - with the remnants of Ersatz army - had made their peace and pledged loyalty to the king. He surrendered his arms and vowed to disown the goblins influence.

Rager and his allies would not accept terms at any cost and had promptly returned to Drone taking the canons with him, giving a warning that he will return with an even larger army. Meanwhile Ersatz was given a chieftains burial - in consecrated ground - by Royal decree. His Tower and Citadel totally destroyed as part of the peace plan.

Evermore was now a much safer place with the demise of the Neandethal warrior - Ersatz: A renewed air of confidence existed too and had spread among the little folk now that D'rasnah and his goblins were not around to intimidate them. The only real cause for concern in all this change was over Brimen. He had found a new level of unrivalled leadership, making him intolerable.

The fact of the matter was, he was feeling pleased with himself becoming, more and more obsessed than ever with his leadership image now that the ultimate victory over the goblins had been achieved. Expecting and organising a next 'Heroes' celebration at the castle was taking up more and more of his time. The idea of having a statue of his likeness erected in the village square, had now gained renewed momentum and others resentment.

Gannon and Olan were determined to put a stop to his nonsense and kept arguing for a medal each and a painted portrait of the three of them. The same could be done for Smarty, Smug and Ankra, they reasoned. Painted as a group, to be hung in the town hall, then everyone else who had taken part - Acktoo and the rest of them could receive a medal to mark their bravery and commitment and if they wanted they too could have a painting hung in the town hall. Unfortunately another snag to these ideas presented itself when Ankra decided that he too wanted a statue of himself.

Distracted when he should be dealing with important matters at hand, Brimen would not consider the new found rumours that D'rasnah and his leaders may have survived the pit. "Impossible! There's no Darkwood anymore," he would rage. "Where would they go?" he would question annoyingly. "Rumours are rumours," he would laugh. Then finish with: "Now that's that and all about it!"

Many more months passed with things swiftly getting back to normal in Evermore. The sisters - Merva and Derva - were now spending a lot of their time with Sprite and the fairy's bringing Darkwood, that would now be renamed – Monkswood, out of its stunted existence, back to its former green and pure, glory. It put joy on their faces that had not been seen for a long time, encouraging Monk to be a little more understanding and friendly.

The lean years were now over and Monk encouraged the king to finance the rebuilding of the Abbey to which he gladly contributed with the Oakmen getting readily and deeply involved in the reconstruction. Ersatz's tower and Citadel had now gone, erased from existence forever, leaving Grondo, Graff and the miners now able to concentrate on filling in the tunnels that had given so much access to the potential destruction of Evermore,

Everything was now on course for the total healing of Evermore. Everything that is, except for strange reports from Bat about hauntings and noises coming from the grave of Ersatz. It was now some time since the burial of Ersatz but a strange haze was seen and a mild heat felt, coming from the freshly dug earth, lingering over the grave. Some had said they heard groanings of an imprisoned soul. Some had said they saw shadows and spectres walking about aimlessly. Once or twice Monk was called upon and attempted to placate the strangeness, without any effect.

One clear autumn night, lit by a full moon, Owl decided to investigate these reports.

On paying a visit he saw a disturbing sight. Looking down from his perch in the church tower he could clearly see shadowy movements coming through the lynch gate. Five 'shadowy' yet! familiar figures were walking down the path making their way toward the grave of Ersatz. As the bell tolled in the tower - on the stroke of midnight - these intuders reached the spot.

Owl was mystified at their appearance and wrestled with troubled thoughts. "How did they survive the pit? – Do the Oakmen know?" Menacingly he could not work it out. "How did they get back into Evermore?" thought Owl. Even more frightful to his reasoning power was to wonder. "What have they come here to do?"

Leading this troublesome group was D'rasnah, carrying an axe in his belt and a sack over his shoulder. The others following him; Trypannon; Atropine; Nescient and Lurker were each carrying shovels and pickaxes.

It was obvious to Owl that they had outwitted the Oakmen as all had survived the horrendous landslip. Frustratingly for Owl, it hadn't taken them very long to regroup after the death of Ersatz. But the biggest problem to solve was – how had they managed to escape that awful landslip.

Owl's, gnawing yet justifiable questions were going to remain unanswered. He watched the five goblins standing around the grave of Ersatz chanting, carrying out some kind of strange ritual. He let out a long hoot to warn them that they were being watched, but they took no notice.

It was now becoming aparrent that the whole purpose of the goblins being here, at this midnight hour when the crescent moon was bright, was centred on exhuming Ersatz from his entombed hell.

They dug with a frenzy to reach their treasure, ignorantly smashing through the bones of Tether that had lay for some months, decomposing on the top of his grave. Tether had never left his master's side and had pined away awaiting his return.

The restless spirit of Ersatz was, for eternity earthbound. Trapped and tormented by its resting place it demanded a way out and the goblins were here to free it. They would then bring back the head to join the other skulls that D'rasnah had stolen from the Citadel. Ersatz's mind was their mind, they all shared the same pain together.

It's muffled wailing, coming from the deeply interred coffin, could only be released by its own kind and that is why the goblins were here. Digging frantically to ease its pain the first shovel released the wrath of the haunted night. Bat was not amused and became angry, dive-bombing the grave robbers in protest at what they were doing.

When at last they had reached their objective they removed the lid of the coffin exposing the decomposed features of what they had come to collect. "The head, The head...Take it, Take it," it seemed to urge. "Part me from this loathsome hell," was its silent request from the drawing power of mind. D'rasnah knew what he had to do and raised the heavy axe with his two hands above his head. Not once, not twice, but three times before the head was severed from the rotting corpse. The weight of the tattooed head took two of them to lift, unceremoniously, by it's long hair, into the sack that D'rasnah held over his shoulder. Once it was secured the goblins scampered off, out of Evermore. Minutes later Nescient ran back to retrieve the skull of Tether.

Owl was mystified as to how they escaped from the tunnels and wanted to find the escape route that they would return to. For some time he followed them through the dense woodland until they arrived at Meadow Steppe and open country. He halted thinking it would be wise to wait until they had crossed such an exposed area.

The open field meant he would have to navigate north and pick them up in the wood on the other side. Unthinkingly he swooped down fast to catch up with them but was then pelted with stones by some goblins that had lain in wait - anticipating his move.

He lay on the ground seriously hurt. And there he would have remained if it hadn't been for Fox and Badger who had been shadowing him. They came to his rescue and returned him to Monks grotto.